Jeana – Michele – Denise

No matter what happens in life,
we will always have each other.
We're bound by blood, our memories, and love.
I'm blessed to call each of you my sister.
I love you.

Namaste

PROLOGUE

Life is not fair. The moment one believes in total bliss, it gets shredded by circumstance and unforeseen accidents. This cannot be my life. It just can't. Shit like this does not happen to good people. Not to someone like James, a man who represents everything good and right in the world.

The words filling the room can't be real. Even as the doctor repeats his prognosis it's muffled, strained, said through a long, dark tunnel. The space around me turns fuzzy, its edges softening like a wall of cotton. I don't know which way is up or down. Tears stream down my face like raindrops in a race to see which can fall the fastest. The severity of what the doctor said hits me. Hard.

"What do you mean less than twenty-four hours to live?" The words leave me in a drawn-out screech.

"Honey, calm down. We knew this was a possibility. My liver…it's just too far gone and without a donor…"

"Take mine!" I scream at the doctor. A long time ago, I watched a television program that said a healthy donor can donate three-fourths of their liver and still live. I hold on to that piece of trivia like a talisman.

"London, you're not a match. We've been through this." James's tone is calm, collected. I don't know how he is holding it together but the cracks in my armor have grown into giant gaping holes. That monster within, the raging scared, psychotic wife is about to break free—until his cool hand grasps mine. "Look at me, I want the last thing I see to be your beautiful face."

I shake my head repeatedly. If he can't look at me, he can't leave me. It's a ridiculous theory, but it's all I've got.

I hear the doctor give his condolences to James and promise that if a liver becomes available from a donor match he's first on the list.

Shivers of grief rip through every nerve ending as I lean over to pray. It's probably a cardinal sin to wish someone else would die, but I'm not capable of caring.

God, if you'll just use your mercy and find my husband a liver, I'll be the best human you've ever made. Please. Please don't let him die. I'll do anything. Anything at all. Be nice to my mother? Done. Volunteer? Consider it my next full-time job. Please, oh God, please bring us a liver. You can do that, right? I know you can. You save people unworthy all the time! Please, please just save James. Take me. Spare him.

"Just take me," slips across my lips. My eyes are closed tight, fingers clasped in prayer.

A tiny featherlight caress runs across my cheek. "My love, never you. You're meant to do great things. You have to do them now. Not just for you, but for me, too." His voice cracks and a tear slips down his face.

Seeing the love of my life cry, the strongest man I've ever known, breaks me. Visibly, I shake. The shock of the situation is setting in, and a deep chill rips across my skin. Bone-chilling cold.

"Come here." James pulls back the blanket, inviting me in to what will likely be the last bed we share. A hospital bed.

Crawling in, I settle next to his warmth. "How can I ever be without you?" Thoughts of the life we planned, the children we'll never have, the things we never had the chance to do together pour through my mind like sands through an hourglass. Regret swirls around us, thick and heavy.

"It will be like before, when we were just friends." He laughs and I snuggle in deeper.

It will never be like before and nothing will ever be the same again. Internally, I know this but choose not to share it with him. He's dying. The only man I will ever love is dying. He has less than twenty-four hours.

Oh God, Jesus, please! Please.

"One day, my love, you will realize that this was meant to be. We don't get to decide. It's all decided for us." Fate and James. Forever the believer in one's destiny. "I was just your act one, sweetie pie. Someday, you will find love again."

"Never." That five-letter word seems to pound through my body like a heartbeat. A proclamation. It's as if my heart and brain made a pact, then signed a contract sealing the deal. James will always be the end-all, be-all.

"Oh, sweetie, don't say that. I'll never rest in peace knowing you're torturing yourself. Promise me. Promise me, when the time is right, you will accept it and not run?"

"How can you ask me this? You're leaving me!" Huge sobs soak his hospital gown as I cry a river.

"Not by choice, London. You know that. If I could, I'd grow old and gray with you just like I promised you on our wedding day four years ago." The image conjures a new bout of Hell. Him in a crisp tuxedo, and me in the biggest, most poufy princess wedding dress the world had ever seen. The best day of my life. "I will always love you, London. And one day, years down the road, when I'm just a memory, you will be loved."

We kissed one last time. It was everything and so much more. I put a lifetime of lost kisses into that press of lips against lips. Heart to heart. Soul to soul.

When he left me, I felt my soul crumble into miniscule pieces of nothing.

James was wrong. I will never again be loved, because I'll never, ever, let myself fall.

CHAPTER ONE

"Bridge, it's time to go. Get that fine ass out here. If I miss out on hot hors d'oeuvres, you're a dead woman!" Tripp's voice jangled through the open doorway. Placing a sheer line of gloss along my lips and with one final flip to my hair, I was dashing toward him.

He held the door open as I ducked under his outstretched arm. His cologne swirled in the air around him, making me want to stop and hug him, rub my body against the heady scent. Inhaling deeply, I passed by him. A stinging smack to my ass jolted me into motion. It burned, and I rubbed it soothingly. The champagne-colored slip dress rubbed against my heated skin enticingly.

"You wanna follow up on that promise?" I asked cheekily.

He rolled his eyes and pushed me toward the elevator with a firm hand to my lower back.

"I'm looking forward to seeing your latest work." Tripp smiled and hugged me to his side. "I'm guessing by the client, you went with an Asiatic theme?"

My lips twitched into a smile, knowing how much he loved to play this game. I shook my head and he frowned.

"Middle Eastern?" His dark eyebrows rose as he tilted his head to the side smiling. "No? Huh." He looked perplexed. Tripp Devereaux was a gorgeous man. Tall, dark, and handsome, a little lost soul that I couldn't live without and I couldn't fix.

"Stop guessing. Part of the excitement for me is seeing your face during the reveal."

We arrived at the client's home, nestled away in the upper-class Park Avenue neighborhood. Tripp clasped my hand and led me up the walk and into the building. Soft music was streaming through the door as we entered.

"London! The woman of the night is here!" a voice bellowed from across the room. In a few long strides, my client Maxwell reached out and smoothed his hands from my shoulders and down my arms until he gripped my hands. That feeling of gratitude hit me hard and washed over my soul like a healing balm. "I have someone I need you to meet," he said, his voice lowered an octave.

It had been two weeks since I left him to move on, to make right what went wrong in his life. I knew instinctively who he'd be introducing me to. He led me over to a pretty blonde who had large brown eyes only for him. I smiled warmly at her, feeling no inner conflict. This was who he was meant to be with.

A fluttering memory rose to the surface sending me back to when Maxwell and I ended our time together.

Strong arms encircle my waist. His chin settling against my neck. Large hands slid up my back, pressing me closer to him. The scent of his aftershave was intoxicating, but that's not what made my heart thump. It was gratitude. The waves of appreciation that leapt off him crash against my soul, bringing with it an incredible sense of peace. That hum of forgiveness, the newfound resolve to fix what went astray and mend his heart, was overwhelming in its goodness. I close my eyes and pull his form tightly against mine, realizing it would be our last real embrace.

"How do I…" His voice cracks and breaks off.

"You love her…you love her greatly," I whisper against his ear. He nods, and I could feel when the moment changes, sizzling with tension when his soul pulls away from mine. It hurt, but it always does.

"Michele, this is London Kelley, designer and life-coach extraordinaire." He beamed. The blonde shook my hand.

"It's good to meet you, Michele." I shook her hand and that tingling essence unique to her soul passed through to me. She, too, was grateful, with no concerns about my stay. Sometimes it was difficult when I moved in with my client and his girlfriend didn't live with him. The green-eyed monster often made itself known, and that bitch had serious claws. To my great relief, Michele wasn't the catty type, and technically, they weren't an item when I stayed or I wouldn't have slept with him.

"You have a gift, Ms. Kelley. Truly beautiful work," she said while glancing around the open space. I had chosen to bring earthy warm tones into the stark white-and-black space.

Max lived like a bachelor before I entered his world six weeks ago. He was unhappy, lost in what to do next with his life. He was good-looking and extremely successful; only individuals making six figures could afford my design services. Even with all his success, he was desperate for something he couldn't quite name. I was able to lead him to what his heart desired.

I thought back to when I first moved into his home, setting my luggage on the bed.

"Will we be sleeping together?" he asked uncomfortably.

"I am not a highly paid hooker, Max."

"No, no, I didn't think you were. I just…you're moving in, sending me signals that you're attracted to me." He shuffled from foot to foot. "I don't know, I just …"

I cut him off. "I understand. And, yes, I am attracted to you on a physical level and that connection could very well manifest during our time together." I shrugged and continued unpacking. "My methods are unconventional. You will understand by the end of my stay."

Back to the present, I watched Max tuck the petite blonde to his side. It made my heart fill to bursting to see him opening himself to the one thing that would make him happy and fulfilled. Michele looked into his eyes adoringly. He needed this woman like he needed his next breath.

"I can't thank you enough, London," he said to me as he squeezed the lovely woman more tightly against him.

"What can I say? I'm good at my job." With a wink, I excused myself to enjoy the party.

Tripp was at the food table loading his plate with crab cakes and puffy morsels of phyllo dough filled with cheese. I grabbed one off his plate and popped it in my mouth. The gooey mixture of cheese and spinach was warm and salty. He handed me a glass of white wine. It was perfectly paired with the food. Being a bartender at a gourmet restaurant in downtown New York City had provided Tripp with the training for incredible skills in the kitchen. He instinctively knew how to pair a meal with the perfect wine.

We ate in companionable silence for a few moments.

"So what do you think?" I asked him.

He crinkled his brow and scanned the room. "Could have been better." His tone was serious with a hint of boredom. I knew by the sliver of a grin across his beautiful lips that he was joking. I pushed against his shoulder and he laughed. "Seriously, Bridge." Tripp always used his pet name for me. *London Bridge is Falling Down.* When we met years ago, I was falling down. Crumbling into small bits of nothingness. "You're incredible. You turned a boring man cave into a home, something a man could invite a woman into."

"That's exactly what the plan was." I looked over at Maxwell and Michele. Even their names together sounded sickeningly sweet. "He needed her." I gestured to the couple. Tripp studied them and nodded.

"A complete redesign of the house didn't hurt either. I love how you went with the large puffy couches with a million pillows. And the bed you chose for the master bedroom? It's magnificent. Where did you find that?" he asked.

"He needed a place where he could be in touch with his feminine side." I lovingly trailed my fingertips along the couch pillows and led him toward the bedroom. Once there I patted the bed and Tripp sat down next to me. We both tumbled backwards, holding hands. "The gigantic bed was designed to empower his ego, make him feel he needed a woman to share it with. Otherwise being in here alone would feel too encompassing and lonely."

We tilted our faces to the side to look at one another. "Bridge, I meant where did you get the bed, literally? Not your psychobabble shit about his inner most desires." His face twisted into a grimace. "I don't want to know that about him, especially while laying on it with you." He rolled over me and straddled my hips. He nuzzled my neck and kissed my cheek. "You did a good job," he said softly and pulled me up into a sitting position. I gripped his outstretched hands. "Let's go enjoy the fruits of your labor. You're moving in with your next client in two days and I want to spend some quality time with my girl." The smile I gave him was huge as he hurled me back into the party.

★ ★ ★

My stomach growled loudly as I caught sight of a stunning dark haired beauty across the room. She sashayed, practically glided, from the bedroom toward the kitchen, stopping at the drink service. I watched her laughing, dazzling crystal blue eyes alive with joy, her arm hooked in the crook of a man's arm. Small hands slid over her hips, then adjusted the tiny straps of her barely there dress at the shoulder. She pulled her long black hair to one side and brushed her fingers through the shining locks as she waited for a drink at the bar.

She took my breath away.

Petite and lean with a perfect hourglass figure, her rounded breasts weren't huge but large on her small frame. My hand gripped into a fist imagining squeezing the firm globes, her nipples scraping against my palms.

I shook my head. My immediate desire for this woman, a stranger, was confounding. I hadn't felt such an attraction to a woman since my last torrential cock up with my wife, technically ex-wife of five years.

"See something you like, Collier?" My business partner

and best mate gestured toward the woman I'd been watching, rather stalking with my eyes.

"Who's the bird?"

"That's London Kelley, she's the reason we're all here," he said mockingly.

"The interior designer?"

"One and the same. I've had dinner with her when she was staying with Maxwell," he finished.

"She lived here?"

He nodded.

"But I thought he was in love with *her*." I pointed to the pretty blonde attached to Maxwell's hip.

"He is. He wasn't in a relationship with London; she just lived here while she worked. It's part of her agreement. She's highly sought after," he continued.

My eyes traced over her curves. "I'll bet."

He clasped me on the back. "Not like that. Blimey! She's the most pursued interior designer in New York City. Everyone wants her to redesign their home. Her waiting list is a mile long and she charges a pretty penny. She's going to redo my flat in six weeks' time." His British accent and perfect English comforted me when the entire city seemed to survive on colloquialisms and bad syntax.

Nathaniel Walker was my best mate and half brother, sharing the same mother but different biological fathers. We left our parents and old lives back in England to open a New York office of Stone, Walker, & Associates five years ago. Our law offices touted clients with recognizable names such as Trump and Gates. We handled everything from extremely public celebrity breakups to million-dollar company embezzlers down to the legalities involved in major corporate acquisitions. Our top clients graced the telly, the big screen, and the leather seats of high-rise offices across the globe.

"So will she be moving in with you, then?"

Nathaniel nodded. "Part of the contract." He took a sip of his wine.

"Is she a beggar? A drifter with no home?" My shocked voice rose.

Nathaniel laughed heartily. "No, you old sod. She's got her own small fortune. Her fee for the four weeks she's moving in is $100,000 pounds." My eyes went round. "That does not include the cost of the actual redesign of the home."

"Interesting. And of course you're buying what she's selling. But you are a master player of the field, dear brother. How will that work?"

He rolled his eyes and sighed. "She's not staying in my bed. Well, maybe." He grinned and waggled his brows.

I cringed. The thought of him and the lovely London almost made me lose my appetite. Then my gaze settled on her across the room. I was once again famished, practically starved. She looked at me, our gazes held. Her grayish-blue eyes, full of light, seemed to call to me. I moved along the room navigating through other guests, eyes tethered to hers. It felt as though I was in a trance, as if my body floated along the room, defying gravity to reach her side.

A large smile split her delicate features, making her impossibly more beautiful when I held out my hand. She clasped mine and electricity sparked and crackled between us. I lifted her hand and brought it to my lips for a brief kiss. She smelled of cinnamon, and I wanted to run my tongue along her wrist and taste the spicy scent for myself.

"Have we met?" she asked. Her voice filtered through the noise of the party, and I could hear nothing but her soft tone. "You seem familiar."

I shook my head. "I would remember you." I placed another kiss on her hand. "Collier Stone. It's good to meet you, Love." The desire to keep a hold of her hand was strong, but I didn't want to appear creepy. Strangely, when I let go, I missed its warmth.

"You're English?" She smiled. Her face lit up. It was adorable and made my groin stir in appreciation.

"Guilty. Though my mate and I left the Queen Mum five years ago. Can't shake off the accent to fit in with you Yanks."

"You should never change yourself for another person. You're perfect just the way you are."

Her words pierced my heart. My ex didn't agree. She wanted to change everything about me.

"I'm sorry, now you look sad." Her hand came up to my cheek. Her thumb skimmed across my cheekbone as her eyes searched mine, swirling from gray to blue to gray again.

I could spend the rest of eternity looking into those eyes, trying to determine their color. Her touch slipped away leaving me feeling bereft. I wanted those hands on me. When I blinked, the man she was with earlier held her tucked into his side.

"You ready to go home, Bridge?" The tall man kissed her on the temple. Jealousy flared in my gut. She patted his chest and nodded. "I'll get your coat, sweet cheeks." He turned and left without an introduction. It irked me.

"Your husband?" The glance down at her left hand was obvious. No ring sparkled back at me. Just long delicate fingers painted with a golden nail polish.

"No," was her small reply.

"Boyfriend? Significant other perhaps?" My tone held a twinge of irritation but I clamped it down.

"Tripp is definitely significant," she answered vaguely.

"Tripp is ready to take home the most beautiful woman in all of New York." The man's arm went around London's shoulders, pulling her closer. Her slim arms encircled his form. Made me wish I had that familiarity with her, that it was my body she was pressed against. He looked at me, his eyes assessing me from my dirty blond hair to my wing-tipped shoes. "Mmmm hmmm, unless you have plans to bed James Bond over here." He blatantly allowed his gaze to look me up and down again.

"Thinking about it," she answered coyly and bit her lip. She did her own assessment, head cocked to the side in thought.

The image of her face, her lips glistening and reddened from the bite of her teeth made me imagine her down on her knees, her head titled just so as I plunged my cock into her mouth over and over again. I took a deep calming breath and stared into her eyes. She must see the desire there; I wasn't trying to hide it. All rational thought be damned, I wanted this woman.

"I sure as hell know what I would do to that fine ass." Tripp grinned. He was a good-looking bloke, but I could hold my own. My dance card was rather full…with women. Now that I was confident she wasn't attached, only one name had just skyrocketed to the top of the list, London Kelley.

"Thank you, I think."

AUDREY CARLAN

"I see you've met my brother." Nathaniel's voice broke the staring contest between London and me. He held out his hand to London's "significant other" as it were, though I don't know how significant he could be if he likes men over women. Maybe he does both?

"Not at all. Collier Stone." I held my hand out to Tripp and he shook it quickly, as if in a hurry.

"Tripp Devereaux. And you are?" Tripp's voice lowered to a gravelly timbre as he openly ogled Nathaniel.

My brother grinned, playing into Tripp's suggestive tone. "Nathaniel Walker. Good to meet ya, mate. London, always a pleasure seeing you." He pulled her into a hug. *Bastard.*

"English hotties, Bridge? Tell me I'm dreaming because I feel like I've died and gone to heaven." Tripp's gaze undressed us with abandon.

All four of us laughed, but my eyes stayed glued to London's. Nathaniel and Tripp started talking about someone they both knew named Hank. I encircled London's wrist and pulled her to the side. "It seems as though your mate and mine are hitting it off quite nicely." I laughed and then held her hand. It was warm and soft.

"Nate works for my sister. He even dated her for half a second," she offered.

"Then your sister does work with me. I'm the 'Stone' in Stone, Walker, & Associates." I smiled and made a point to touch her forearm. I couldn't not. The woman's skin, body, and simple being called to me. Made me *need* to be near, *want* to hold her.

She gasped as I held her wrist. "Are you a couple?" I tipped my head toward Tripp and Nathaniel.

"Not exactly, but I couldn't live without him." She got a glazed look in her eyes.

My hopes plummeted. Her tone made me wonder if maybe they were, in fact, a couple in a twisted weird new age way. I couldn't blame her if she was. Since my breakup with Claire, I'd bedded more women than I'd ever willingly admit to. Though bonking tens of women didn't wash away what my ex did to me. Unfortunately.

"He's not my lover if that's what you meant to ask." The spark was back. Though talking to her was like a ping-pong match. Just when you thought you were about to make the winning point, she whipped the ball back with a zinger. "Tripp, I'm ready." He nodded. She smiled at me and then asked, "walk me out?"

"I'd be honored." She glided alongside me, her hand at the crook of my elbow. It felt good there, right somehow. I led her through the room.

She briefly stopped and said good-bye to Maxwell and his girlfriend. They both hugged her and then she placed her hand back on my forearm as we went down the lift and to the curb. A black town car waited when we exited.

Tripp trailed behind us, not interfering with our moment together. He passed us and jumped into the car. She turned and looked at me.

"Will I see you again?" I asked.

"If you want to," she whispered and leaned up. Her lips brushed mine, hands clasped around my neck. Her fingers dug into my nape and tickled my hair.

My mouth opened in shock and her little pink tongue entered swiftly, melting along mine. She tasted of crisp white wine and I wanted to drink. Hell, I wanted to consume. The synapses in my brain finally clicked, and I gripped her body tightly against mine and took control of the kiss, melding my mouth to hers.

She moaned, and I sucked her tongue into my mouth and then nibbled her plump lips. My hands tunneled into the silky strands of her hair and settled at the nape. I tightened my grip at her hairline and with a tug, deepened the kiss, ravishing her mouth, pulling her head where I wanted it.

Bone-deep lust plowed through me. Savagely and desperately, I tried to stake my claim on her, out in the open, on the busy streets of New York City. My hand slid down her spine and landed on the slight swell of her bum.

She started to pull away, but I planted my hand on her sweet arse and ground my erection against her, knowing it hit her at the perfect spot. She groaned and, with a renewed interest, gripped my face with both hands and devoured me.

"Get a room, you two! Jesus, Bridge, you're fucking making me want to jack off as I watch the show." Tripp's strangled voice came over London's shoulder.

We both pulled away, startled expressions our faces. Her hand touched her swollen lips, her eyes widened in surprise. She was beautiful, effervescent in an unearthly way. She walked over to the town car and got in without a word.

I'd just shared the best kiss of my entire life with the most mysterious and unusual woman I'd ever met. And she was just going to walk away? *Hell no!* This could not happen. *What is it about me and women? I always seem to screw something up?*

"London, wait. I'm sorry," I said as she closed the car door.

She smiled so sweetly I wanted to melt into the

pavement where I stood. "Don't be sorry. I very much look forward to seeing you again."

"May I have your number?" I desperately needed proof in my hand that she was interested.

Her lips twitched and a perfectly sculpted dark eyebrow rose. "If it's meant to be, you will find me." The town car roared to life and drove away. Find her. In a city of over eight million people, she wanted me to find her. My grin widened at the challenge presented. The chase was on.

CHAPTER TWO

Collier's breath was raspy and thick with lust against my ear. "Holy shite! That's so uh…good, London." His breath came in feverish gusts along the sensitive skin of my neck. "Love, just a little more…" His entire body was strung tight with pressure, legs entangled with mine as my hand stroked him up and down, harder and harder. Not only could I feel his release coming through the tension in his body, but also pure ecstasy rippled off of him, turning me into a blistering pot of desire. When in the throes of passion, being able to empathize and feel the pleasure of another made my gift bearable. Beautiful even.

The surroundings blurred. Shook. "Fuck, Bridge! Yes, yes…" came the voice of my best friend as globs of sticky cum coated my hand. My entire body accepted his pleasure with a euphoric rush of adrenalin. Realization dawned and I became aware of what had just taken place.

Not again.

Tripp's breath was labored against my neck. He kissed his way to my mouth, gliding along my skin until he reached his goal. His lips covered mine, and for a brief moment, I allowed it, appreciating the softness in his kiss. Then the real world crashed down, splintering into a million tiny shards of irritation. I shoved his large body hard, almost pushing him off the bed.

"What the hell, Tripp!" I yelled. "Not cool!" The wood

floor of my apartment connected with my bare feet, sending shards of ice through my instep and up my legs as I stomped into the bathroom on the cold hard floors.

"Come on, Bridge. I needed you!" His voice came across sounding like a wounded puppy.

Washing his release off my hands in the bathroom sink, I took a long hard look at my face in the mirror. My sleep tussled hair would take a miracle to tame. I had rosy cheeks from thinking I was having a private moment with Collier, *not* Tripp. The pupils of my eyes were dilated, so black with lust over the Englishman I could barely see the blue of my irises.

"Are you mad?" Tripp's voice was small and I hated it instantly. He leaned against the door, a defeated look plastered across his gorgeous face. I was not going to be another person who screwed him over, literally or figuratively.

"Yes." I looked him in the eyes, expressing my irritation. His features were drawn and apologetic. "So, how was it?" My lips twitched into a smirk.

His answering grin was huge and spread over modelesque features. It was hard to stay mad at such a lovely creature. My best friend was beautiful. Inside and out, though he would disagree with my assessment. His dark chiseled bone structure and light eyes made him the perfect playboy and he lived up to his title. Tripp was the definition of a man-whore. He loved men and women alike.

Often when I'd come home to spend time away from my clients, I'd find him sprawled across the furniture with a new piece of arm candy, looking freshly fucked. I stopped asking names long ago. They rarely were invited for a second go-around with Tripp.

Then again, I was no better in many ways. I took my pleasure when and where I wanted it. The "who" seemed to differ quite often as well. Traditional relationships were not my thing. Aside from Tripp. He was the only constant male in my life besides Daddy and my brother, Rio.

"Bridge, baby, sometimes it's hard for me to keep my hands off you." He leered and gave me a full head to toe Tripp once-over. My nipples hardened against my camisole, more because of the feelings I felt pumping off of him like a firehouse shooting water at a burning building than my own attraction.

"Tripp," I warned. "We've had our fun in the past but…"

"I know, I know. We're friends. Best friends. I can't help it sometimes. You're fucking hot." He came and put his arms around my waist and hugged me, my back to the solid muscle of his bare chest. He inhaled against my hair. "You smell so good." He nuzzled my neck then slipped his hands up my waist and over my breasts, firmly gripping each globe. "And your body is fucking incredible." He tweaked my nipples through the fabric of my camisole and I pushed him away, shaking my head.

"You and I both know this never works. We both have issues…" He nodded in full understanding.

"I don't want to screw up what we have. But that doesn't stop me from wanting to fuck you." The man was nothing if not honest.

Every few months, he would make sexual advances toward me again. We'd had sex *many* times in the past. It was phenomenal. We're very compatible as sexual partners. It's real life we couldn't handle. Each and every time we had sex in the past, we both became distant toward one another. It ruined our easygoing friendship for a solid couple months. The problem always seemed to be that we loved each other; we just weren't in love.

Tripp and I wanted to be with other people. Monogamy was not an option. That's a fact we had in common. So we agreed to stop having sex and focus on the genuine love we had for one another. The best friend kind.

Real lovers, the kind of romance that lasts a lifetime, don't allow for other relationships. Tripp and I wanted both. I'd had the real kind once. Never again.

"So where are you staying this month?" he asked, changing the subject.

"Dylan Matthews is my next client. Investment banker."

Tripp pretended to yawn. "Boooooorrrrriiiinnngggg!" His smile was infectious, and I snickered along with him.

Turning on the water for the shower, I removed my clothes and stepped in. Tripp hopped up on the bathroom counter and watched me. He'd seen me naked more times than I could remember. I wasn't shy. "So what about Double O Seven from last night?"

"Collier Stone?" My tone sounded sultry, even to my own ears. "He's who I thought I was giving a handy to this morning when you so rudely interrupted my dream fantasy."

"Really? Interesting. You dreamt about a man?"

"Yes. Don't sound so surprised. I have the occasional wet dream." Not really. Usually I sleep like a rock, a dreamless rock.

"Since when? You never once told me about your dreams. I actually remember you saying you don't dream."

The damn man had a perfect memory. It was tiring. You could never pull one over on him. "That's ridiculous. Everyone dreams, Tripp."

"Yeah, but you never remember them. Now you're dreaming about a man you met last night, and kissed, I might add. That was a little fast, even for you." He laughed loud enough for me to hear it over the running water.

He was right. Kissing Collier last night was an unusual response, even for me. Typically, I'm not shy around men I want but generally not so aggressive. I practically devoured the man on the sidewalk after barely meeting him. He tasted good too. Everything about the man was rich and thick, like a full-bodied cabernet.

"I was really proud of you…and turned on. Hence the need for the hand-job." He lifted both arms and made a jazz-hands movement. "Thanks for that, by the way."

"I hope you enjoyed it because you're not getting another one." The moment I turned off the water, he opened the door and held a towel open for me. I stepped into it, and he wrapped it around, drawing me into his arms.

"So are you considering making a change from your normal MO?" Tripp asked as I tucked another towel around my wet hair.

"In what way?"

"Well, it's probably about time you let a man in."

I shrugged and shook the towel around my hair squeezing out the wetness. "You know, I'm happy the way things are. I don't need a man to be happy. I'm in control of my life and most importantly, my heart." Tripp's question struck a chord that hadn't been played in a long while. Since James died, I'd worked hard to glue the pieces of my broken soul back together. For the most part, I'd done well. I get what I physically need from the men I bed casually, and I have emotional companionship in Tripp. "Besides, I have you. Why would I need anyone else?"

Tripp smiled wide and shook the towel in my hair and then pulled it off. He pushed the wet hair behind my ears running his fingers through it and down my scalp. "And you always will have me." He ducked his head down so we were forehead to forehead, gazes locked. "You know I love you, right?" His voice was sweet and tender. He was trying to make amends for taking advantage this morning. This habit was old and worn through many years of trial and error. If Tripp did something to upset me, he'd immediately need to re-establish our connection and confirm my love. That screwed-up bitch of a mother of his tortured him into believing he was unlovable. "More than anyone?"

"More than anyone," I assured him. He smacked my towel-covered ass. "Ouch!"

"Good. Now get moving. We have one full day together, and I'm not letting any of it go to waste. "

I heard the shower turn back on as I entered my walk-in closet. My relationship with Tripp was unconventional, but it was mine and I wouldn't change it.

Instinctively, I thought back to last night when I kissed Collier. Gooseflesh broke across my skin. Just the memory of the man's lips and body against mine had my nerve endings thrumming. I could imagine his essence surrounding me, making me feel whole again. It'd had been a few weeks since I'd been with a man. Briefly, I wondered how long it would take him to find me. Would he even seek me out? I had a strong feeling he would. That kiss was memorable to say the least.

★ ★ ★

London Kelley. I couldn't get the bloody bird out of my head. Visions of her invaded my thoughts throughout the horrendous week. For days, I'd dealt with a celebrity debacle with one of our rock stars destroying a New York hotel suite. Apparently, daft, coked-up rock stars thought it funny to use a flat-screen telly to slide down the stairs of a posh two-story penthouse in downtown Manhattan. Same blokes escorted slappers scantily dressed through the hotel lobby and proceeded to publicly shag them in the lifts. Each member of the band was arrested on public indecency and vandalism charges after the hotel concierge called the cops on them. Of course, we settled out of court and paid the hotel off, leaving me with a mountain of paperwork, but they will pay the firm for it in spades. It reminded me I needed a legal assistant.

Hearing a soft knock on the door, I lifted my head to see Nathaniel standing with his overcoat, ready to leave for the day. "Cheerio, old mate."

"Hey, Nathaniel, I need a favor."

He entered my office and sat in one of the plush leather armchairs. "Anything, old chap."

"Bollocks, I'm not that old!" Ever since we were little boys, he would complain that he was younger. Now that we're adults, he constantly reminded me of that fact, though lately I've felt well beyond my thirty years.

"You act old. When was the last time you had a good shagging or went off on a bender?"

"The former is none of your business, and the latter,

well, I could use a good night with me mates, yeah?"

"This weekend, we'll call a couple lads, maybe pick up some ladies, and have a good time. I want to introduce you to a new buddy of mine, Hank Jensen. He's dating a client of ours, remember Aspen Reynolds?" His light brown hair fell over his forehead as he waggled his brows and grinned.

"You're incorrigible. But speaking of women, I'd like to get in touch with London Kelley." I focused on the papers in front of me and tried to look as nonchalant as possible.

"You fancy Ms. Kelley, yeah?" His smirk was undeniable as he pulled out his cell phone. He grabbed a note card and pen and copied her telephone number onto it, along with her address. "Just call that number there, and Bob's your uncle! You've got her."

"Thanks, mate. I think I will. There's just something about this girl."

"Well, she's a fit bird," he said. "Brilliant choice. You know, Aspen Reynolds is her sister. If calling doesn't work, maybe I could plan a meeting with Hank and Aspen, have her bring along her sister." With that, he stood and saluted as he left.

I stared at the phone number on the note card. Brilliant choice indeed. Scanning the number, I made the call. A deep male voice answered on the second ring. "Hello?" It surprised me because I thought London was unattached. It was entirely possible, bloody likely, that she had a man in her life.

"Hello. Yes, I was hoping to speak with Ms. Kelley." A glance at the clock told me it was six in the evening. Perfectly respectable time to receive calls.

"She's with a client. Is this her James Bond?" the man

asked. I now recognized the voice as Tripp Devereaux.

"I'm sorry?" I answered, confused.

"You're the Brit we met at the Maxwell reveal last week, right? The one who had his tongue down my girl's throat if I remember correctly?" His tone was filled with mirth but it jangled my nerves, making me feel the need to explain.

"Tripp, she made it clear that the two of you were not a couple, mate. I'm sorry if I misunderstood." The pencil I was holding was neatly broken in half.

Did she lie to me? Why would she lead me on if she was in a relationship? Perhaps she wanted to make him jealous?

A full-bellied laugh came across the phone line. "We're not a couple." His voice still contained hints of humor, which had my ire building. "London doesn't do the couple thing, Mr. Bond."

"It's Collier, Tripp. What do you mean London doesn't do the couple thing?"

"It means she is not in a relationship, nor does she do relationships. She prefers to stay unattached."

"I see. When will she be home?" I didn't really see what he meant. Far from it, actually. The little bits I picked up about Ms. Kelley only gave me introspection on how complex the woman was.

"Don't know. You've reached her home and office. However, when she's staying with a client I'm not sure when she'll be home. If you'd like to give me your number, I can get her a message."

I rattled off my phone number and rang off with Tripp. Such an odd duck, that one. If she's not home, why was he answering her phone? Did he live with her? Everything about this woman was a mystery, one I was becoming more and more determined to solve.

★ ★ ★

"Sweetheart, I know you're hurting." His eyes held a longing that would not be fulfilled.

"James, I just… this is so unfair. There hasn't been enough time…"

"London, you have to be strong. I know you can. You're going to be fine. And one day, you will see our time together as a beautiful memory."

"No. I'll never get over you."

His eyes smiled until it reached his lips. *"Sweetie Pie, it's not fair to hold your love away from another. I don't want that for you."*

"It's true; you've ruined me for all others. I wish…"

"Shhhh, London, don't waste wishes that were not meant to come true. Someday, you will be loved."

"London, are you hungry?" Dylan's voice cut through my daydream.

My newest client was the perfect gentleman and host. And as Tripp expected, boring. Investment banking did not provide much excitement in his life. He lived a sheltered, mundane lifestyle. His world had little entertainment.

I smiled to myself. This was going to be so much fun. The man needed excitement in his life and I was just the right woman to give it to him. He had no idea what he was in for but he'd love every minute of it, once I got past his reserved nature.

"I asked if you were hungry." Dylan smiled wide when he found me sitting on the bed in his guestroom.

"Sorry, you caught me daydreaming. Yes, famished.

What did you have in mind?" I stood up and took one last glance at the journal I'd been reading when the memory overcame me. No more thoughts of James today. Time to have a little fun.

"Oh, I'm open. You're the guest." His gaze skimmed my body so quickly I almost didn't notice it. His breathing became labored. Every so often, he'd take a deep breath. Desire filled the room like a hazy smoke around him. He wanted me. It was a heady feeling knowing a man wanted to mate with you.

I tilted my head to the side and gauged his vibe. Telltale waves of his desire prickled the hair on the back of my neck. Oh, it was going to be fun getting him to loosen up. Besides, best way to get over a man was to get under another. At least that's what I kept telling myself. When I was with a man, feeling his pleasure, receiving my own…I wasn't alone anymore.

"What if I told you that I was hungry, but not for food?" My hands found their way to the tie at my neck holding up my halter dress. I pulled the string and let the fabric fall, exposing my bare breasts. I slid my hands over each globe massaging and tweaking the nipples to elongate and darken them. His eyes filled with heat and need.

He groaned. "Uh, uh, shit!"

The inability to form actual words versus caveman-speak was a good sign. He was interested. And I deserved a little slice of relief and distraction. The man wasn't gorgeous but he was very good looking. Tall, handsome and he had a great big heart. I'd enjoy his body, help him find his way, fix his disastrous home, and be gone in four weeks.

His green eyes sparkled when I shimmied out of my

dress, leaving only a wisp of lace covering my lady parts. "How about this? Let's satisfy one hunger and then I'll let you buy me a fat bowl of pasta! Whaddya say?"

His head moved up and down as he licked his lips. "I can't believe this is happening."

"Well, believe it, buddy. It's time you had some fun." I climbed on the bed and lay down. "Come here, big guy; show me what you've got."

After we'd sated one hunger, he took me to a little hole in the wall, mom-and-pop Italian restaurant. The food was served "family style" which I appreciated, not ever having family style dinners at the Bright-Reynolds home. Mom and Dad were not the type to sit around a table and share a meal. They had servers and perfectly polite dinner conversations each night as if it was pre-planned and read from "The Guide to High Society Eating."

My sister, Aspen, and I railed against the debutante lifestyle. My brother, Rio, on the other hand, was the perfect little rich boy snob, making my mother's crusty heart swell with pride.

Out of all of us, Aspen was the impressive one. She was worth billions but currently was on the outs with Mommy Dearest due to her choice to live out of wedlock with a country boy from Texas. I didn't blame her. Hank was hot and loved her enough to move to New York to be with her.

Thinking of Aspen reminded me how much I missed my sister. I hadn't seen her in weeks. She'd had a falling out with Hank and then reconciled a couple months ago. I felt bad for not having reached out to her sooner. I'm sure Hank and work was keeping her very busy. An uncomfortable feeling crept up my spine, reminding me to reach out to her later this evening.

"So, do you always do what you, uh, did?" Dylan pulled me from my thoughts. He seemed nervous, which was funny seeing as we'd just licked and kissed every surface of one another's body less than an hour ago.

"Do what? Sleep with my clients?"

He looked down at his bowl of spaghetti. His face turned beet red. "Yeah."

I laughed long and hard. "No. Not all of them. I have many clients. I've had sex with a few over the years. If I'm interested, they're unattached, and it feels right, then sure. Why not? I'm pretty sure you had a good time." My lips twitched, remembering how his body arched and tightened with release.

"Fuck, yeah!" he half-yelled.

I smiled. He was already losing some of that reserve. Profanity was only the tip of the iceberg.

"I just didn't know how this works," he continued.

"Well, let me explain it to you. I spend the next twenty-six days living with you. I follow you around, figure out your likes and dislikes, in the home and in your life. It helps me design a space that will provide you with what you need to add more value to your inner being. Today, you needed to get laid and I wanted to get laid. That was a bonus." I shot him a wink and he grinned. "There's really nothing more complicated than that." I took a big swallow of my water and waited for him to respond.

"So does this mean we're dating?"

Oh no. Not a good sign. The last thing I needed was another stray following me around like a long lost puppy dog. It reminded me of the Andrew debacle all over again.

Mentally I added a reminder to make sure that restraining order was still in place. He hadn't cropped up in the last couple months so maybe he'd finally gotten the hint that he was going to go to jail if he kept up the stalking.

"No. Absolutely not. I do not date. Relationships are not an option."

Dylan looked away and winced.

"Dylan, it's not you. I plan on fully enjoying our time together, but you cannot get attached to me romantically. Do you understand?"

"Not really. But I did have a really good time." He smiled, presenting even white teeth. He was getting more handsome by the moment. I would definitely enjoy breaking him out of his shell.

"I did, too. And if we're going to continue to have good times like this afternoon, I have to know you understand there are no strings attached. Once our month is up, I will leave and hopefully we can continue to be friends."

"So, you're offering a month of guilt-free sex and a redesigned home?"

"Exactly. Now you're getting it." I was proud of my ingénue. When I was through with him, he will have matured, have a better understanding of what he needs to move forward in finding his heart's desire. On top of that, he'd have a lovely renovated condo to come home to. "Just remember, what we have is casual. You're free to date and be intimate with whomever you want. As am I. We're not in a committed relationship. We're just friends...with benefits." His brows crinkled and then a slow grin slipped over his lips. "Understood?" I had to clarify with him. I might enjoy men, but I didn't want to lead him on. Besides, a sexy

Englishman's sculpted face kept coming to mind, reminding me of new possibilities.

"Clear as day. I'm in, baby. Let's finish up; I'm ready for another bout with my newest guilty pleasure."

"Now you're talking!" The waiter came at just that moment. We both said, "Check please!" and laughed all the way back to his apartment. We spent the rest of the night screwing until dawn.

After the first week, I called to check in with Tripp. He answered on the fourth ring, completely out of breath.

"Hello, handsome. Did you take up running in your spare time?" I asked, knowing full well what he must be doing.

I could almost hear his grin through the phone. "Yeah, and I'm enjoying a tall blond drink of water as we speak. What's up? Kind of in the middle of something."

"Just checking in with my best man. Anything to report on the home front?"

"Mmmm that's…fuck yeah…right there…" He groaned into the telephone.

"Tripp! Push the blonde off your cock and talk to me."

"You're killing me, Bridge. Hey, baby, you gotta hold on. I need to talk to…" A rustling sound could be heard and then, "Oh, fuck baby…" he started again. I decided it was easier to wait it out. "Uh…oh yeah, fuck right there, uh, uh…" A constant strand of moaning, then, "Yeah, suck it all down like a good girl."

Holy hell, I was getting horny just listening to my best friend get off. Looked like I'd be jumping Dylan when he got home from work. I waited a couple more moments for Tripp to get his crap together.

"Tripp, you done now, Casanova?"

"Wow, uh yeah. Damn. I might have to keep this one, Bridge. She sucks dick like a Hoover." He laughed.

I rolled my eyes. "Man-whore."

"Takes one to know one!" he shot back. He had a point. I definitely enjoyed myself.

"All right, enough sparring. Anything going on?"

"The dry cleaning service picked up your clothes and unmentionables. Aspen and Hank are officially engaged. Your bills are paid up for the month. Oh, and James Bond called."

Too many thoughts scrambled for attention at once. "Pen's getting married!" I screeched. "I knew it!" Those two didn't stand a chance away from one another. My freak-o-meter called that connection immediately. "Oh, that's fantastic. Did she say when? I'm hoping for next September." New York was lovely in the fall. "Hey, wait a minute, how did you find out before me?" A sense of sadness swept across my heart squashing the excitement. I shouldn't have waited so long to call Aspen.

"Ollie. He was bursting at the seams and couldn't keep a secret. Aspen was yelling at him in the background as he spilled the beans." Tripp laughed. "Anyway, according to Ollie, it's going to be fast, as in right between now and your next client. About five weeks. I wrote it on your schedule. It's the week before the Walker design."

My brain stopped functioning for a second. "I'm sorry. Did you say five weeks or five months? Hell, both are too damned soon. What's the rush?"

"I don't know. She said Hank was adamant, and they were getting married at his ranch in Texas, second week in

November. She's flying all of us in her jet."

"Wow, I'll have to call her. Find out what the hell is going on. I mean, I'm happy for her. She found her soul mate." I had found mine too…then he was gone.

Shifting gears was necessary. "So what about James Bond?"

"Surprised you didn't clue into that first." He chuckled. I love hearing my guy laugh. "He called and was all thinking we were a couple. Tried to apologize with that sexy-assed accent of his."

"Did you set him straight?" My voice was clipped, worried.

"Pretty much. He wants to talk to you. I told him I'd share the message. I'll text you his number. Are you going to call?"

Was I going to call? It was a damned good question. I'd thought about the man on and off for over a week now. Dreamt about him most nights, which was unusual for me. I didn't dream often and when I did dream, it was always about James. That's why I never talked about it. Tripp would think I was backsliding again.

That kiss last week was scorching hot. If that was a precursor to what he could do in the bedroom, we'd light the sheets on fire. I couldn't say no to that chemistry. Just thinking about him had my blood boiling and my body coiling with tension. Yup, was definitely going to jump Dylan when he got home. Burn off some of this excess energy.

"Earth to Bridge? Hello?" Tripp's voice cut through the line.

"Sorry. Yeah, I'll call him. There was something about

him that deserves a little investigating."

"Investigating or sex-tigating?" He was making up words again.

"Stop it," I teased. "Hey, how about lunch tomorrow? You, me, and Pen? Think you could set it up? I'll be home for the night tomorrow. Client has a business trip to Iowa. Not interested in hanging around while he attends boring meetings surrounded by corn fields."

"Excellent. I'll see what Pen's doing…probably Hank though. That big manly cowboy is hot."

I giggled. "You're right, he is. But I love how he adores her. I can't believe they're getting married. Anyway, find out and text me. Maybe we can eat at The Place downtown. You know those people go gaga over Pen eating there. It's like they're feeding royalty."

"I know and I love it! We get to enjoy their worship of her by default, and I'm not too proud beg!" He snickered. "Speaking of begging, the hot blonde's beckoning me. Bridge, her legs are wide open. Mmm, she's dripping wet…"

The door slid open behind me, and Dylan walked in carrying two bags of Chinese. "Dinner?" he called.

"Gotta go, handsome. I love you." Saved by the boy!

"More than anyone," Tripp said, breathing heavily yet waiting for my reply.

"More than anyone."

CHAPTER THREE

"You're going down, mate!" Nathaniel gritted his teeth and smashed his racket against the bright blue ball.

The ball bounced on the left wall, then the right and back toward us. I held my position, pulled my right arm back, tightened my grip on the wooden handle, and smashed the ball with all my might. Tendons strained, muscles flexed and sweat trickled down my neck as my racket made contact with rubber. The satisfying *swak* echoed off the white walls.

Nathaniel ran to the side, his sneakers screeched across the reflective paneled floor leaving a gritty black smudge across its surface. He flew toward the ball, his arm stretched to the max. I held my breath. The ball swooshed past the tip of the racket as his body fell to the floor in a heap of limbs.

Instinct sent me jumping into the air in an ungentlemanly display of victory. Choking back the smack talk I felt bubbling to the surface, I dodged the ball as it bounced back and made my way over to Nathaniel's limp form.

He had rolled over onto his back. His legs crooked up at ninety-degree angles with his arms out in a wide T shape. Nathaniel's chest heaved awkwardly as he tried to catch his breath.

I leaned over and held out my hand. He opened and closed his eyes a couple times. "Hey, brother, you okay?"

"Aside from the deep mortification of losing to my

older brother? Yes, mate, I am." He grinned and took my hand. I pulled him up and we did the manly hug-pat thing, reinforcing our connection.

My half brother and I got along brilliantly. Ever since Dad died and I was forced to live with the Walkers full-time when I was a teenager, we'd been inseparable. We had two little sisters who were married off and making their lives back home. Their husbands seemed nice enough. Both hardworking but one had shifty eyes, a true sign he wasn't the gentleman he claimed to be. He made me uncertain about his intentions with my baby sister. However, sweet Emma always believed the best of all beings. Evan claimed to be a stand-up guy, but Nathaniel and I didn't buy it. I'd check in on my baby sister this weekend, make sure everything was roses and rainbows back home. Ella, the second youngest, was madly in love with her husband, Ethan, and had just had her first child six months prior. The fact that they all had E names was endless entertainment for Nathaniel and me.

"Hey, you heard from Em or El?" I asked.

"Yeah, actually, I spoke with Ella. She was really tired. Said the baby was colicky and she and Ethan were having a time of it."

"I'll send her some flowers, let her know we're thinking about her."

"Brill, mate! She'll adore that." His smile turned into a frown and he looked stroppy as we walked to the lockers.

"What is it?"

"Emma seemed out of sorts." He opened his locker and pulled out his towel for the showers. I did the same.

"How so?"

"She didn't say anything. It was just a feeling. She

shouldn't have married that wanker." He said aloud what the entire family thought but wouldn't dare mention to her. She was too proud and too young to listen. She had to learn on her own. But if that bugger hurt her, he'd have two very brassed-off brothers to deal with.

I nodded as he sighed. "I'll call her. Find out what's going on. Maybe have her come to the States, pay us a visit?"

"Agreed." My phone pinged, signaling I had a voice message. "I'm going to hit the showers. You coming?"

"In a minute. I've got a voice mail from an unknown number."

"Okay, brother. I'll catch you back at the office." He headed toward the showers.

"Hey, Nate." I used his nickname even though I made it a point to use his God-given name most of the time. I expected the same of him. He turned around. "Good game, mate." He smiled and waved over his head as he left the lockers.

I typed in the code to my voice mail and heard the loveliest sultry voice. She spoke with an American New York accent that sent pleasurable chills down my spine.

"Hi, Collier, this is London. London Kelley. I received your message and was hoping to catch you." Her voice pitched and glided like water flowing down a babbling brook. "I'm heading out to lunch with family and friends but would love to meet up with you some time. I think we have some unfinished business…" She let that word dangle and drift off. "Feel free to text me your availability at this same number. Have a lovely rest of your day."

The call ended, and I listened to it one more time, just to hear that voice smooth over my senses like chocolate drizzled over a sundae.

She asked when I was available. I scrolled through my phone planner. Tonight was the only night this week I didn't have an engagement. It would seem presumptuous or eager to ask her out tonight. But there wasn't another option unless I waited until next week. Finishing what we started last week sounded so very appealing. A week would be torture to my hardening prick.

Blimey! To hell with it.

I edited her phone number, filling in her name, and then hit the text icon.

To: London Kelley
From: Collier Stone

I received your message. Fancy a meeting tonight? My schedule is booked through the next week. Collier

After taking a rather cold shower to rid my burgeoning desire for a petite tanned goddess with a name that matched my former home, I checked my phone.

To: Collier Stone
From: London Kelley

What did you have mind? I may have an opening this evening. LK

To: London Kelley
From: Collier Stone

Dinner perhaps? Does 7 suit?

A smile split my face. This was the first time in a long time I looked forward to seeing a woman for an official date. Bonking a woman I met in the local pub had become commonplace. Downright humdrum. Anticipating taking a woman out brought me back to my college days when I was courting my ex-wife, Claire.

Back then, I was less wise in the ways of wooing a woman, though the chilling, creeping tingle of nervousness pricking the nape of my neck was familiar. The mere thought of being near London's perfection had me blooming with need. In seconds, her return text rang through, clearing my thoughts.

To: Collier Stone
From: London Kelley
You want to date me? Based on our last encounter, I expected a booty call. ;-)

Bloody Yanks and their funny symbols and euphemisms. My fingers raced over the keys.

To: London Kelley
From: Collier Stone
You want me to ring your bum?
To: Collier Stone
From: London Kelley
LOL That's an interesting idea. Dinner it is. I can meet you. Where?
To: London Kelley
From: Collier Stone
A gentleman picks up the lady he is courting at her residence.

Chivalry is not dead. I'll be damned if it dies with me.

My mum would kill me if she'd heard I met a date and didn't properly knock on her door. Growing up, my mum was everything you'd ever want out of a mum. She was kind, gentle, and always smelled like cookies. Baking was her hobby. I thought about the first time I caught London's scent. She smelled of cinnamon. Familiar, yet sexy. My suit smelled of her for days after her body had pressed against it street side. I'd stashed it in my closet, waiting to send it to the cleaners so that the scent would waft over me again in the morning when I started my day. The smell had just started receding. I needed a fix and I'd have it tonight.

To: Collier Stone
From: London Kelley
You surprise me…and confuse me. I'll see you at 7.
To: London Kelley
From: Collier Stone
May I have your address?
To: Collier Stone
From: London Kelley
I'm sure you'll find me. <swak>

"Oh bloody hell!" The bird was a piece of work. She seemed to enjoy toying with me. Even still, I couldn't shake the smile that spread across my face as I strutted into work, a full spring in my step. My secretary stood and followed me into my office.

"Here are your messages, Mr. Stone. I rearranged your afternoon meetings as you requested. Was there anything else you needed before I take my lunch?"

"Yes, actually. I need you to make dinner reservations

for seven thirty at a nice place downtown."

She took down the note. "For how many? And who will be in attendance?"

"Just two. I'm entertaining a beautiful woman named London Kelley this evening." I smiled. Her eyes met mine and widened. It wasn't often that I surprised her. She took the new information in stride. A consummate professional.

"Business or pleasure?" She bit her lip and focused on the notepad in front of her. I enjoyed riling her.

"Oh, pleasure, my dear Jane. And I want to impress, so pick a romantic location."

My secretary was tall and thin with no body to think of. I wouldn't call her a great beauty, but was extremely competent with lips that stayed shut. She was not one to gossip, and I appreciated her honesty and work ethic.

"Thank you. That will be all." She turned to leave the office. "Actually, Jane?"

"Yes, Mr. Stone?" Her pale hand held the door handle like a lifeline.

"When an American ends a communication with the letters SWAK, what does that mean?"

Her cheeks pinked, and her lips lifted in a hint of a smile. "Sealed with a kiss."

★ ★ ★

"What are you doing?" Tripp asked accusingly as I shoved my phone back into my purse.

"Nothing. Just texting with Collier. I have a date." Already, I was imagining the ways in which I'd defile that beautiful man. My hands itched to be all over him.

"You're kidding? You have a date? A bonafide sit down

and eat, go to a show, dancing kind of date?" He cringed. "With a man?" His expression clearly shocked. He leaned forward and gauged my reaction.

"Who has a date?" said a voice I knew as well as my own from behind me. Aspen sauntered in, her long blond hair blowing in the wind as if she just came out of a shampoo commercial, which actually could have happened. She does have a huge modeling agency as part of her empire.

"Bridge!" Tripp hollered with delight. My best friend was a riot. A true funny man. *Not!*

My sister stopped dead in her tracks and pretended to almost faint. "No way!" I rolled my eyes.

Tripp pulled out her chair and kissed her cheek. "You look gorgeous as usual, Pen. Love suits you."

She offered Tripp the biggest smile I'd ever seen. I loved Aspen's boyfriend, Hank, more and more for making her so happy. She deserved it even if the odds were against their relationship. With her being a top performing billionaire workaholic, and he a laid-back cowboy construction worker, a love match was not in their favor. However, it just proved that no matter the odds, love always prevailed. Except for me. Love was a bitter, cold bitch that I stayed far away from.

"So tell me more about you going on a date. An official date? The kind one has when they've first met someone they may be interested in getting to know, in case you don't remember what that is," she added.

"Ha ha. Real funny. Yes, I'm going on a date. Not a big deal. Just dinner."

Tripp and Aspen looked at one another and rolled their eyes.

"Bridge, when was the last time you were on an actual

date?"

"I go on dates all the time with my clients. What are you talking about?" I knew what they were talking about, but they didn't need to make it something it wasn't.

"That's work!" Tripp chided.

"It's more than work sometimes." I winked. He knew my sexual proclivities; they were the same as his. All work and no play made London a dull girl. I made certain there was never a dull moment between me and clients, especially the ones that were worthy of bedding.

"Fucking your clients or boy toys don't count and you know it!" he accused.

Aspen nodded and waved the waiter over.

"Martinis?" she asked us brusquely. Tripp and I nodded and then continued our heated glares. "We'll take two Stockholm seventy-fives, and I'll have iced tea," Aspen ordered.

"Very well, ma'am." The waiter scurried off with her order. It was strange that Aspen didn't order herself a drink. Before I could ask, she started in on the third degree.

"All joking aside. Who's the mystery man?" Aspen asked.

"You probably know him. Collier Stone."

"My lawyer?" she laughed. "That's rich!"

"No, you're rich. Collier's a sexy man who asked me on a date and I agreed. We're going out to dinner tonight."

Tripp and Aspen shared a knowing look. Tripp took a deep breath and then continued. "James Bond is hot, I'll give you that."

Aspen snorted at Tripp's nickname for Collier. "I haven't actually met him. I always work with his brother, Nate. But, are you ready for a real date?"

"You act like I haven't been with a man in ages. As a matter of fact, I had Dylan just last night."

"That's sex, not a relationship," she chastised.

"I don't do relationships." My tone was scathing, harsher than I intended.

Our drinks arrived, and Aspen took a healthy sip of her tea and continued, "Exactly our point."

"Look, guys, I know you're just trying to make sure I'm happy. Believe me, I am. Very much so. Collier asked me out. I said yes. At this point, I'm going to dinner with the guy, not marrying him." That reminded me of why we were having lunch today. "Speaking of marriage…you're getting married?"

My sister flung out her left hand and bright as the sun stood a huge diamond ring.

I gripped her hand to inspect it, and my body started to tingle. An all-encompassing tickling sensation ran up and down my spine. It was as powerful as full-body laughter or one of the most earth-shattering orgasms. You couldn't help but be swept away by it.

Instantly, I felt sheer joy pump off her like sound waves encasing me, lulling me into a happy stupor. She was throwing off some intense vibes. My empathic ability struggled to accept it all. Even when she admitted to being in love with Hank, it was never this concentrated. Something had changed. It was as if she was a giant force and anything that touched her couldn't help but be affected.

"Aspen, what's going on?"

"I'm getting married in five weeks!" she squealed like a five-year-old little girl, something I'd never seen her do. My sister was always in complete control.

"It's more than that. Why are you in such a rush? Just a couple months ago, you two were on the outs. Now you're rushing into marriage?"

Tripp's head volleyed from side to side, watching us. "Hank is the one pushing it. Not me." That was an odd admission, even for my sister, who tended to be brutally honest.

I rolled my eyes. She was being vague, and it annoyed the hell out of me. I watched her sip her tea almost nervously and stop making eye contact. She was hiding something. I knew my sister as well as I knew the backside of my hand.

"Out with it." I crossed my arms, tilted my head, and stared her down. I was prepared to wait all day if I had to.

She looked at me, then at Tripp, and bit her lip. "Okay fine." She took a deep breath and then blew me away with her next words. "I'm pregnant."

Tripp and I looked at one another, grabbed our glasses, clinked them together, and then swallowed our entire martini down in one go. It was how we dealt with crazy information. Knock one back when you don't know how else to deal with what life has served you.

"Now that…I didn't expect." I shook my head and smiled.

She watched us closely to gauge our reactions.

"Looks like we need more drinks, Bridge. You're going to be an auntie!" Tripp laughed.

"I can't wait," I said. Aspen clasped her hands together and took a deep breath, obviously worried what my reaction would be. "Just one favor, Pen. Just one is all I ask."

She looked puzzled. "Anything."

"Please let me be there when you tell Mom."

She threw her napkin at me, and we all howled with laughter. Our mother was a stuck-up mega beast who hated that Aspen and Hank were together. I could only imagine what she'd say when she found out they're getting married in five weeks. Add a baby to the mix? That's a whole new angle, and this information would send Mother into a manic-depressive state. I wanted front row seats to that show.

"You're terrible, Bridge!" Tripp grinned wickedly.

"No, our mother's terrible. Watching her face twist and contort when she hears her daughter is marrying a blue-collar man *and* pregnant with his baby…before the wedding! Oh seriously, Pen. I need to be there. I'll do anything!"

"Two things?" She tilted her head and grinned. "Be my maid of honor and decorate the baby's nursery in the penthouse, maybe even at the ranch, too?"

I jumped up and instead of sitting in Pen's lap like I always did—fear of crushing the baby prevented my usual antics—I hauled her into a great big hug in the middle of the restaurant. She squeezed me, and once again, I felt extreme happiness surrounding her. It sunk into every one of my pores, filling my dark with light.

"Can I pick my own dress?" She laughed, but I was dead serious. There was no way in hell I'd be wearing some ridiculous bridesmaid dress. We needed appointments with Vera Wang ASAP. It was a good thing I'd done her office design last year. I could pull a few strings.

"Whatever you want. It's going to be really simple though, London. Only you, Ollie, and my soon to be sister-in-law, Jess, on my side. On Hank's, it will be his brother, Heath. Also Dean and his best friend, Mac. We're getting married at Hank's ranch in Texas. I've hired a wedding planner to handle all the finite details. I do not have the time nor the desire to plan a wedding. I just want the man. Besides, *Bright Magazine* is going live the first of the year and there is so much to do before it launches. If Hank hadn't demanded we push up the wedding when we found out about the baby, we'd be doing all this next year."

"You sound stressed. That can't be good for the baby. How far along are you?"

She smiled and glowed a little when she pulled out a little black-and-white photo. "Officially, I'm eleven weeks. I'll be four months along by the time we get married. I have to find a dress that can hide a small bump if I have one by then." She clasped her hands over her belly thoughtfully.

My big sister was getting married and going to have a baby. Incredible. She was with the man of her dreams and was the happiest I'd ever seen her.

"Do you want to go look at dresses? I'll set up something with Vera. She owes me a favor."

"That would be heavenly. Thank you." She looked at her watch and stood. "I have to go. Meeting at two. Enjoy your evening with Collier. If he's anything like his brother Nate, he's a good guy. And if he's as good-looking as Nate and has the same accent? Wow. Gotta love a man with an accent, right, y'all?" Her joke was lame, referencing Hank's southern accent, but I appreciated how love can make you silly. Once upon a time, I, too, was a lovesick puppy. "Lunch and drinks on me. They have my tab. Enjoy!"

Tripp and I watched her leave. "Wow. That was unexpected news, eh, Bridge?"

"You're telling me. I barely digested the fact that she

was getting married, and she drops the baby bomb."

"She dropped the bomb on me…baby. She dropped the bomb on me… "Tripp sung and I chimed in.

Things were changing for the better for those around me. I wonder if Tripp and I could somehow carve out that chunk of happiness where we wouldn't be hurt anymore and we'd live happily ever after. We'd spent the last few years resigned to the fact that we were not the people who found happily ever after. We'd both actually believed the concept was more myth than reality. Aspen and Hank's Cinderella story changed that thought process. Besides, I'd been in love once, and it was ripped away prematurely. One day four years ago, my time ran out.

CHAPTER FOUR

London seemed like the kind of bird that fancied men who dressed to impress. The pitch-black suit jacket I'd pulled on made me feel like I had secured my armor and was ready for battle with a sexy vixen. I'd paired the jacket with light gray slacks, a white dress shirt, and a deep purple tie, making an additional effort for the evening.

Boy, did I want to impress her. The woman was more than beautiful. She was ethereal and unlike anyone I'd ever dated. Something about her called to me. It was more than the fact that she was the exact opposite of my ex-wife, Claire, a fact which made me appreciate her physical qualities even more.

Claire was definitely attractive and when we'd met in college, I chased her endlessly until she finally gave in. We dated for a year and then got married. I spent five years trying my best to make her happy. It was a valiant effort, one I lost miserably.

In the end, my work and lack of all-encompassing attention drove her away. She wanted the man who fawned over her boundlessly. I couldn't give her that and the lifestyle she required, on top of building Stone, Walker & Associates from the ground up. From the start, we were doomed. A woman like her could never be satisfied.

When all was said and done, she left me for a filthy rich man whose family had money and owned hotels across

Europe. Over the years, I'd heard a little about her through mutual friends we'd had while we were married. They claimed she wasn't happy and regretted her decision to end our marriage. It didn't matter. The damage had been done.

After I moved to the States, information became less forthcoming and now it was practically non-existent, an ideal situation to be in when I was contemplating starting something fresh and new for the first time since my marriage failed.

Before I headed out my phone pinged. It was a text from London.

To: Collier Stone
From: London Kelley
Something came up. I'll meet you at the restaurant. Text me the name. See you there.

After texting the name of the restaurant and the address, I made my way out of my flat and into the garage. I waved to the attendant and slipped into my beloved Porsche 911. Even its name implied a sense of urgency. When I'd seen the deep slate-blue paint, its sleek curved lines, I knew she had to be mine. A similar feeling came over me last week when the crowd thinned and I'd spotted Ms. Kelley at Maxwell's housewarming.

Making it out of the garage, I downshifted and the engine purred, as if it enjoyed the ride as much as I did.

When I reached the restaurant, the valet took my beloved. "Be nice, she bites," I warned the young man, who smiled widely. The kid probably enjoyed his job immensely, getting to park striking cars all evening and getting paid to do it. He couldn't have been a day over eighteen.

"Yes, Sir!" he answered and sped off with the love of my life. I sighed.

A glittering spot of light caught my eye down the street and I knew it was her. She was bent over paying the cab driver. Her legs seemed impossibly long in her short dress, even though she couldn't have been more than a few inches over five feet. She stood and her gaze caught mine. One delicate hand pulled her dark hair to the side then ran her fingers through it. I could have walked the thirty feet and escorted her but I stood still, watching her come to me. She made walking seem like an art form. It wasn't so much that she walked but rather glided down the sidewalk toward me.

The sheen off her skin dazzled and toyed with my vision. My hungry gaze swept over every bare expanse of skin, her graceful neck, bared arms, tanned thighs. Her breasts, high on her chest and rounded to perfection, were encased in a silver sequined cocktail dress. She looked smart and utterly edible.

Those blue-gray eyes twinkled when she stood in front of me. Even with ungodly tall heels, she still had to look up at me. It made me feel powerful, in charge, and protective over her much smaller frame.

"You look good enough to eat," I whispered into her ear as I leaned down to kiss her cheek.

"Shall we skip dinner then? Go right to dessert?" Her eyes held a challenge.

"Cheeky, are we, Ms. Kelley?" I clasped each bicep and swept my thumbs along her buttery soft skin. She smiled but didn't back down.

"Cheeky? I'm sure a bit of cheek is doable." She pursed

her lips and slid around me, toward the restaurant door. Her hand trailed skillfully along my waist as she went. Tremors zipped from my abdomen and to every neuron, filling me with energy and life. A simple touch had me primed at the ready, physically needing to shag her. If I wasn't careful, I'd be sporting a solid stiffy in no time. I took a deep breath and willed my body to relax.

I caught up to my raven-haired beauty and escorted her with a light touch to her back through the frosted glass doors. She felt warm and firm, and I imagined touching her skin to skin. I closed my eyes for a moment and took a breath, trying to calm my desire for the bird. Her mere presence wrecked me.

We were led to a quaint booth. The seat was high back and made of a rich dark purple velvet material. Tiered candles encased in purple mosaic glass ran along the edge in varying heights casting a lavender glow onto the white linen tablecloth. Crystal wineglasses were preset alongside heavy silver flatware. A piano sat across the room and a man in a tuxedo tinkered out a soft tune, accompanying a seated violinist. The music added to the luxurious theme.

"You okay? You seemed to have a moment back there?"

When we sat, my thigh grazed hers, sending bolts of electricity through me. I focused my attention on her eyes instead of the pulsating need that hummed just below the surface. "Your beauty astounds me. That's what happened back there." I covered the hand on top of her thigh. Her breath picked up and her eyes changed color. In this light, they looked a mossy green.

"Oh." She looked around. "Nice place."

"It is." I watched her features and something akin to

nerves seemed to preside over her mood.

"You come here often?"

"First time." I gave the room a once over. "Jane chose well."

"Jane?" Her question held a twinge of speculation.

"My secretary." I smiled and she returned it.

"Do you always have your secretary set up your dates?"

"Again, first time. I don't usually date."

"Me neither," she whispered. Her shoulders relaxed, and she moved her hand to clasp mine. Then her eyes widened. "Then we have something in common." I squeezed her hand, and she brought her other hand up to clasp both of mine. Her widened eyes marred the delicate soft features with hard edges. She held my focus and my hand as if it was a life raft and she was up to her neck in water.

The waiter arrived, but she didn't move, didn't release her grasp of my hand. If anything, she held it more tightly between her smaller ones. Her gaze never wavered from my face. The waiter must have noticed the tension because he averted his attention and quietly walked away.

"You were hurt by love," she said as if she simply stated the temperature outside. A gut-wrenching cold ripped through me at her words. How was she able to hit the nail so evenly on the head and cut me to my core? It was as if she had some type of magic or telepathic ability. Then it dawned on me. It took one to know one. I knew it as well as I knew my own pain. I could see it cross her eyes, briefly, but it had been there. She expertly masked it to focus on me.

"As were you." It wasn't a question but rather a statement of fact. Instinctively, my heart knew I'd met a kindred spirit. Someone who understood what it felt like to lose everything you ever held dear.

She stared into my eyes. The shadow of hurt that lay beyond those crystal depths was staggering. In that moment, she was the most striking woman I had ever known. Then, she bared her soul with a simple nod of her head.

Leaning forward, I pulled my free hand up to her neck. With the tips of my fingers, I traced the long column of her neck from her ear down to the flimsy strap at her shoulder holding up her dress. She shuddered and gasped at my touch. My hand wove into the thick dark mane of hair at her nape. Her gaze traced each of my features, jumping from my eyes to my lips and back.

With my mouth close to hers, my breath fanning her face, I whispered, "Never again."

She closed her eyes as if she was about to pray. Then I kissed her.

It didn't matter where we were or that we were surrounded by a room full of people. All that mattered was this woman, this moment, this need to connect with her.

Her lips were as soft as the petals of a rose and just as moist. As I kissed her, one of her hands left mine and glided along the side of my face, from my temple to the dip in my chin. She opened her lips just enough for our tongues to graze one another's in a sensual flirtatious dance. She smelled of cinnamon but tasted of mint tea. With one more press of my lips to hers, I grudgingly pulled back. Her eyes stayed closed for a moment until someone cleared their throat and startled us both.

"Excuse me," the waiter said and I chuckled. Back home the British only said "Excuse me" when they belched. Same goes for "pardon me," only that phrase meant one has passed gas. It cracked me up how Americans were always talking about their digestive tracks. It took Nathaniel and I months to figure out they weren't constantly apologizing for burping and farting. To this day, it is endless entertainment. "Would you like to start with something to drink? See the wine list perhaps?" The nice fellow in a white sport coat handed me a book rather than a list. It was filled with the wine they offered.

"Beauty, do you have a preference?" She smiled at the nickname I had inadvertently given her. I always used a man or woman's God-given name. With her, the pet name just popped out. And boy did it fit bloody well.

"Actually, I had martinis with Tripp earlier. I'd like a cosmo, please." She handed the wine book back to the waiter.

"And for you, sir?"

"There is obviously no need to impress the lady with my lack of wine knowledge." She giggled and shook her head. "I'll go the unpretentious route and order a glass of your house cabernet."

"As you wish, sir. I'll be back momentarily with your drinks and to take your order."

London and I reviewed the menu in a comfortable silence. "So have you decided what you fancy eating?"

She twisted her lips, grabbed a lock of her hair, and twirled it around her finger as she studied the menu, deep in thought. The act was so naughty schoolgirl it triggered my shaft like a beacon. I warred with my thoughts, trying to get the idea of shagging her out of my mind for the hundredth time this evening.

"I think I'll go with the filet." She nodded and then

snapped the menu shut. She caught me staring at her. "What?"

"Oh love, you break me with your beauty."

★ ★ ★

I leaned over and whispered into his ear, making sure to trail my lips along the curl of flesh. "You know, I'm a sure thing tonight. You don't have to keep complimenting me." Purposely I placed my lips just under his ear and licked the salty skin there.

He sighed and stiffened. Pure lust poured off him like a tsunami ready to hit shore. It soaked into my pores and made wetness pool between my thighs. There was nothing that was going to prevent me from drowning in him tonight. With one last drag of my lips along the tender skin of his neck, I told him what I'd been dying to say to him since we met. "I want you."

"Shite." The word slipped from his lips as he adjusted his pants. I looked around and it seemed everyone was in a world of their own. The tables were tall with long drapes that fell over our laps. No one could really see what I was about to do. In a bold move, I placed my hand on his thigh and slid it up to cup and fondle his package. The desire to touch him intimately was overwhelming.

"Christ, beauty, you'll be the end of me." He thrust his hips against my wandering hand. My fingers reached deep between his legs to cup his balls through the texture of his slacks and rub him from root to tip and back down. In this position, his cock was thick and long, reaching up to his waistband. My mouth watered, wanting, no *needing* to taste him.

"God, I want to taste you."

"Shite, woman. You're sex on a stick!" He gritted his teeth then buried his face into the crook of my neck, breathing heavily and nibbling on the skin he found there. I continued to rub him over and over, effectively making him insane with lust. A litany of small groans left his lips as he thrust several times against my palm. I had the Englishman exactly where I wanted him. Too soon, the waiter approached with our drinks.

Immediately I backed off and his lust-filled eyes cleared. The caramel brown in them swirled. He ran both hands through his wheat-colored hair. It landed in sexy layers against his scalp and reminded me of bed hair after a good hard night of fucking.

The waiter took our order, and we spent the rest of dinner making small talk, learning more about each other. The sexual tension between us never left, just simmered, steadily bubbling just under the surface.

I learned he was obsessed with rugby and watched it on the telly late into the evenings. He preferred live games, but they were few and far between in the States.

I shared my affliction for sexy shoes, colorful fabrics, and my love of anything handmade and artistic. He seemed to appreciate that most, asking questions about things I mentioned and wondering what museums I preferred.

"Why do you do what you do?" he asked out of the blue.

"What do you mean? Interior design?"

He nodded.

"Well, it seemed to fit. I've always had a knack for entering someone's home and intuitively knowing how the furniture should be re-arranged to maximize space. Colors and textures are fun to play off one another, but the real fun…"

His eyes twinkled as he focused intently on me.

"The real fun is learning what it is people need in their life besides the design. If the home needs the new look, usually it's the man, woman, or couple that needs the resurfacing."

"How so?" He took my hand and made endless infinity doodles on the top and wrist.

God, he's sexy.

"People have an innate inability to not do right by themselves. Sure, there are egotistical people out in the world who are very 'what's in it for me,' but usually they're hiding their insecurity over something else. Sometimes a person stays at a job for the money, not for the love of the work. It depends on the person."

"So you move into their flat to learn about them personally along with their likes and dislikes for the design aspect?"

I nodded eagerly. "Exactly. When I move in with them, I have an 'in the trenches view' of how they live their life, what makes them tick, what hurts them, what heals them. I work with them to see those things themselves and make the required changes. On top of that, I give them a new look and feel on their home. Kind of like stepping into a new world, or at least a new lease on life."

"That's blooming incredible. The way you see things is fascinating." His head shook, but his eyes blazed with intensity. He licked his lips and bit down on the plump flesh.

I closed my eyes and took a deep breath to let his

emotions trace over my senses.

"You're not so bad yourself." I placed my napkin over my plate signifying that I was ready to leave, take this party somewhere more private. He'd been sending me sex-laced vibes all evening. I'd had enough.

When he'd paid the check and we stood, a brief moment of uncertainty came over me. This was the point where we moved forward or turned back. I'd wanted him to make that choice, not let my oversexed mind make that decision. He led me to the street and handed his ticket to the valet.

I stood clutching my handbag and looked around, not sure what he intended. Would he take me home or want to go to his place? I knew I hadn't read him wrong. The man wanted me. The bulge in his pants through most of dinner confirmed it.

Two hands came around my waist from behind, and he pulled me back against his solid chest. "Penny for your thoughts, my beauty." His nickname for me was sweet. I found I rather enjoyed it, made me feel special somehow. Besides Tripp, the only other man who had ever given me an intimate pet name was James.

James. I pushed the thought of him to the furthest recesses of my mind. Nothing good would come of bringing up that wound now—especially when I was about to get me some of a hot Englishman.

"Just wondering what happens next?" My voice was smooth and strong, hiding the fact that I was actually somewhat nervous he'd reject me.

"We go back to my place where I plan to shag you for hours. Then I'll make you breakfast come sun up." He gripped me against him, my back to his front. The steel of his erection pressed against the heat of my ass.

"And what if I want you to take me home?" I teased, but in a serious tone to keep up the charade.

He growled into my ear, fingers digging into the flesh at my hips. "Then I'll take you home and shag you for hours at your place where your roommate can hear how many times I make you scream. Then *you'll* make me breakfast at sun up."

"Your place, please," I confirmed, though, it could have been mistaken for begging.

"Oh, beauty, the ways in which I'm going to make you come…I can hardly wait." He thrust his rod against my ass. His heat left when the valet strolled around one of the most beautiful cars I'd ever seen and handed him the keys. It was a grayish-blue Porsche. I knew that much. It had only two doors, and he opened the door for me like a gentleman. I slid in, enjoying the feel of the cool dark gray leather against my fiery skin.

"This is a hot car."

He looked at me, a sexy grin plastered on his handsome face. "Isn't she?"

"She?"

"But, of course!" he continued excitedly. "All cars are female, that's why men are so gobsmacked by them."

"Gobsmacked? You come up with the most interesting choice of words."

"That's because I speak proper English, my beauty." His tone was light and filled with humor.

"And I don't?"

"Not even close." He laughed. I opened my mouth but he continued. "Actually, gobsmacked is a British slang term for amazed or astonished."

"See, I knew it!" We both laughed.

Collier was more than just a fine male specimen. He was funny, easy to be around and his British accent brought me to my knees. The moment we had in the restaurant worried me though. I'd not felt connected to a man on that level since James. It was confounding.

It's that second when a man looks into your eyes and not only sees your soul, but identifies with it, a rare connection of two persons who were fated to meet, to know one another intimately. It dawned on me. I was so ready to jump into bed with him, not because I needed sex—I'd had it pretty recently with Dylan and never lacked for a willing participant. It wasn't the physical contact that had me hanging on Collier's every word or mindlessly touching him in subtle innocent ways. It was the buzzing and thrumming, the halo of light I felt moving in the air around him. It sucked me into its vortex and I wasn't prepared to leave until I'd gotten my fill and understood why it had a hold on me.

"Having second thoughts?" Collier asked, concern evident in his tone.

"What? Uh, no. Not at all. Just thinking about what happened in the restaurant. That doesn't usually happen to me. Well, actually that's not true. It happens all the time, me, being able to feel and empathize with others emotions, but it doesn't usually mirror my own."

He took a deep breath, ending it with a sigh. "Yeah, that was a bit peculiar but not altogether uncomfortable. At least for me, anyway. I've had a long time to accept the things that hurt me in my life. Now it's just a matter of getting past them."

"Is it too soon to ask who she was?"

He smiled and brushed his fingers though his hair. "It's not too soon. It's just not pleasant."

"I understand if you don't want to tell me." Mentally, I chided myself. I shouldn't have asked something so personal so quickly. Damn curiosity.

"No, no, it's okay. It's not a secret. I was married just out of college. Did everything I thought was right. Worked hard, tried to give her all she ever wanted. Started a company with my brother, Nathaniel. You know him." I nodded but didn't want to interrupt for fear he wouldn't continue. "I was loyal and I loved her. Probably more than a man should." He stopped talking and shook his head.

"Then what happened?" My voice was soft and sympathetic.

"It wasn't enough. She found someone with more money and more time. Left me for the bloke. Been about five years now."

"I'm sorry." There really wasn't anything more I could say. The man had been cheated on by the woman he loved.

"It's life. It is what it is." He brought his hand to cover mine in my lap. Immediately the sizzle and thump of our connection leapt from my hand to my heart, filling it with something I couldn't define. "What about you?" His voice was soft.

"What about me?"

"What sort of daft bastard would leave a bird as lovely as you?" He squeezed my hand reassuringly.

"He didn't mean to leave me. He died."

Normally when a man finds out I'm a widow at

twenty-six, he has a freak-out moment, one in which he either decides the waters to this woman's bed are too treacherous to wade, then bails. Or the alternative: offering me a sympathy fuck to make me feel better. Neither is desirable. After years of dating, I realized men just couldn't deal with the fact that I didn't choose to leave the man I married, nor did he choose to leave me. It was decided by an innocent but tragic accident, which left me unwilling and incapable of loving another ever again. That part of me died when my husband died.

"I see," he said.

Quietly, we both chewed over the thoughts, a heavy brew based on the information we'd both shared. The air around us was thick with tension.

Finally he asked, "So what happened to your husband?"

I liked that he referred to James as my husband. It reinforced the importance of that relationship even though he was gone.

Collier had a way about him that put me at ease. Usually, I refrained from telling people about James. Tripp was constantly telling me I had to let it out, let the ghost of James rest. Maybe this would put me one step closer.

I took a deep, calming breath. Collier waited patiently, eyes glued to the road ahead. Not looking in his eyes made it easier to share somehow.

"It was raining out. The first rain of the year. The pungent scent of the newly wet roads in New York City was stifling. I remember the humidity being unbearable. James was driving home from work. His car was T-boned at a light. The driver lost control of the vehicle; bad tires with little tread didn't stick on the slick oily streets. It catapulted the car into cross traffic."

"Was the driver bombed?"

I shook my head. "No. He was sixteen. Just got his driver's license. It was his first time on the road by himself. He was driving home from studying at a friend's house. He didn't have a drop to drink."

"Was it instant?"

"Unfortunately, no. The accident broke a lot of his bones, did a great amount of damage internally, but all that could have been cured. What couldn't was his liver. He needed an immediate transplant, but one didn't become available in time. He died within forty-eight hours of arriving at the hospital."

"In my experience, beauty, it's better to have loved and lost than to have never loved at all. Our past makes us who we are today. I, for one, think you're incredible." He said it with all the conviction of a man who'd gone through it himself, which I now knew he had.

It was refreshing. Collier didn't apologize for my loss. He didn't tell me that everything would be okay or look at me as if I were a broken woman. His brown eyes gleamed with understanding. Like he'd said to me, when he reiterated his tale, it is what it is and he truly believed that. We couldn't change what the universe doled out to us, but what we could change was how we dealt with that experience.

"You're a wise man, Collier Stone."

"Indeed." He waggled his eyebrows, breaking the serious mood. "You still want to stay the evening with this wise-arse, I mean wise man?" He chuckled and I laughed with him. He was good for me. At least for tonight he would be.

"More than anything."

CHAPTER FIVE

After parking the car and taking the lift to my flat, a bit of melancholy wafted in the air. Her admission about losing her husband had been tough on her. I wondered how many people she'd told the story to. By how she was responding now, not many.

She stood ramrod straight. Desire drove her to follow me, but the walls she'd dropped during dinner were firmly back up. It would be my duty to drive the wrecking ball through them and bring her back to the present. In order to do so, I was going to be bold. This woman demanded a hefty dose of truth. It wasn't hard to tell that she dealt in honesty and no bullshit. She wasn't expecting or wanting prophetic love declarations. Physical release was clearly the only item on the evening's agenda.

For now, I was on board with that plan, knowing it would never do in the long run.

Recently, settling down again, stopping the vicious circle of bedding dozens of women, rarely ever the same woman twice, was what I was after. No longer was I interested in one-night stands or women who were disposable. It hurt my pride even knowing how I'd treated too many lovely ladies as a mere shag, just a tool to get my jollies off. A change would occur now and regardless of what London said, she responded to me. Her body responded to me. Her mind responded to me. Now I'd work to get her soul to respond.

We entered my flat, and she set her things down on the leather couch. Hands on hips, she turned her head, those gray-blue eyes assessing what little I had to offer in my living space. The apartment was large with a wall of windows that overlooked the city. There wasn't anything hanging on the walls aside from a flat-screen TV. The couches were black leather and barely used. I never entertained here. With all of the women I'd bedded, she was the first I brought home. Seeing her scope out the space almost made me regret the decision.

She turned around and her cool gaze held mine. That pink tongue slid along her lips, making them glisten enticingly. After taking a long look around, she cocked her head to the side. "You need me."

Those words were a powerful aphrodisiac, going straight to my cock. With both hands, I shuffled my fingers through my hair, a nervous habit I'd picked up during long hours in law school. "Indeed."

She glided toward me, one foot in front of the other, almost predatory. Without missing a stride, her fingers slipped under each tiny sparkling strap at her shoulders, pulled, and then her sliver of a dress slipped to the floor as if a million tiny stars rained down from the sky all at once.

A guttural growl escaped my lungs as she stalked toward me in nothing but a strapless white bra and high-cut panties. I bit the inside of my cheek to the point of pain, trying to keep my inner Neanderthal in check.

The desire to push her into a fireman's over the shoulder hold, rush her to my bed, and throw her down and make her mine was strong. Slow deep breaths. *Get it under control,* I reminded myself, though I had a sneaking suspicion she wanted to catch me off guard. This woman liked being in charge. Maybe it had to do with losing her mate so suddenly and outside of her control.

"You need me in more ways than one," she said, referring to my lack of creature comforts and the hardening shaft tenting my trousers. She trailed her index finger down my chest to the thick buckle at the top of my slacks.

I nodded and placed my hands on her barely existent waist. She was so tiny.

Nimble fingers loosened the tie around my neck. It fell to the floor in a wisp of fabric. With excruciating measures, she drew out the task of unbuttoning my shirt. Smooth lips trailed light kisses along each new expanse of skin she exposed. With a little effort, she tugged and pulled my shirt from the tuck in my trousers. Cool fingers slid against the bare skin of my abdomen, continuing their journey over my pecks and shoulders. The fabric seemed to float away and fall to the floor.

"You're beautiful." Her lust-filled eyes took in every inch of my skin. Her tongue retraced the same path.

"Isn't that my line?" I laughed, but it was cut off with a moan as her teeth bit down on the tender flesh of my nipple.

"Christ, beauty," I whispered as she twirled her tongue around the peak, soothing the ache. Tunneling my fingers into the hair at her nape, anchoring her chin with both thumbs, I lifted her head to mine. Unmasked desire shone bright in her blue eyes. "I want you," I admitted, swiping my thumb against her plump bottom lip. She pulled the digit into her mouth and swirled her tongue around it.

A fresh wave of heat ripped through me, making the

steel rod in my pants even harder. I thrust my hips against hers and she gasped.

"Then take me," she challenged.

"Not here."

She cringed at my words.

"I want to enjoy you. Gorge on this body until we're both gasping for air, and you're begging for me to stop."

Her eyes widened and then closed. In one swoop, I scooped her up. She weighed next to nothing. Her mouth attached to the skin of my neck as I brought her to my room and laid her in the center of the bed.

She was stunning. A work of art. Her tanned skin against the stark white of her lace underthings was right out of a Rorschach inkblot test. The black waves of her hair fell dark as night against the gray of my duvet. Those eyes. Shite, those eyes of hers beckoned me as I slid off my belt and shoved the straining fabric of my trousers down. I stood at the edge of the bed and surveyed her gorgeous form in nothing but my jockeys.

She leaned up, her chest puffing out in a full-body inhale, breasts straining against the fabric. "Now that you have me here, what are you going to do with me?" The coy remark was playful yet needy.

"Ravish you. I want to become intimately familiar with every inch of your beautiful body, starting right…here." I leaned over and picked up one dainty ankle. She had a tiny chain encircling the delicate bone. I ran my lips against the chain, tugging it with my teeth. Her eyes glowed in the low light of the room as she watched me trail my tongue along the side of her small foot. I nipped and kissed each one of her red-tipped toes. Taking my time, I placed long drawn-out kisses against the skin of her calf.

Her eyes fell closed and gooseflesh rose to the surface of her skin when I licked the crevice behind her knee, a sensitive spot I promised myself to explore more fully later. Repeating the process with the other leg, I continued my journey, rubbing my lips along the silky expanse of her toned thigh.

Her legs shook as I sucked and bit the fleshy patch of skin just under where the top of her thigh and her sex met. She mewled and shimmied her hips. Long fingers tunneled into my hair as I feasted on that spot. That cinnamon smell that was uniquely her swirled all around me as if I was bathing in the scent. It was so strong on her bare skin.

When I'd made a quarter-sized cherry-red mark in *my spot,* I happily moved on to the Promised Land. With great care, I slipped my fingers into the sides of her lacy knickers, dragged them down, and off her legs.

Thank God I hadn't removed them prior to enjoying her long legs and scrumptious hips. I'd have never completed. To my extreme pleasure, her mound was completely bare. Not a speck of hair tainted its surface. She restlessly moved her legs from side to side. I longed to see her, uncovered and open to me.

"Let me see." Her eyes met mine in warning as I placed the palms of my hands on her knees. Something in her changed. She relaxed and with a firm grip, I massaged down the insides of her honey-colored thighs until I had her spread before me. A veritable feast waiting to be devoured. I could feel her muscles strain against my hold, but I wasn't having it.

This was honest. Her baring it all for *me.* The petals of

her sex glistened with arousal. Her spicy scent was strong. The banquet before had me starved, salivating, ready to feast. With a well-placed tongue, I licked her from her pink rosette all the way to her hooded nub. It peeked out between her wet lips, and I zeroed in on that spot as if shooting an arrow directly in the center of a bull's-eye. Clamping my lips over it, I hollowed my cheeks and sucked. Hard. Relentless lashes from my tongue had her screaming as her first orgasm ripped through her.

"You're enchanting," I whispered against her thigh, kissing my mark on her skin as she calmed down. Once those beautiful eyes opened, half-hooded, she peered over the large mounds of her breasts. That's when I started to enjoy her again.

Always was a greedy man, one taste wasn't even close to enough.

She tugged on my hair and tried to pull me up, probably really sensitive. I didn't care. I wanted her out of her mind. "Collier," she said, breathing hard. "Oh, God…mmm." I delved my tongue deep into her core. She tasted like the finest, sweetest cream. Her head fell back, and her hands came up to cup and squeeze her breasts through her bra.

"Show me."

She looked at me as I sat up, changing my position. Within seconds, I was two fingers deep in her wet heat, my thumb circling the tight knot of her pleasure. She lifted on her elbows, her gaze focused between her legs. For a minute, she tipped her hips up and circled them around and around pressing against my hand, pushing me deeper into her body.

"Oh yes, shite, that's good," I encouraged her.

She licked her lips and held herself up, braced on one

hand as the other bent behind her. All the while, I continued fucking her with my fingers. Her white bra slacked, and she pulled it off and threw it aside. Her breasts were full and large, a perfect handful with rosy tips that seemed to tighten the more my gaze devoured them.

She held herself in a semi-seated position, her body rocking effortlessly against my hand. "Kiss me," she said, quite breathless. Her hips lifted and she moaned when I added a third finger into her tight channel. "God, it's never been like this. So, shit, so—"

"Passionate," I finished her sentence before I took her lips.

I was surrounded by cinnamon and sweet, uncertain which I liked more. The sugary taste of her tongue as it tangled with mine sent me spiraling. With my fingers burrowed into her core, I hooked those three digits up to rub against the bumpy patch along her internal wall.

She went crazy. Gripping me, biting my lips, scoring my back with her nails. I didn't stop. Couldn't. Hearing her blast into her second orgasm by my hand alone was like a healing balm to my soul, righting all the wrongs of the past few years. All the one-night stands were gone from existence. Now it was just her.

I vowed in that moment as her body trembled and shook that she would never be a mindless shag. This was something more.

She was different.

★ ★ ★

I spiraled into the abyss a second time. At first, I was scared. This felt like nothing I'd ever experienced. I didn't fear because Collier's warm body encased mine as I fell back against the sheets. He swept his hands up and down my naked back, hips, and thighs as I panted into his rock-solid chest. Who knew the man had the body of a Greek god under those suits? I had an inkling he was built, but the surprise of just how lovely he was bare was a gift I enjoyed unwrapping.

His chest was broad and tapered into a perfect "V" shape. The abs…God, his abs were like parking curbs, perfectly spaced and ready for me to park my lips and tongue.

As my breathing slowed, I thought about what had transpired. We hadn't gotten to the main event yet, and the score was two and zero, with me leading in orgasms and Collier falling behind. This was new territory for me. Usually I was the one who took charge, controlled the man into doing whatever I wanted.

With Collier, relinquishing control came without a second thought. What was most mind-boggling was what I could feel and sense in his emotions. He was happy, even elated that he pleased me. He wasn't boasting, bragging, or requiring I reciprocate. He just held me tight, perfectly warm and safe within the comfort of his strong arms as the fire he'd lit dissipated.

It made me feel sad and disjointed that the smaller Brit wasn't getting any attention. I knew I needed, *no wanted*, to rectify that situation. It was time for me to level the playing field.

I started by kissing my way up his chest. He shifted, allowing me to flop a leg over his hip and push him on his back. He groaned.

Teasingly, I sat over his length and used my hips to thrust

up and down against his ridged member, coating his boxer briefs with the wetness between my thighs. His fingers dug into the sides of my hips as he rocked forward, pressing that long erection perfectly against my oversensitive clit.

Before I could I take over, one of his hands cupped my breast and the other dived between my thighs, circling that talented thumb around my clit once more. Shivers ripped through me, and I arched into his hand. As I tipped my head, my hair fell in tumbling waves along the bare skin of my back.

"So perfect," he whispered, then leaned up and took my nipple between his lips. The warmth spread through me, centered at my heart, then bled through every neuron and pore until it turned into the most pleasurable tingles. He was perfectly content to take his time, spread out the pleasure instead of racing towards the finish line. I respected that but I needed him. Wanted to fill my body with his essence.

I shook my head, but he continued to nibble and pull with his lips, elongating my nipple into a wickedly tight, sensitive peak. His tongue flicked the tip in maddening whirls, his other hand moved to its twin, mimicking the movement of his mouth with his fingers. In seconds, he had me wanton, grinding my sex against his cock.

"I need you inside," I pulled his mouth away from my breast and searched his eyes. The brown and sparkling gold flecks I saw earlier were replaced with dark pools I'd willingly drown in. He was as far gone as I was.

"Condom?" I questioned, breaking through his haze. He gripped me to him, reached one long arm out, and riffled through a side table drawer. I grabbed the foil packet and kissed my way down his long body.

Taking just a moment before I undid my present, I nudged my cheek along the fabric of his boxer briefs, inhaling his musky scent through the material. His hips jumped. I swept my hand over the hard bulge between his thighs, tracing its length, driving him insane with lust. He hissed and his hands tightened into fists at his sides. The emotions he emitted pounded the air around us, hitting me with immense pleasure. It was like rolling around naked in Egyptian cotton. Smooth. Delectable. Enchanting.

I could feel his desire, his lust. It consumed him and was about to be released onto me. This was why I sought sexual relief so often. Being empathic and able to share in this experience on a completely visceral level was earth-shattering. With Collier, the feelings were heightened a million times over, ready to explode into something I'd not experienced, or at least I hadn't in a very long time.

Pulling his boxer briefs down his long muscled legs, I made quick work of sliding the condom over his impressive length. I stroked him a few times, becoming more familiar with this sensual piece of him. The man was scrumptious everywhere. I knew he was going to feel good buried deep inside me. Choosing to draw it out, I thumbed the wide crown, enjoying the surge of heat and wetness that seeped between my legs when he moaned.

"Any more of that, beauty, and we'll be over before we've begun," he warned. "Come here. Bring those sweet lips to mine."

I crawled up his body and took his mouth. He still tasted of the berry notes from the wine and something a little darker, richer. He sucked my tongue and nibbled my lips. "Now, my beauty. You take me," he offered.

I shook my head and stared deep into his dark eyes. "Together."

His tongue swirled with mine, and then he went deep, kissing me with intent and fervor. His wet, dizzying kisses held promises of things to come, things I knew I wasn't ready for, but I dived in anyway, giving as much as he gave. Then his hand slipped between us and I leaned up.

Our eyes met when he centered his cock at my entrance. I pushed the first inch in and we both gasped. As his fingers tightened around my hips, I pushed down and he pushed up. The moment our bodies met and he was seated completely inside of me, tears sprung to my eyes. I hadn't cried during sex since my wedding night. *What the hell was he doing to me?*

I looked down at Collier, and he was holding himself stiff as a board. The tendons in his neck stood out, strained tight with the effort not to move. The death grip he had on my hips stung, but wasn't hard enough to bruise, just tight enough to hold me in place. The muscles of his abs were bunched, coiled, and ready to thrust. Everything about him was strung tight, honed in on the target between his legs. He was glorious in his nudity, downright magnificent.

After a couple breaths, he opened his eyes. They shone so bright it almost hurt to look at them. "You're divine," he whispered. I closed my eyes, letting the feeling of complete and utter bliss sink into every pore. Then I lifted slowly, dragging his length along the walls within. When I got to the top, I opened my eyes, smiled wide, and slammed down his shaft, forcing him as deep as the position would allow.

"Shite!" he cried out as tears fell down my face. "You little minx. My turn." With a couple quick movements, I was on my back and under his large body. His lips came down for a scorching kiss as he pulled back and plunged into my core over and over. A fine sheen of sweat broke across his hairline and chest making him slick and salty. I licked the length of his neck, biting the tendons there. He groaned, hooked my right leg up and over the crook of his elbow until he could hold my leg behind the knee with his palm. He pressed it up and toward my shoulder.

"I want to crawl inside of your perfect body," he said on a particularly deep thrust. The new position opened my body fully and he ground deeper into me, bumping against the walls of my cervix, touching me in unchartered places. A fire built deep within and started to spread out to each of my limbs. I was burning from the inside out. He was the fire.

"Never again," he grated through his teeth on another brutal thrust to be farther inside me than anyone before him. I moaned in response, completely taken away with his need to take me, mark me, make me his.

"As long as we're together like this"—he gasped and ground his pelvis against my throbbing clit, sending sparks in every direction—"we'll never feel alone again." He said it as if it was a promise, a benediction. As he pounded into me, pouring every ounce of affection and desire into his thrusts, I knew he meant it.

I went screaming over the edge, calling out his name, begging for him to take me, take me away from it all… life, heartache, the grief over missing James. Everything. He made it all go away. And in that moment, his body turned rigid, and he bit down on my shoulder, teeth piercing skin. I climaxed again, taken by his primal response. It wasn't just the release of his body—it was the release of his essence.

In a heap of limbs and naked skin, his soul made me a

promise. One I didn't know if I could return.

Much later, we were still in bed, sated and spent. His tongue made lazy circles around the mark he left on my shoulder. A perfect set of tiny imprints in the shape of teeth marks made two small half-moons that didn't quite meet at the ends on the rounded skin. I would be wearing shoulder-covering attire for the next couple weeks. The thought made me smile.

A little marred skin was a small price to pay for four mind-altering orgasms.

He definitely wasn't all talk. By the time I was coming off my fourth orgasm, I begged him to stop. I physically had to remove his mouth from my left nipple, but not before allowing him to kiss and suckle its mate. He had a theory about things needing to be balanced.

Collier held me close, and I snuggled just under his chin. The crook of his neck smelled so yummy. He was all musky, with hints of sex and sandalwood. I lay there wondering what tomorrow would bring. I had to go back to the job. Back to my client…*Dylan*.

"I can feel you thinking."

I smiled against his neck.

"I thought I'd shagged all thoughts out of you for the night." His hand slid between my legs. Immediately I started to moisten. Two of his fingers stroked my clit in a small circle. "Looks like you need another go. I want you completely mindless, thinking of nothing but our brilliant night together."

He slid down my body, and I sighed and stretched my legs. He parted them and went to work on me with his tongue. I could get used to this.

"Your taste…" *Lick*. "It's like…mmm…" *Lick*. "The most decadent dessert."

In minutes, he had me arching, slamming my thighs around his ears. He held my legs apart, using his strong arms to keep me splayed open for him. As promised, he ravished me. Between his tongue, lips, teeth, and his fingers, I lost track of how many times the tight-assed Englishman made me come, the pleasure rolling them into one another so fast it was like one long drawn out peak. After what could have been hours of pleasing me, he finally entered me again. A full-body sigh of relief settled over me when we were connected. He had held himself off for a long time this round.

"Use me. Oh God, Collier, please, please use me. Find your pleasure in me," I begged and finally, he listened. He plunged into me with deep, hard strokes. He was relentless, seeking his release.

Holding my face between both his hands, his tongue sought mine. With a deep growl, he surged and came. His body heaved and wound tight as he shook and trembled. I held onto him with everything I had, whispering words of affection against his temple as he came down.

"London, I…I n-never knew it could be like this." The words choked and broke as he breathed against my sweat-dampened hair.

"I know. I didn't either." Instead of drowning in the negative aspects of how much of myself I gave to Collier tonight, I just held him close. Before long, sleep took us both.

The morning brought another round of intense sex.

Me lying on my stomach while he nipped and bit the fleshy skin of my ass. Then he entered me from behind. Collier was a talented lover, stroking my clit as he pounded his length into me. One hand held the tender column of my neck from behind while the other was anchored to my clit, pressing, circling, flicking until I lost it and came. My voice was raspy from sleep and last night's sexcapades. A hoarse cry spilled from him. A few more deep strokes and he, too, came, his body falling over my back.

"Bloody brilliant," he said, trying to catch his breath.

I smiled and giggled.

"Best way to wake up, thank you." I turned my head and he kissed me.

"Agreed." He lifted up, tied off the condom, and tossed it in the trash near the bed.

I wondered if he threw out his own trash or would an unlucky maid find proof of our night of debauchery.

He smacked my ass and I whooped. "I'm going to hop in the shower. Then I'll make you some tea and biscuits."

"How very English of you," I joked.

He smiled and entered the bathroom, leaving the door wide open.

If that wasn't an invitation to join him, I didn't know what was. I debated a few minutes but chose to enjoy stretching out my sore overused limbs in his bed that smelled of him and sex. Two of my newest favorite smells.

He came out of the bathroom with a towel draped low on his hips. Water dripped down his chest and it took everything I had not to jump out of bed and lick them off. Lucky droplets. Before I made my decision, he pulled the duvet off my naked body. He whistled as his eyes scoured every inch of my bare skin.

"Feel free to use the shower while I start breakfast." He turned to go through a door next to his dresser. I assumed it was the closet, but I hadn't spent much time checking out his house when we arrived last night, preferring to check him out instead.

I took an extra long time in the shower, letting the heat loosen up my muscles. Looking down I did a survey of my body. Shit. I was littered with reminders of our night together. Bite marks, finger print sized bruises on my thighs and hips. This was going to put a damper on me bedding Dylan this week. Though after last night, with Collier, I wasn't sure I wanted to continue screwing around with Dylan. The boy was good in bed, but he was a boy compared to my Englishman. Jesus, I lost count at how many times we pleased each other last night and then again this morning. As much as I didn't want to admit, it was more than the physical.

Confused, I scrubbed my body clean while my mind felt twisted and dirty. For the first time in four years, I didn't want to have sex with anyone else. Last night with Collier, something clicked, like a deadbolt locking into place. The tide had shifted and the beach was scattered with remnants of what once was normal for me. Fear and uncertainty filled my thoughts.

Normal. What was normal? Being with a variety of men, having a good time with whomever I wanted to on a whim? Yes, that was normal. Now it seemed as though my normal was obliterated. Shattered into a million tiny pieces. Still, I had no idea how to handle it. It was one night. I was still me. London Kelley.

I couldn't deny that something happened last night, putting a chink in my armor. What I experienced with Collier was beyond anything I'd ever felt with another man, including my husband James. And I loved him with my entire body and soul. So why did I have a sinking feeling in my chest like I'd cheated on James? He's been dead for more than a few years now. He wanted me to move on. He told me to find someone else. To fall in love again. He said it right before he took his last breath, "Someday, London, you will love again." I needed to get out of here. Think this over. Figure out what took place last night.

After I dried off, I slipped into one of Collier's clean dress shirts and my underwear. My dress was in a heap on the floor in the living room. If I went out there naked, it sent a message that I was ready for more and right now, where my mind was at, I knew I needed to be alone.

Collier, however, had other plans.

"Oh, beauty, come sit down. Have some tea and a biscuit." He really did have honest to God tea and biscuits, which he delivered on a very traditional English-style tea set with a saucer and small teacup. The biscuits were actually cookies.

"I thought you were kidding," I joked.

"Us English chaps never joke about tea. It's sacrilege." He turned and with a whip of a spatula, turned over four fried eggs. Bacon sizzled in a pan next to the eggs. With a stretch of his arm, he pressed two slices of bread down in a toaster. Fascinated, I watched him work.

Never before had a man I slept with made me breakfast, aside from Tripp, and he didn't really count. Technically, I hadn't shared a bed for the night with any of my previous conquests. Once the sex had finished, I'd leave their apartment or they'd leave mine. Even with my clients, I'd get up and sleep in the bed assigned to me, not wanting the intimacy of sharing a bed with a fling.

Collier set a steaming plate in front of me. "Do you like marmalade?"

I nodded, and he spread some of the orange jelly substance along a piece of bread and added it to the feast before me. I waited for him to sit and then clinked my teacup with his.

"Cheers," he said and took a sip.

We ate as if it were going to be taken away any moment. I hadn't realized how hungry I was. A baker's dozen worth of orgasms will do that to a girl.

Collier seemed to feel the same. When he finished off round one, he plopped another heaping pile of bacon on his plate and another piece of toast.

I eyed his toast lustfully. He looked at me and held the toast in front of my lips. I took a gorilla-sized bite, and he snorted and choked on his food, obviously surprised by my audacious response.

"In my defense, that's some damn good marmalade!" I pouted, and he placed the rest of his toast on my plate with a sexy grin. I leaned over and gave him a sticky kiss for his chivalry.

"It's so easy being like this with you," he said around a bite of bacon.

"Don't get used to it. I have to go back to my client today for another three weeks."

His eyes narrowed. "Will you sleep with him?"

And there they were. Strings. Our very no strings

attached relationship now felt like a cross stitch with tons of yarn ready to be woven into something crafty. Only I wasn't crafty and strings of any kind were cut the moment they were visible.

"Collier, I'm not prepared to answer that right now. Maybe not ever."

His lips tightened. "I see." He stood and cleared our plates. Tension clouded his brow and our easy morning. The tight line of his shoulders made me want to rush over and massage the knots away and go back to our happy, easy-going vibe.

Only, it wasn't so simple. It never was.

While he cleaned, I grabbed my dress and shoes and ran into the room to change. I had myself almost completely back in order when I felt his presence. He was leaning against the doorjamb. "So, that's it? An incredible night, a handful of orgasms, and you're off to your next guy?"

Embarrassment burned low in my gut and probably reddened my face. I felt as though he emotionally punched me in the gut. "I didn't say that."

"Then what do you say? Will I see you again?" His voice was low and filled with emotion.

"I don't know. Do you want to?"

"Of course I do. Last night…shite, London. Last night was different. I know you felt it, too."

I stared at his brown eyes for what seemed like forever. "It was different."

"Okay then." His voice was calm, more soothing. "Then we start there. Do you want to see me again?" That was the question.

He wasn't a client, so I didn't have to spend any more

time with him if I didn't want to. But damn it all to hell, I wanted to. So much. "Yes," I whispered.

"What was that?"

With more confidence, I said the words I knew he wanted to hear. "Yes. I want to see you again."

His chest broadened, seemed to puff out and expand. "When?"

"I don't know when. Call me," I answered quickly, needing to put space between us. I slipped around him and headed for the door.

"No."

I swung around with my hand on the doorknob. "No?" I said confused, hurt creeping into my bones and chilling my spine.

"No." He put a thumb to his chest. "You call or reach out to me. If you truly want to be with me, you need to take that leap."

No man had ever given me an ultimatum. I didn't handle it well. I looked into his beautiful brown eyes, thinking that maybe this was the last time I'd gaze into them. Instead of speaking, I nodded and left, closing the door firmly behind me as I went.

CHAPTER SIX

It's official. A woman has made me crazy. Certifiable, shoulder-biting, crawling out of my skin nutso. I can't get the bloody bird out of my mind. Over and over, I replayed our evening of pure bliss and then spent the last hour trying to figure out how the morning went to hell.

We spent hours glorying in one another's bodies. I feasted on her beautiful curves to the point where time ceased to exist within our bubble of pleasure. Everything seemed to go smashingly. We made love long into the night, until we couldn't move and completely passed out, our bodies still wrapped tightly around each other.

This morning, everything changed. She turned cold, distant. It was as if something wiggled its way into her mind and turned our night of passion into something unsavory. I couldn't fathom how it occurred. The only thing I was certain of was that this was not the end. No. London Kelley was not waltzing out of my life so easily. There was something between us. It wasn't easily definable, but I knew she felt it, too.

I picked up the phone and called Nathaniel. It rang a few times before he answered.

"You better be dying to call this early, mate." Nathaniel's voice was groggy and rough.

I glanced at the clock. The dial read six a.m. "It's not that early. Whatever happened to the early bird caught the worm?"

"That was me, last night. Only the worm was in the bottom of the tequila bottle." He groaned. "Was out celebrating with a couple blokes. Remember I mentioned Hank Jensen?"

"Yeah, that's the guy you said is dating our client."

"That client is the sister of your London."

"Is that so?" I briefly recall him mentioning the relationship. I think I was more focused on getting the delectable Ms. Kelley's information. "What were you celebrating?" I pulled out a suit and threw it on the bed. Another day, another quid.

"Turns out the sod is going to have a baby and is shacking up for the long haul with Aspen."

"You don't say? Did the bouncing bundle of joy bring on the engagement?" I asked with a chuckle. I know if Claire and I'd had children together, I'd have never let her go. No children of mine would be raised in two homes.

"Nah, he's been smitten with her since the start. Either way, I've been invited and you're coming as my date to the wedding. It's in Texas in five weeks."

"Texas?" I groaned. "You go. I'll hold down the fort."

"London is Maid of Honor," he said, his voice holding a tone, something between Don't-be-stupid and Opportunity-doesn't-knock-twice.

"So how's the weather in Texas this time of year? Will I need a jacket or a snow suit?"

"That's what I thought." I could hear his grin through the phone line. Bastard knew he had me by the balls.

★ ★ ★

What the hell was I thinking?

Simple answer. I wasn't. Collier did that to me. An evening of pure sexual delight and I was contemplating more. More! I didn't do more. More made people fall in love and I most certainly was never going down that road again. That road was unpaved, had huge potholes, and jagged rocks that would fly out and break your heart as easily as an unsuspecting windshield.

When James passed, I made a promise to myself. Nothing would ever hurt me like his loss. Ever again. If I was going to feel that kind of pain, I'd learn from it, and learn from it I did.

Relationships were not for people like me.

I decided to go home to think awhile before heading back into Dylan's world. It was important I had a clear head and heart to do my job effectively. And he wouldn't be home from his trip until later anyway. Maybe I'd get him to scout furniture with me. A solid find always had a way of picking up my spirits.

The apartment was silent when I got there. It was still early. Tripp would be in bed. His door was wide open and I prayed he'd be alone. Usually if the door was open, it was our signal that we weren't entertaining.

Typically, I didn't bring men home with me. They didn't often take kindly to Tripp, and he enjoyed playing with my dates the moment they entered our sanctuary.

I, on the other hand, ignored his toys. They rarely were invited back, and I found it unnecessary to get attached to disposable bedmates.

I slipped off my dress and bra and then grabbed the T-shirt I saw crumbled on the floor. It smelled of Tripp.

Like fruity and delicious green apples. DKNY Be Delicious was the brand. The sweet scent of apples combined with his herbal undertones was like taking a step into your home after a long trip. He'd always be a safe homelike place for me. And I endeavored to always be one for him.

The last few years it had only been the two of us. We met in the hallway at the local community center. James had passed a few months before, and I was attending a meeting for grieving widows. Tripp was attending Narcotics Anonymous. He was only a few months into his own recovery. Between us, we were like the walking dead. Two lifeless shells, devoid of any real feeling. Then we teamed up. Together we were able to stick a Band-Aid over our past wounds. Sometimes it was in one another's bodies, but mostly it was through a deep friendship. He helped me live again. And I helped him have a reason to live.

I threw the shirt on and slid into bed next to him. He slept naked and his warmth was the most comfortable place in the world. Well, that and the crook of space where my head fit perfectly into Collier's neck and shoulder.

Tossing out that thought I snuggled closer to my best friend. His arm flung over my waist pulling me close, chest-to-chest. He burrowed his huge arm under the back of the shirt I was wearing and rubbed my spine. I arched and purred into his caress. He kissed my forehead, eyes still closed as if asleep.

"What's the matter?" His voice was groggy. He didn't open his eyes, just held me and rested against my body. The tips of his fingers massaged my scalp, soothing the stress as I held onto him.

"I screwed up." The words came out small and quiet,

but I knew he heard them.

He mumbled something against my forehead. I only caught the last bit. "...did something with Bond," he finished.

I nodded against his chest. Tears pooled and slipped down my cheeks wetting his skin. That got his attention.

"Bridge, baby. What happened?" He held me as the dam broke and I sobbed, unable to bring forth the words I needed to say.

"Did he hurt you? I'll fucking kill him." His entire body tightened like a rubber band pulled too far at opposite ends. I clung to him, wanting, trying to get the words out.

"No, h-he didn't h-hurt me," I whispered as more tears streamed down my face. He kissed them away.

"Did you hurt him?" Tripp knew me too well. Sympathy poured from him as he clenched me tight against his body. "It can't be that bad. You only had one night."

"It was the best night of my life."

It hurt so much to say that. So many nights I had with James ought to fill that spot so high on a pedestal, but it was true. One night with Collier surpassed even the height of the nights of my marriage. Maybe I was starting to forget. My wedding day, the first time James and I made love, all vied for clarity, but the memories were growing old, worn from overuse. Now they seemed as if they happened a century ago. Only the memory of feeling happy could be brought to the surface with ease.

His eyebrows rose and shock plastered his face. "That's a strong statement."

I nodded and sighed.

"Then why are you upset? What brought you to my

bed? Not that I mind. I love snuggling with my best girl." He pulled me up and over his naked body. Sprawled across his chest, I placed one hand on top of the other on his chest and then rested my chin on him. I couldn't stop my lips from quivering or the tears from spilling as he searched my eyes for the answer.

"I gave him hope."

★ ★ ★

A week later and nothing. I've worn a hole in the carpet in front of my desk pacing. I obsessively checked my phone for recent or missed calls, a text, an e-mail perhaps, anything to prove I hadn't lost her. I'd gone over that morning ad nauseam. There's nothing I'd change, save for the moment when I told her to call me. Then I wouldn't be feeling like a bloody idiot for the past week.

"Bugger! I can't take it anymore!" I pulled at the strands of my hair, making an arse of myself.

"What has your willy in a wrinkle? You've been a bit of a prick all week." Nathaniel's cheery English timbre broke my brooding.

"You want the truth or the twisted happenings I've got going on now in my head?"

Nate unbuttoned his sport coat and sat down. "Truth." He nodded.

"You remember that woman London Kelley?"

"'Course. A bloke would have to be blind to forget her." He grinned and I sneered.

"We had a date last week."

Nate slapped his knees and leaned forward. "Bloody wanker, that's brill!" His smile was bright, his dimples clearly displayed. I help up a hand to hold off his congratulatory talk. His smile waned. "What?"

I sat down, sighing heavily, not knowing how to put what happened between us into the right words. We'd had the best blooming night. Enjoying one another until the wee hours of the morning before starting all over again. Then it all went downhill.

"I don't know. We had a date. A really good time. Made it back to my place. Best bloody shag ever." I shook my head then held it in my hands.

"Better than, you know…" I nodded into my hands. "So where's the problem, mate?"

"I'm doing a piss-poor job of explaining. She left the morning after. We had a bit of a row. God, it's Sod's Law."

"The relationship area is not exactly my cup of tea, brother, but I'm still not following. You had an argument after a lovely night and an even better night of bonking and you argued?"

Exasperation took hold. "I told the bird I wanted more than just a one-night shag, and she took off. I scared the girl, and I have no idea how to fix it!"

Nathaniel tilted his head back and laughed. Loud. Heat rose in my chest and up my neck. I knew my ears were tinged red to match the fire inside my gut. "I pour my fucking heart out to you and you laugh. Stuff it! You're no help, brother mine!"

Charging around my desk, I tried to pass the snickering hyena otherwise known as Nathaniel. He shot an arm out to stop me. "No, Collier, I'm sorry. Brother, I'm sorry!" I smacked off the hold he had on my sport coat.

"You're an arsehole!"

"Guilty! And a bugger, a wanker, a sod, a daft bastard, but you've caught me at a disadvantage."

"How so?"

"I've not seen you knackered about a bird in ages. Since the queen-beast Claire. Excuse me if I find it a bit humorous to see your panties in a twist over a girl."

"So, what do I do? I gave her an ultimatum. Told her I wouldn't call her, that she had to contact me if she wanted to see me. Now it's been a week and I'm wrecked!"

I slumped into the chair next to him. He put an arm on my shoulder. Its weight was a great comfort. Reminded me of our teen years back home. We'd spend nights sneaking out, getting pissed, seeing what type of horseplay we could get into. No matter what happened, if we got caught, we always took the punishment together. Mum was ruthless with the chores, and my stepfather always gave us the long talk. We didn't care. At least when we were cleaning the garage or taking out the rubbish bin, we'd sneak looks at one another and laugh it off. Life seemed easier then. Nothing but curfews, shenanigans, and rugby. God, I missed those days.

"Find out a way to run into her. There's Hank and Aspen's wedding but that's in four weeks." He twisted his lips and steepled his fingers under his chin.

"Would you consider hosting a dinner party at your flat? Invite Hank and his fiancée, get her to bring London?"

Nate's smile was huge. "Brill, mate! I'd love to have them over, cook for everyone. Of course, Aspen rarely goes anywhere without Oliver. He'll bring his boyfriend Dean and then we'll have them invite London."

The cloud of doom dissipated as the plan came together.

This would work. She'd come to dinner, be forced to spend time with me. We could slip aside and talk, clear the air as it were.

"I'll owe you for this, Nate."

His grin was wide, his eyes laced with an evil glint. "Yes, you will, brother mine." He laughed sinfully.

Owing Nathaniel was like playing cards against the Devil. Only worse because he'd come back with a zinger that puts your lousy favor to shame. Last time I owed him one I was stuck on a date with a six-foot-two amazon woman who thought bench-pressing young uni blokes was a fun pastime. The bruise on my hip lasted for weeks when the giant unexpectedly pulled me off my feet and into the air. Someone made her laugh, and there I was, a crumpled heap of gangly limbs and sore bones. I was lucky not to have broken anything when my hip hit the pavement.

"So it's settled then. How fast can you plan this and what can I do? Call a caterer?"

Nate scoffed. "I'll cook. Besides, I have this new little thing I was hoping to impress…"

"No, no, no! Not again. Do not use this dinner party to put the moves on some tart you'll toss away after one night of shagging."

Nate had the presence of mind to look a tad trite. "You're a funny one to talk. Isn't that exactly what you are doing with the lovely Ms. Kelley? Trying to woo her?"

"Yes, but I plan on keeping this bird around. You, on the other hand, change bedmates more than you change your jockeys!"

He waggled his eyebrows. "Jealous?"

I rolled my eyes. "Hardly. I just…look, let's try to make

this as civil as possible. She means something to me. I can't explain it."

Nathaniel put his large hands out in front of him, which mimicked the universal sign for "say no more." "All right, we'll have it your way. No sexy vixens to keep me company." He pursed his lips then pulled out his phone hitting a sequence of buttons. "Aspen love, how are you this fine chilly day?" The beat of my heart seemed loud against my chest. "Yes, well, I was wondering if you and the gang would fancy a dinner party at my flat this weekend?"

He waited a moment, drumming his fingers against his pant leg. After what seemed like eternity, he clasped a hand over the speaker portion. "She's asking Oliver about her schedule," he whispered to me, taking the edge off a bit.

"Why?" I ask.

"He is her assistant and her best friend. I told you, they are two peas in a pod." He rolled his eyes and then smiled into the phone. "Brilliant, love! Dinner it is. Do you think it would be possible to invite your sister, London? She'll be redesigning my flat after your wedding and I'd love for her to get a quick run-through prior to the move in."

Ecstatic didn't begin to explain how I felt. I was amazed at how easily Nathaniel was able to come up with something so clever to bring the black-haired beauty around. At the same time, I fought a deep-seated anger all at once. I'd forgotten his plan to have her design his flat.

That was not going to happen. Over my dead body would he be in a confined space with *my* beauty for any length of time. That tidbit of information could be discussed at a later date. First priority, get the bird to dinner. Next, get the woman in my bed. Lastly, convince her to give us an honest shot at something more.

"All sorted." Nathaniel pocketed his phone and stood. I held out a hand. He shook it and smiled. I gave him one of my own.

"Dog's bollocks, brother."

"As the Yanks would say, now don't screw it up!"

"I don't intend to." I looked at my desk and took a seat as Nathaniel reached the door. He held onto the door handle and stopped.

"She's special, this one. True?"

I slid on my spectacles, clasped my hands in front of me, elbows on the lacquered surface, and looked over the rims of my glasses at Nathaniel. He wasn't only my brother, he was my best mate. His tall built frame filled the space, though the daily swimming he did kept his body from being too bulky. He waited for my response. I took a deep breath and let the air flow slowly through my too-dry lips.

His gaze met mine. A hundred thousand words were said, ones only brothers, kindred spirits, could express without speaking. The word slipped from my lips, heavy with a deeper meaning.

"True."

CHAPTER SEVEN

Aspen yanked my hand so hard she almost pulled my shoulder out of socket.

"Ouch! Stop it already!" I tried and failed to smack off the viselike clamp she had on me.

Her grip tightened on my hand as we made our way into the sitting room in my parent's mansion, a posh and prestigious nightmare of social grace. Everything perfect, nothing out of place in the Bright-Reynolds home. The couches were sparkling white. The type that made you afraid to sit on them if you weren't careful. Holding a glass of wine or cookie from the gold-tipped china plate bought to show off Mother's expensive taste was a risky move, one I constantly enjoyed making. I loved freaking Mother out. Grabbing a cookie as I sat, I made a point to bite hard, allowing the crumbs to fall onto the floor. Her perfectly sculpted brows knit together in clear disdain. Point one for me.

My sister slowly sat next to me, crossing her long pale legs with grace. Her blond hair hung like a golden sheet across her back. Aspen was a magnificent woman, not only in beauty but in all things. Her stature was strong, she was poised. Her gray-blue eyes assessed our mother with a twinge of distaste. One of the things we had in common was our dislike of our she-devil mother. The woman was insufferable. But today was the day I was waiting for. Aspen was going to drop the bomb and I couldn't wait. I was barely able to contain my glee. Mother would flip over this information.

"Mother, I have news." Aspen adjusted her suit, carefully pulling the blazer over her swelling breasts and stomach. Tension rippled the air around her. Poor thing. Even though Mother was a bitch on wheels, Aspen still wanted to please her. She had always hoped our mother would give a shit about someone instead of social niceties and the who's who of New York City. Fat chance. Nothing my wildly successful and model-beautiful sister could do would change Vivian Bright-Reynolds.

"You've come to your senses and dropped the silly relationship with that construction worker?" She sipped her tea and tipped her chin up, a mocking gesture if I'd ever seen one. She held her pinky out as she drank, the pale pink polish of her manicure catching the light for a moment.

"Quite the opposite actually," Aspen said, taking a slow calming breath.

"Oh?" Mother's eyebrow pointed to the sky.

"Hank's asked me to marry him and I've agreed." Mother's hand shook. The teacup clacked against the tiny saucer. It was the only indication she felt anything. Her face stayed stoic, unmoved, still pinched in her usual reserved pout. I was practically bouncing out of my seat with joy as the wall of angry emotions flooded my way from the woman sitting opposite us.

"Is that so?" Mother's voice was tight and held no emotion.

"Yes. We'll be married next month at Hank's ranch in Texas. I'd love for you and Daddy to come."

"A month?" The first hint of stress entered Mother's tone. "Why so soon? Shouldn't you spend more time getting to know one another?"

I had to give it to her. Mother pretended to be concerned for her daughter's well-being, but both Aspen and I knew she had other reasons. More time meant she had longer to meddle and attempt to break off the engagement.

Aspen reached for my hand and I held it tight. Sister solidarity.

Our father took that moment to enter the room. His dark suit jacket flapped as he bounded in. William Reynolds was a force of nature. His dark good looks, salt-and-pepper hair, accompanied with our same gray-blue eyes were dominant traits that had women everywhere falling at his feet, though he stayed true to the she-bitch. Never could understand why. Tripp was convinced she had a golden pussy. *No man could handle such a stuck-up bitch unless she was a tiger in the sack*, he'd said.

"Girls! Sorry I'm late. Business. You know how it is." He leaned down and clasped my cheek and kissed the opposite and then did the same with Aspen. "Stunning beauties. To what do we owe the pleasure of your visit?" Daddy asked happily.

The way Daddy just sat heavily next to Mother and put his hand high on her thigh, much higher than her social graces would normally allow, made me think Tripp could be right. Blech.

"Aspen's getting married, William," Mother answered before my sister could. The tone that slipped from Mother's lips was deadly cold, clearly showing her true feelings about the pending nuptials.

Our father hopped up out of his seat and pulled Aspen into a big hug. "Pen, my darling. Congrats are in order. We should have champagne!" Daddy and Aspen's happiness filled the room as they hugged, essentially putting a blanket over Mother's negative vibes. Point two goes to Daddy.

"Tell him how quickly you're marrying, dear," Mother encouraged.

"Next month, at Hank's ranch in Texas. Really small affair. Just close friends and family. I want you to walk me down the aisle," Pen said, tears in her blue eyes.

He swiped them off her cheeks. "I'd love nothing more to give your hand to Hank Jensen. He's a good man. Solid. Hardworking."

Aspen's smile glowed so bright it was blinding and infectious. I could feel my own cheeks splitting the seams with my wide smile, watching my sister and our father embrace. Not to mention how disgusted and angry Mother was. She hadn't even told them the best part. I could hardly contain my excitement. I tugged on Aspen's white blazer.

"Pen, you forgetting something?"

She wiped her eyes and then took another breath. "There's more." Her voice was a little choked. Daddy went back to his seat and put an arm over Mother. He gripped her to him, a huge smile on his face.

"What more?" he asked happily. Clearly, our father approved of Aspen's decision to marry the hot cowboy.

"You're going to be grandparents!" Aspen's tears fell down her cheeks, and I stood and gripped her shoulder, comforting her while our parents took this information in.

Dad's smile went from happy to utterly ecstatic. Mother's eyes were so wide, I worried they'd pop right out of her head. Her mouth was open in what could only be shock.

"You're pregnant!" Dad jumped up and put a hand over Pen's waist to feel. If anything, she only had a tiny miniscule bump. I'd know. Every chance I'd had, my hand was feeling that belly, measuring its elasticity. Hank was convinced he could feel his baby growing. I was bound and determined to not be left out. This was probably the only time in my life I'd experience a pregnancy, not ever planning to go that route myself.

I'd wanted children with James. We talked about it all the time, how they were going to have his green eyes, my black hair, and be the most precious things in the world. One girl, one boy. James William Jr. after him and my father. Collette Aspen after his mother and my sister. Now, it was another thing I threw into the never-to-be box of unfulfilled dreams.

"Isn't it amazing? We're going to have a baby running around the mansion!" I squealed, throwing my arms around Dad and Pen. Mother sat stewing, trying desperately to find a way to make this information untrue.

"Are you sure it isn't Grant's child?" Mother asked, hope tinting her tone.

All three of us looked at Mother as if she'd just lost her mind. Which she had. Sick bitch.

"You were together almost a year. How would I know you weren't still seeing him when that cowboy fella was off gallivanting back in Texas with his ex-girlfriend? I heard the story. Very uncivilized, if you ask me."

"I didn't. It's obvious you didn't hear much of the real story," Pen said, biting back her anger. "Hank pined over me the entire time we were separated. His ex made a play for him that I misinterpreted. Almost lost the man of my dreams over it!"

We all sat down. I held her hand, trying my best to put all the love and support possible in my touch. "Don't ever mention Grant to me or my fiancé again. He's liable to go insane. Hank is very protective of me and our child. I would hope you could support the decision I've made to marry and have his baby, Mother. So help me God"—she choked back a sob—"you'll never see or know your grandchild." She stood up abruptly, pulling my hand. "London, time to go."

I nodded and grabbed my purse. Daddy stood and took a hold of Pen. "Darling, my darling Pen. I am through the moon over this news. You tell me where to be, what to wear, and where to stand. I'll happily do it." She nodded, tears pooling in her eyes.

"I love you, Daddy," she whispered as he hugged her.

"I love you, too. Both of you." He let Pen go and embraced me. His long arms pulled me into the warmth of his chest. His essence washed over the situation, coating it with love.

"Me, too, Dad. Please talk some sense into her." I tilted my head to our mother. She squinted, her irritation clear in the tight way she held her shoulders and pinched her lips together.

"I always do." Dad laughed.

Aspen and I made our way to the limo. Sadness flowed over me as I hugged her. She cried into my shoulder.

"Why can't she be happy for me?"

I shook my head and petted her hair. It felt like the finest silk. "You can't make someone happy who isn't happy with themselves. She had a plan for you, me, and Rio. Wanted you and me to marry some rich pompous asshole and have the perfect three socialite kids. Just like she did. Remember how angry she was when she found out James and I were getting married?"

Aspen's shoulder shook, and I could tell her tears turned to laughter. Pregnancy hormones made normally calm people a bit wacky. "She was so angry. You'd just turned eighteen, and James claimed he was marrying you and that was that."

We both giggled as I thought back to that day. James had bought me a thin gold band. Like Hank, he didn't come from a family with money. Love, but not money. We were both college bound, and he wanted us married and living together, going to school, and coming home to one another each day. At the time, it was everything I'd ever wanted.

James got down on one knee at an ice-cream parlor the day we graduated high school. His brown hair had flopped over into his green eyes, and he shook it off in that way that made my knees weak. Daddy paid for us to get married in a garden wedding on our estate, much to Mother's chagrin. She pretended like a perfect actor that day. Daddy made certain she was on her best behavior. There were more people at our wedding that I hadn't met than had. James and I didn't care. As long as we had each other, nothing else mattered.

We had barely finished college when the accident happened. I was twenty-two, a design school graduate and a widow. Without Mother's knowledge, Daddy paid for my schooling and ensured James had gotten scholarships approved from New York State University. Then it was all over.

Pen and I stayed silent, remembering James. "He was a light in a dark world, London."

"Yes, he was. My light. It's still hard to accept he's gone."

Aspen hugged me tighter and we both cleared our eyes of our tears. "But you're moving on, right? Did you have a date with Nate's brother, Collier?"

Collier. I hadn't seen the gorgeous Englishman in a week. Staying away from him had been harder than I expected. My body yearned for him, for his touch. But I fought it. Had to or he'd get hurt.

"We did. Had a great time, too, but it won't work."

She pulled her hair over her shoulder and threaded her fingers through the long blond strands. Her eyes met mine and I quickly looked away. "You had a great time but it won't work? Why not?"

"Because." I took a deep breath. "He just... I don't know." I shook my head.

"He what? Made you feel something?"

I nodded. "Yeah, too much."

"Don't do this to yourself, London. You are not an island. James would not want you to go through life alone." Her tone was soft and pleading as she gripped my hand.

"I can't," I whispered.

"You can, and eventually you will. You don't have to let your love for James go, but you can't keep forcing people to stay at arm's length. It's unhealthy. It's been four years now. Time to move on. Let someone in." Aspen was not only big in business, but she also had a way of making sense, convincing others to follow her. It made her a great leader in all things.

I shook my head, clearing it, letting the idea of Collier and me float off into the sky. I rolled my eyes. "You're saying that because you're happy and in love. Everyone who's found their soul mate feels that way, Pen. But I already had mine. You don't get a second shot at it!"

"That is such bull." Anger and concern seeped into her tone. "When it's the right person, it will happen. You just wait. Please, just please promise me you'll try. Let someone in…just a little?" Her gaze pierced mine, pleading and intense.

I wouldn't back down—the decision had been made. She didn't need to know that. "I'll try."

Images of Collier flashed across my mind. His chocolate-brown eyes bored holes into mine as he hovered above me, filling me, completing me in ways I hadn't wanted or expected.

★ ★ ★

A knock on my door startled me. I paused the rugby match I had DVR'd on the telly and went to answer. I was not prepared to see my sister Emma at the door, tears in her eyes.

"Colly!" she screeched and flew into my arms.

I held her petite form as she sobbed. "What happened?"

"Evan. H-he…he…oh, God," she cried, wetting my shirt. "He cheated on me." She sniffed and I held her tight.

"That fucking pissant! I'll kill the bastard." I shuffled her into the room and settled her on the couch. She pulled the arm pillow into her lap and buried her face into it. I hustled into the kitchen, giving her a moment as I whipped up a spot of tea.

She hadn't moved when I returned. I eased down onto the glass coffee table sitting directly across from her, our knees touching. "Tell me," I urged.

Her brown eyes, same as my own, same as our mother's, were filled with unshed tears. "Baby girl, please." She closed her eyes and held my hands as she lost the battle, and they spilled over the edge. The torrential proof of her pain and suffering was as effective on my big-brother-kick-some-arse-nature as a scalding pot of hot water over an ice cube. The wanker was mine, though Nathaniel would want a shot and he'd have his turn too. There was plenty of that cocksucker to go around.

Emma straightened her shoulders as if preparing for battle and took a deep breath. "I went to his work. You know, in Dartford?"

I nodded.

"He'd been different lately. Not wanting to you know…"

I closed my eyes, really not wanting to hear what that bastard did with my sister but allowed her to continue anyway.

"…share the marital bed as it were."

I rubbed her hands back and forth, calming her. "Go on." The tension coiled tight in my gut, and anger seeped into my veins.

"So I showed up in a saucy dress. I'd been working out a lot, trying to get him to look at me the way he used to. And I brought him some supper and that's when…" She choked back another round of sobs. "That's when I walked in and saw him!" Tears streaked down her face so fast it was as if she'd turned on a faucet. "He had his face…his face,

Collier! B-between his secretary's legs! All spread out like a holiday dinner!" she screamed and threw herself back into the couch, hands over her eyes.

That's it. Forget the arse-kicking. Evan was a dead man. D-E-A-D M-A-N. I moved to the couch and pulled my baby sister into my lap, hugging her close.

"Baby girl, it's going to be okay. You'll stay here in the States. You can stay with me or Nathaniel, or we'll get you a place of your own. Don't go back to that wanker. He's… You're so much better than him. A man should worship you, not walk out on you. It's unforgivable."

She nodded. "But what about work? My life? Mum, Dad?"

"We'll handle it all. You have a degree. We can put it to use. You can stay in the States if you'd like. Work at our firm. I really need an assistant. Remember those years you helped Nathaniel and I out with our proposals and getting the books together at our first office while you went to school? I'll pay you twenty times that to work for us. We need someone we can trust. Someone with brains." She pulled back and looked at me, her eyes a tad less teary.

"You'd do that for me?"

"Baby girl, of course. Besides, you'd be doing us a huge favor. You're perfect. Would you like to work for Stone, Walker, & Associates?" She tilted her head and bit her lip, so I continued, "It will give you the time to figure out what you're going to do about the daft prick who's going to be a dead man when your brother and I get our mitts on him."

The most beautiful sound came out of her mouth. She giggled. It reminded me of when we were kids. Nathaniel and I would chase our sisters around the house, tackle them, and tickle them until they'd wet their knickers or begged forgiveness.

"I'd like that, Colly. Thank you. I'm so glad I came to you first." She snuggled into my neck. "I'm such an idiot."

"Shhh. None of that. You are pure and beautiful and sweet. One day you will have real love, the kind they write about in those chick flicks you adore. You know, the ones with that sod, Hugh Grant?"

She laughed.

"I never understood why they paired up a great beauty like Julia Roberts with the likes of him." I pretend shivered. She continued to laugh, and then smacked at my arm.

After holding her for some time, she stopped crying completely. "I'm so tired, Colly. I left the moment I caught him yesterday. I just went home, packed a bag, and showed up at the airport. No one knows I'm gone. Will you tell Mum and…you know, everyone?"

I nodded and lifted her to her feet. "Come on now. I'll get your case, settle you in the guest room. It has an attached bathroom so you'll have privacy."

"You're the best, brother mine. Why hasn't some great beauty scooped you up since you escaped the queen-beast?"

"Working on that, actually."

She sat on the bed in the guest room. "Is that so? You met someone?"

Instead of lying to her, I went with the truth. "I did, but we've only been on one date and she's very skittish. So we'll see."

"I'm glad. After what that bitch did to you, it's time you found someone who will make you happy." The waterworks built in her eyes again. "Look at us. Two siblings both cheated on. What is wrong with the sanctity of marriage these days? Is nothing sacred?" She sounded indignant, and with great reason.

I sat down next to her and blew out a long breath, thinking back to when Claire left me. She'd been with the rich hotel entrepreneur for the better part of a year before I'd had a clue she was gallivanting around on me.

"Apparently not. But I will tell you this, sister mine, every day it hurts a bit less, until you forget why you even married that person in the first place."

She nodded. "I hope you're right."

"If they were the ones we were supposed to be with, they'd have never left us."

"I love you. Thank you for…this." She held an arm out to the room and bed. "And for, you know, everything. If Nate agrees about the job, I'll take it. Stay awhile. I need time away from Europe. Find myself. Figure out what to do next."

"Okay, baby girl. I love you, too. I'll take care of everything."

"You always do."

I smiled at my sister. She had bags under her too-young eyes. "Get some rest. We'll talk more in the morning. Things will seem better then."

Once I'd settled her, I grabbed the phone. I did the time conversion in my head and figured it was around eleven in the evening back home. Mum would still be up. She was a night owl. The phone rang and then her worried tone came across quickly. "Colly, what's wrong?" She'd obviously read the caller ID.

"Nothing, Mum. Well, nothing that can't be fixed."

"What happened? Is it your brother? My Nate."

"Mum, Mum, no. Stop, don't worry. No one's hurt. It's Emma."

"Emma, love? What do you mean?"

"She's here in the States. My flat, actually."

"Come again?" Her tone was confused.

"Mum, Evan cheated on her. She actually caught him in the act with the tart at his work. That young secretary."

"Oh, goodness, no." She tsk-tsked through the line. "How is she?"

"Hurting. Sad. You know the drill."

"I knew Evan was no good. That boy has shifty eyes." My mum was ever the good judge of character. "I wish I'd tried harder to get her to wait to marry him. At least she's still young and doesn't have children with the wanker." Hearing my mum cuss stopped me dead in my tracks. Eleanor Walker did not cuss. It was so rare that I wasn't sure I'd actually heard it.

"Well, I've got her here with me. I've asked her to come work for me. Be our assistant."

"Assistant? Colly, that's beneath her. She's got a degree in business—"

I cut her off. "Now, now, Mum. This is just for the time being. If she likes the legal field like she did back when she was studying for school, we'll come up with something more fitting. Maybe our head office administrator. I can't offer her more than I know she's capable of. Her mind is not in the right place now. Busy work will keep her...well, it will keep her busy and not worrying about the sod who went out on her."

Mum sighed deeply. "You're right dear. Always thinking.

My Colly, so bright. Just like your father." Another long sigh came through the receiver. "He'd be really proud of you." She sniffed, and I could tell she was thinking back to when she was married to my dad. Even though they didn't get along well enough to stay together, they always were civil when it came to me. Made sure I was loved and had a good home, wanted for nothing.

"Just, do me a favor. Tell Dad and Ella, okay? And if Dad wants to go say his piece to Evan, that would be brilliant!"

"I fear brilliant is the wrong word. This boy hurt our baby Emma. He's in for a beating, I'm afraid. Lord on high, I hope your dad doesn't go to jail over this. Thank you for taking care of our girl. You okay, poppet?" She used the first nickname I'd ever had, one she reserved only for me. I claimed to hate it, but secretly, having anything special with a woman who had three other children screaming for attention made me feel unique.

"I'm good, Mum. I'll call next week after this has had time to blow over a bit. I'm going to ring off."

"Okay. And Colly?" I pressed my ear tight to the phone.

"I love you, my darling boy."

"I love you, Mum."

It had been a long day and an even longer week.

Last weekend, I was here shagging the hell out of the beautiful Ms. Kelley. God, I'd give anything to go back to that morning and take back what I'd said to her. I'd love to hear her voice right about now.

Instead, I poured myself a pint and hit the telly once more, unpausing the rugby game. Watching men beat the living shite out of each other while chasing a neon-colored ball would help my newly acquired aggression. I wasn't prepared to call Nathaniel tonight. I'd tell him what occurred when he was back from the case in California.

At least there was a light at the end of the tunnel. Saturday evening I was going to see my beauty again. Someway, somehow I'd convince her to give me another chance. Everyone deserved a second chance.

CHAPTER EIGHT

"Still sulking, I see." Tripp tugged on my ponytail and sat in the chaise behind me. I twirled around in my office chair, knees tight to my chest, his huge sweatshirt covering me and my legs like a sleeping bag.

"I'm not sulking. I'm thinking." I tipped my chin up to prove I was perfectly centered.

His eyes assessed me. The moment he saw through my bravado, his lips tipped up at one corner. "Yeah, thinking about the sexy Mr. Bond and how you blew it last weekend?" He leaned back and unfolded his long frame onto the tiny chaise. "Why don't you just call him?" he added for what seemed like the millionth time.

"You know why." I threw ice-cold daggers his way.

This was not the first time in the past week we'd had this particular conversation. My Englishman had been on the regular loop of conversation with my best friend. I could just stay at Dylan's and avoid Tripp, but I didn't want to do that either.

The client, though sweet, wanted to jump me. Unfortunately, I'd made it perfectly clear in the first couple weeks that I was game for it. Now things were different. I'd changed. Anxiety now filled my head-space when I was at his apartment, giving me the desire to run off to my hideout. Not so lucky for me, I had my very own self-proclaimed six-foot three-inch therapist in residence.

"Bridge, this conversation is tiring." He yawned for emphasis.

"Then stop bringing it up."

"I would if you'd stop acting like the dog died!"

"We don't even have a dog!"

"Exactly. Stop sulking and being down. You chose to ignore him all week. It's up to you to change that."

"I can't!" I groaned, frustrated with the added dose of lying to myself.

"Give me one good reason why and I'll never ask again."

Tears swelled and blurred my vision. "You promised, Tripp," I whispered. "You said we'd never get hurt again. We'd be there for each other…" The few tears I'd tried to hold back slipped down my cheeks.

"Jesus, Bridge. What the fuck?" He stood and wrapped me around him as he sat back on the chaise. "I had no idea this was so serious. Forget everything I said." He took a breath and petted my hair. "I just want you to live a little. There's nothing wrong with starting a relationship with a man other than me, you know?" His strong arms held me as I thought about his words. "We'll always be there for one another, and I will kill any man who harms you, but dating someone isn't unusual. Having feelings for the opposite sex is okay. It really is." The way he worded it made me feel he was convincing himself as much as me.

I laughed into his chest. "Since when did you get all feely-mick-feelerton? Feelings for the opposite sex?" I mocked him, making an ugly face and sticking out my tongue while rolling my eyes. "Really, Tripp?"

He grinned and kissed the edge of my mouth. "Really.

According to my sponsor, it's time for the both of us to make some changes. It starts with us relying on others now and again, and not just one another." He pointed to his chest then mine.

"I think I read a book on that once," I said dryly, with an eye roll.

"Be serious. We are completely co-dependent on one another. For everything."

"But I trust you." I bit my lip and grabbed a hunk of hair to twirl it around my index finger.

"And I you." Tripp hugged me tight. "But it's time we take baby steps. I'll do it, if you will?"

"You're not moving out are you?" I stared into his light eyes. There was something there I couldn't get a good read on. Usually his emotions were all over the place and easy to identify.

Normally, I didn't need the vocal answers to questions. I knew the answers in the emotions that poured off him. Right now, I felt…nothing. It scared the hell out of me. Heat rolled through me as I pondered the concept that I'd be alone. Without Tripp. Prickles of panic sneaked up my spine and sent gooseflesh to the outer edges of my skin, tickling and uncomfortable.

Tripp cupped my cheeks. "Baby steps, Bridge. Shit, relax, breathe for Christ's sakes!" I let out a huge lungful of air I hadn't realized I'd been holding. "I don't know how to start either," he finally admitted.

That's why I couldn't feel anything. I took a deep breath in and out slowly. He honestly didn't have any emotion tied to the concept of moving forward, moving on. Probably because for so long he believed he'd end up dead in the gutter like his bitch of a mother told him he would. And it actually could have happened had he not cleaned up his act and gotten off the drugs.

"Look, Bridge, I'm not asking you to make a life change here. God knows, I'd prefer to be the only man in your life. But we know we have to let others in at some point. Now when you've got a sexy Mr. Bond of your very own, you might as well take advantage. Hell, if you don't, I will!"

"I think that new sponsor is helping you." I giggled and squeezed his hands.

He nodded, pulled me into a standing position, and gave me one of his megawatt, model-bright smiles. "I think so, too. How about we go get your client and start filling his house with what he needs!"

Tripp was the best thing I could ever hope or wish for in a best friend. He was kind, loving, more concerned about my needs than his own and a tiger in the sack, though we promised no more of that. We have kept that promise for the past year aside from the little handy a couple weeks ago. We've both been on our best behavior. Our friendship has never been stronger. He threw an arm over my shoulders and walked us to my room.

"So what's this guy Dylan's problem, anyway? Besides that, he's no longer getting laid by you, poor guy. That makes two of us." He pouted, sticking his full pink lip out, looking adorable.

I narrowed my eyes at him and pulled some clothes from the closet. "Believe it or not, he actually needs to be a bachelor. A real bachelor. Live on the wild side, have some parties, experience life. He's too stuck on being a Goody-Two-shoes."

Without paying attention, I grabbed a pair of skinny jeans and a tank top that crisscrossed in the back.

Tripp shook his head and grabbed the blouse from my hands. "You can't wear that, unless you're putting this sheer thing over it." He held out a teal-and-purple peacock-inspired blouse. It looked best with a tank under it, but sometimes I rocked a teal bra and showed off my assets.

He didn't normally make a point of picking out my clothes. That sounded more like Aspen's bestie, Oliver, not mine. Her BFF moonlighted as her personal assistant, fashion stylist, and second in command of her company. Tripp was more man than she-man. Women's clothing was not his thing unless he was stripping it off said woman.

"What do you mean I can't wear this?" I pulled the white silky tank from his grip.

"Are you trying to confuse the guy? You know longer want to fuck him, but this says 'Here, look at my perfect tits in this top.' It's cruel, Bridge." He grasped the peacock shirt and tank and shoved it into my chest. "Give the guy a break and cover up the precious, will ya?"

I laughed. "You did not just call my boobs 'the precious,' Tripp Devereaux!"

"Oh yes, I did. I've had them every which way you can get 'em, and they are worth all the gold in China and then some." He put his hands under each globe to test their weight. "Yup. And still perky as hell."

"Cut it out!" I smacked his hands away. "I'll wear the damn blouse, okay? Jeez, you're worse than my mother. I don't know why I put up with you," I grumbled and threw on the tank, adjusted my boobs and slipped on the sheer overlay. The deep purples, teals, and blues contrasted with my black hair and light eyes. It really worked for me. I actually *felt* pretty.

"Perfect, now call your client and tell him to meet us downtown. I want to check out that hidden away furniture emporium you found last month by accident."

"Ooh, good idea! I didn't get a chance to really check it out. They have a little restaurant close by. We can hit that afterward for drinks and appies!" I pulled my hair into a thick ponytail, slicked my lips with some pink gloss, pinched my cheeks, and added a quick layer of black mascara, and then we were off.

Dylan met us just outside the furniture store as we pulled up in my BMW. It was a gift from Aspen for my twenty-fifth birthday last year. It matched hers, only she chose a dull, boring gunmetal gray for herself. Mine was candy-apple red, loaded, with high-performance tires and a smooth black leather interior.

Tripp told Aspen the gift was TITS! Meaning it was as great as a nice pair of breasts. Men were weird. I named her "Samantha" after the erotic vixen in Sex in the City.

The Furniture Emporium was a huge metal warehouse, ten times bigger than any of those box stores in suburbia. It hadn't spread its wings as one of the mainstream retailers, but I knew a guy, who knew a guy, who got me access.

The last time I was here, I briefly drooled over the supply. They catered to clientele that specialized their designs with furniture from India, Europe, and Asia. They also had a solid amount of US products that were considered 'boutique' pieces made from local woodworkers and whittlers. Everywhere the eyes roamed, new and beautiful art was proudly displayed. The place was Heaven to an interior designer.

I couldn't wait to show Tripp and Dylan, though I didn't think Dylan would much care one way or the other. He wasn't big on sharing his opinion. Part of why I needed to bring Tripp along for this experience. Tripp was Tripp. Forever the bachelor. Honestly, I hoped Tripp could give the guy a lesson or two on how to let go, live in the now instead of planning his stock portfolio for when he was going to retire. The man was in his twenties for crying out loud.

We got out of the car. Dylan stood, looking incredibly young, having traded in his suit for jeans and a polo shirt. He approached me, placed a hand around my waist, and leaned in for a kiss. I backed away and Tripp stepped between us, introducing himself.

Dylan's eyes followed me as I walked around him. I knew it wasn't fair, avoiding him like this. Originally, I set the rules. Now, I had to suffer the consequences. Tenderly, I gripped his hand and brought it to my lips for a kiss. Confusion seemed to pump off him. It tapped a hasty beat against my heart, making me feel like utter garbage for leading him on the way I had.

"Hey." I kissed his knuckles keeping the hold on his hand. His eyebrows knit together at the gesture. "We need to talk, later okay?"

Dylan's eyes brightened. I could feel acceptance and loss transmitting to my empathic feelers. He looked resigned but smiled and kissed the outside of my hand. "Sure, whatever you say, London."

"Let's have some fun. I'm about to change your life," I said whimsically.

I tugged him through the warehouse style store as I

heard him whisper, "You already have."

★ ★ ★

"I'll fucking pummel the bloody wanker!" Nathaniel strode into my office. He must have seen Emma sitting at the desk opposite my receptionist. "You, you!" He pointed a thick finger at me as he strode in like a knight in shining Armani. "You should have called me." He pointed that same finger against his chest.

I stood and held out my hands to cool him. "Agreed. I'll start now by saying I'm sorry. You had a lot on your plate in California with that actress client you like so much."

He smiled briefly and then sat heavily in the chair across my desk. I followed suit and waited for him to continue. "That Evan is a piece of shite! Pure dog shite!"

"Yes, he is. But what are you going to do about it, being over here and him being back home?"

Smoke seemed to swirl around his head. "I don't know!" He took a deep breath.

"I've offered Emma a job. Assistant to both of us."

"And she went for it?" His voice rose in surprise.

"For now. She needs to work and wrap her head around something other than her husband."

"Soon to be ex-husband!" Nate added.

"One can only hope. As much as we'd like, we don't get to choose for her. She has to come to that conclusion on her own."

"Like hell! I'll draw up the papers today!" he growled. "That bugger thinks he can cheat on my sister. I'll show him," Nathaniel grumbled.

It was almost comical, seeing I'd been accused of doing

the same thing just yesterday when Emma brought me a cup of tea. Then he stopped and a smile broke across his clean-shaven face. "What did Dad say?"

"I don't quite know. I spoke with Mum when I called to tell them she was here and what happened."

Nathaniel nodded and got up. He pressed the buzzer for Jane. "Jane love, can you send our sister in please? Thanks."

Not knowing what his intentions were, I responded to an e-mail while we waited, letting him stew in his anger. I'd had a few days already to get past the initial fury.

Our baby sister entered, her brown hair pulled into a bun at the nape of her neck. She wore a variation of the suit she'd had on Monday. I needed to have Jane take her shopping or at least set up an account for her at Niemen Marcus so she could get a wardrobe. If she was going to live here awhile, she'd need more than what she packed in one suitcase.

"Baby girl." Nathaniel opened his arms. She rolled her eyes and sighed but settled into his embrace. "I'm going to draw up some papers for you. Let's get this situation handled immediately."

She pushed out of his arms. "What do you mean? What papers?" she asked, her voice high-pitched.

"Divorce papers, of course!"

Her eyes narrowed and her hands went to her hips. Her fingers gripped so hard they turned white. "Did I ask you for divorce papers? You're not Evan, Nate. And if I wanted to get a divorce, I'd *ask* you for help."

"So you're going to stay married to the cheating prick, then?"

"I don't know what I'm going to do. This just happened.

Stop your macho shite and give me a little credit. I need some time. Colly?" She looked to me for help.

"Look, I agree with Emma, Nathaniel. She needs to do this on her own. She knows we can handle her divorce easily enough but she needs the time to make that decision."

Nathaniel started to pace the room like a caged, ferocious wild animal. "No man hurts my baby sister and gets away with it!"

Emma deflated and stopped him in his third full circle around the room. "Nate, I know you are worried about me. Hey, I'm worried about me. But this happened to *me*." She pointed to her chest. "Not to *you*." She pointed to his. "Please let me deal with it my way."

Our baby sister was growing up beautifully. She didn't need two hotheaded brothers fighting for her honor, even though we'd both love to wrap our hands around the dirty prick's neck and squeeze until his last breath. Find me a brother who wouldn't want to do the same in the circumstance.

"Okay, Em, but we're revisiting this conversation in a month. And *every* month after that until you make up your mind."

She smiled and hugged him. "You brute! I agree to your terms. Now can I get back to work?"

"Oh yeah, Collier tells me you've been offered a job. Are you okay with being assistant to your two overbearing, though smart and incredibly handsome, brothers? We really do need the help. You'll whip this office into shape in no time."

"For now, I'll accept the assistant title. But, and that's a big butt"—she slapped Nathaniel hard in the arse. He yelped and I laughed—"if I stay on and clean this place up, you'll offer me a pretty penny to stay and a title of my choosing."

She was definitely related to us. Our sister was a tough negotiator. Having her here would be a blessing.

"Are you okay staying with Collier?" he asked.

"Yes, for now. If I stay more than two or three months, Colly already offered to get me settled in an apartment close to work."

"Remember that row of apartments we bought a couple years ago?" I reminded Nathaniel and he nodded. "Two of them have leases that are coming up. One already mentioned they are planning on moving out. It's a perfect flat. Two bedrooms, two baths, a balcony with a view of the city."

"Sounds like a dream. If, and that's still an 'if', I stay," Emma reinforced.

"Okay, sister mine, have it your way." I came around and hugged her petite body against me. "I'm going to have Jane set you up an account at Niemen Marcus. If you're going to work here, you need to dress the part. I've seen that suit twice and it's only Wednesday." I playfully shook her shoulders back and forth until she smiled.

"You think anyone else noticed?" she asked worriedly.

"No, but we want you to be comfortable. Right, mate?"

"Right. I'll have my doorman send over one of my cars. Since Collier's housing you and the business is clothing you, it's my duty to set you up with some wheels and take you out to dinner to feed you. How does that sound, baby girl?"

She launched herself into Nate's arms and pulled me in for a group hug. Nathaniel and I didn't make a show of hugging, but we did the man hug thing around our little sister's body. It was actually really nice. It would be great having Emma here permanently. The more family around us the better.

"You guys are the best. I'm going to owe you big."

"Yes, you are. And I expect it in home-cooked meals. You know I can't cook worth a shite." I poked her arm and went back to my desk. "Now that we've got everything settled. Can we get back to work? I'm bombed and want everything settled before the weekend."

"Oh yeah, why? You have a hot date with that girl you mentioned?"

Nathaniel's eyes went round. "That's right! Dinner on Friday. Oh Em, you must come to dinner. The bird Collier's hooked on is going to be there. Also, my client Aspen Reynolds and her fiancé, Hank, her assistant Oliver and his boyfriend, Dean. All a great group. Recently I've started hanging out with them. I think you'll really like Aspen and our brother's love interest, London."

"You're a wanker, you know that?" I threw a pen at him.

"He's getting grumpy. He must really like this girl," Emma added teasingly.

"Both of you, get. Scat! I have work to do and so do you!"

"All right, all right. Em, you want to help with dinner on Friday?" Nathaniel asked as they headed out the door.

"Sure. What we cooking?"

"Cooking up some love, baby girl. A whole pot of love," his voice trailed off as they closed the door.

"Arsehole!" I yelled, hoping they could still hear me.

CHAPTER NINE

"Stop fidgeting with your dress." My sister's lilting voice reached me over the sound of the heater blasting warm air against my bare legs from the car's unit.

"You got ants in your pants?" Aspen's fiancé, Hank, asked with his sweet southern accent. God, I love a man with an accent.

I glared at both of them, tugged on my skirt one more time, and then flicked my hair to the side. A nice fat lock twirled perfectly round and round my index finger as I stared out the window.

"Oh no, she's doing the hair twirl. Why are you nervous? We're going to dinner at *your* client's and my attorney's house. Don't you do pre-dinners all the time to check the place over?" Aspen tilted her head to the side, her lips curling at the edges. A set of blue eyes and a set of greens focused solely on me.

"Maybe I'm wondering if Collier's going to be there?" I half-asked, in case they knew and would spill the beans. And if he were there, Tripp wouldn't be there to keep me balanced.

Tripp was finishing up his day shift at the restaurant and mentioned he'd be late to dinner but to let Nate know to leave him a place setting. I planned on leaving him a setting right next to me. Close enough to allow a distance between me and any potentially sexy Englishmen I'd been avoiding.

I just knew *he* was going to be there, too. It's his brother's house. He's having a dinner party. Of course, Collier will be in attendance.

Twinges of excitement and panic warred in equal parts as the limo arrived at the curb. A taxi pulled up directly behind the limo as the three of us shuffled out. Our friends Oliver and Dean looked dashing in long wool matching coats as they exited their taxi. I held my tongue at the instant jab that wanted to tell them how cute they looked as twinsies. Though one twin was a massive six-foot-something firefighter with a body that showed he spent long hours in the gym and the other was very trim and sleek for a male. Oliver's boyfriend, Dean, was the dichotomy in that relationship but helped prove you could never judge a book by its cover.

Oliver hugged me tight, and then fawned all over me and my sister's clothing choices.

"I see you went with the slinky purple number," Oliver fluttered over the tiny strings cinching the waist of the cocktail dress my sister wore to hide the tiny but growing bump. I held back the urge to stroke her stomach. It was starting to annoy her, and she complained that she wasn't far enough along to warrant a belly rub.

"Buddy, how many times do I have to tell you to keep your hands off my woman?" Hank growled and clapped a hand on Oliver's shoulder. You could tell Hank was holding back his laughter but trying to hold onto his mock anger. It was an ongoing joke between the trio. Aspen's best friend fiddled over her constantly, and Hank was always thwarting his efforts. Oliver looked over at Aspen, his eyes narrowing, then back at Hank.

"You like the dress a lot, I see?" Oliver's eyes were calculating. His lips twitched into a knowing grin. Aspen fluffed her hair.

"I warned you. I like it down," Hank said, his tone serious and flat.

Oliver huffed and blew out a frustrated breath. "Seriously? You already scored the woman, impregnated her, yet you still have to go all cowboy caveman?"

Aspen's hands flew to her mouth, holding back her laughter as Ollie ranted.

"Do you know how long it takes me to make those perfect French twists with her baby fine hair?" He pointed at Aspen's hair that was around her shoulders in pretty golden waves. Apparently, it wasn't down when Ollie left her earlier. I snickered internally. My prim and proper sister was really a dirty bird who obviously had some wicked sex this evening. Go Aspen!

Hank shrugged, slid a huge paw into the hair at my sister's nape, and tugged her into a wild kiss. She didn't even try to pull away. He owned her, body and soul. It was clear as day to any onlooker. Hank's hands tunneled into her hair as he slanted his mouth over hers, gaining deeper access. I could feel the love pouring off those two like a wall of hot air hitting me in the face, burning with intensity. Once Hank pulled away, he nuzzled Aspen's nose with his and gave her one last peck.

"Down." He pointed to Oliver and, with a firm hand around my sister's waist, tugged her toward the doorman. She giggled, hot on his heels like a silly teenager with a boyhood crush. I totally got it. Hank was a hunk. Also a running joke in this group.

"Neanderthal," Ollie shouted after him. We all laughed. Dean gripped Oliver's hand and crooked his elbow for me. I took his arm and together we all crowded into the elevator.

Hank knocked on the door and we were greeted by a stunning brunette in a gold satin blouse tucked into a black pencil skirt. Her eyes were dark and familiar, blazing with an intensity that spoke of an age well beyond her obvious youth.

"Welcome." The petite woman smiled sweetly as she held open the door. The gang shuffled in. "Wow, Nate, you have some beautiful friends." She eyed each of us individually and chuckled.

Nate's head popped out over a counter and waved. "That I do, sister mine."

Ah, Nate's sister. That means she's related to Collier as well. Bristles of nervous energy shot up my arms, leaving gooseflesh in its wake. The lovely woman came right over to me and grabbed my hand. "You must be London. Colly has told me so much about you."

"Colly?" I grinned, realizing I just was given some excellent blackmail material.

"Yes, my brother, Collier."

"We don't really know each other that well. And you are?" I held out my hand to her.

"Goodness. I forgot my manners." She threw a dish towel over her shoulder after wiping her hands and stuck her hand out. "Emma Taylor. Come on in. Have a drink."

"Ah, I see the gang is here," a liquid deep voice came from over my shoulder. I closed my eyes to let the rumble and his nearness fill my senses. A warm hand encased my shoulder and turned me around. Eyes the color of brown sugar glinted and swirled with something akin to desire.

Collier cupped my cheek, his thumb lightly sweeping along the skin before he laid a whisper-soft kiss against first my left, then my right cheek.

"London," spilled from his lips as if they'd been said in prayer, calm yet filled with intent. A shiver scuttled down my spine as he pulled away.

Nate made his entrance from the kitchen and introduced Collier and Emma to those they hadn't met.

It was just the right amount of time needed to pull myself together. The connection between Collier and me had not dimmed in the two weeks since our evening of pure bliss. If anything, it was stronger, sizzling between us like a live wire, ends exposed and ready to burn anything in contact with it.

Nate handed me a glass of white wine, and I gulped the first half down greedily, hoping to cool my jets. I made a point to hang out near Aspen, though the second we arrived, she and Ollie started talking to Nate about an issue with one of their clients. They needed to have Nate look into it. Bored to tears, I skated around Collier and made my way to where Hank was looking at the artifacts and books lining the living room wall. It reminded me to give the place a once over. I'd be here in a few weeks. Might as well get my pre-run done now.

The room wasn't bad, I decided as I did a cursory scan. Nate obviously had some definite pleasure pieces, thought his things weren't placed in a cohesive way. Nothing I couldn't fix. He'd have to let go of some of the art pieces or place them in other rooms. He mixed textures, colors, and styles that jolted the eye and forced a person to look around the room sporadically. It made me feel dizzy and unbalanced. Not the feeling you wanted a guest entering your space to have.

It was obvious Nate was edging toward a more elegant approach in his home design. Certain pieces were very expensive and definite eye-catchers, things that he noticeably adored but didn't know how to place. On one of the bookshelves stood a solitary piece. It was a telescope from the eighteenth or nineteenth century. It wasn't as archaic as being from the sixteen hundreds when Galileo created the first telescope but it had the curved glass and had likely only modified three times. It was a stunning piece and would look amazing on the mantel with protective hardware and appropriate lighting to give it the attention it deserved.

"That was passed down generations in the Walker bloodline," Collier said leaning into my back, pressing his sculpted chest against the exposed skin.

"It's lovely," I heard myself say, though it was barely a whisper. I was too focused on the feel of his body touching mine, creating that ever-present energy that was impossible to ignore.

"Not as lovely as you are." The tips of his fingers trailed from my neck down my spine, my dress leaving complete access to his bold touch. I gasped. "Hadn't heard from you in a couple weeks, been busy avoiding me?" There was with a hint of laughter in his tone.

I shrugged and turned toward him. "I have been busy. With my *client*." The word "client" came out tight and bitter.

His eyebrows rose. "Ah, I see. You've been entertaining your *client*, forgetting all about the incredible night we had." His lips curled into a small frown. "I hoped I'd see you this evening." His hand came out and lightly rested on my hip, pulling me a bit closer to his warmth. Every instinct told me to run far away, get away from this man. If I didn't, I feared he'd never let me go. My body yearned to be closer, slide up against him, reenact that evening we shared all over again. Wash, rinse, repeat. *Yes please!*

"Oh yeah? Why?"

"Because there's something between us. You feel it. I feel it. I, for one, would like to explore it. Go out with me again?" He crowded my space, leaving only an inch between us. His breath lifted the small hair on my neck to tickle and taunt.

"Not a good idea."

"And why not?" His hand rose and he tucked a loose strand of hair behind my ear.

"I'm no good for you. Trust me on this." Finally, I'd admitted the truth. He was not safe getting attached to me. I was incapable of giving him what he needed. In the end, he'd always want more, to settle, to build a life with someone. With me, that was not an option. Sex and a good time were all I was willing to give. The sooner he understood that, the better off he'd be.

Collier's head tipped back and he laughed. I stared at him in confusion, trying to figure out how being brutally honest with him was funny.

"Do you think this is a joke?"

"More like a tragedy. One, my beauty, we will survive. Maybe a bit battered and our hearts bruised, but once we let the tender bits heal, it's going to be so good. I feel it. It's fate." He used the one word I never expected a man to say to me again. Fate. Thoughts of my dead husband careened to the surface, muddying the sensation between Collier and I with heartache and grief.

I shook my head and pushed at his chest, forcing him to give me a couple feet of space. "You're insane. We just met. Had one date. One fan-fucking-tastic night, emphasis on the *fucking*, but that's all there will ever be. I am not your destiny." I pointed at him and slipped away as Nate opened the door and my savior walked in. Tripp. God, his timing couldn't have been more perfect. I needed him like I needed a stiff drink.

"Bridge baby," he said, arms opening up. I slumped into his embrace calming the jittery hopped up energy that came with conversations with the sexy Englishman. That man confused and confounded me. Everything I knew and understood about myself, about how I wanted to live my life was in a state of juxtaposition when near Collier. I didn't like it. In fact, I loathed it.

★ ★ ★

It took every ounce of my energy not to pound the bastard with his arm over the back of London's chair. Tripp. Her supposed best friend. Right now, he looked very friendly indeed. If I didn't know better, I'd be convinced they were lovers, definitely more than friends. Tripp easily touched her in very overt personal ways, as a lover would. What was it she'd said about Tripp? That he was *significant* in her life, that she couldn't live without him.

My heart ached as I watched him tickle her shoulder, the shoulder I once sunk my teeth into during the height of passion. Her gorgeous body withered under mine, just a scant couple weeks ago. How did we get here? Her stunning eyes met mine across the table. I put everything I felt into my gaze, trying to tell her what words couldn't.

I missed her.

I wanted her.

I needed her.

London made a move to stand. Tripp stood and pulled out her chair for her. At least he was a gentleman. Wanker.

Three of the men at the table stood when she did, my brother and I's manners called for it. Hank's did as well. I liked the bloke more and more. Even though he was a Yank, he had a distinct southern accent. Reminded me how very similar Americans were to their British allies. Back in my mother country, different sections carried different dialects just as in the US.

"Um, restroom?" London asked Nathaniel.

Before he could tell her, I walked over and took her dainty wrist. "I'll lead her." I wanted to end that comment with "anywhere" but I kept that to myself.

"I'll just bet you will," Tripp whispered. I responded with a glare. The man licked his lips and shook his head, turning back to our dinner companions.

What the hell was the bugger's problem anyway? When we'd met, he was overly friendly. He seemed to encourage our kiss on the street. Then when I called, he seemed to genuinely give advice, made it known he was not with London. So why the anger now? Oh bother. Maybe he just woke up on the wrong side of the bed.

I led London down a long hall. Instead of heading to the bathroom closest to the dining room, I brought her through a second guest room that had a combined bathroom.

She turned around and before I could contain myself, I

had her in my arms, back plastered against the door and my lips slanted over hers. She opened, immediately filling my mouth with the taste of white grapes. The unique smell of cinnamon filled my nose, making my knees quake.

I pressed my body into hers, and she groaned into my mouth. Slowly, I slid a hand up her tanned thigh to palm and squeeze her luscious curves.

"Jesus Christ, you undo me," I spoke into her open, panting mouth, and then sipped more from her lips.

Her hands plucked at the belt at my waist, pulling it from the loops and unzipping my slacks. Too quickly, the fabric pooled at my ankles. Using both hands, I slipped her dress up her legs and yanked at the wisp of fabric she called underwear. The lace shredded on both sides in less than a second. A harsh tug on each side and nothing was between me and her bare pussy.

"Need a taste." I slid to my knees at the sound of her groan.

"We really shouldn't be doing this right…" Her words fell to silence as the taste of pure honey exploded in my mouth, tongue fully entrenched between her thighs. I lifted her leg and urged her to slip it over my shoulder. She did, giving me perfect access to the sweet essence that was unique to London. I was ravenous, starving as I pulled the petals of her sex open and dived in. She cried out when I inserted two fingers deep into her and back out. The walls of her sex pulled and griped at my retreat.

Finding the wall within that made her wild, I clung to her clit and manipulated her until she was straining, holding my head against her sex roughly, uncaring how tight she gripped my hair. I fucking loved making her lose control. As her breathing changed to a heavy pant, signaling my beauty was going to fall over the edge, I flicked at that little fuck button and gazed up. Our eyes met. She was luminescent. Her body shook as I stroked her and sucked her into a powerful orgasm.

"Collier!" she half-whispered, coming down slowly. Her orgasm subsided while I kissed my way up every piece of exposed skin. Pulling at the neck of her dress, I licked and kissed the tops of her breasts, relishing the scent of her, wanting more of it invading my nostrils, filling my lungs with its sweetness.

"God, you smell so good." I laved at a nipple and pushed her tit up and out of her bra. She moaned when I sucked her hardened peak, flicking the sensitive flesh. She gripped my face and pulled me into a bone melting kiss.

Her hand trailed down and pushed at my jockeys, pulling out my prick. "Fuck me," she begged, lifting a bare leg over my hip. "Now." She licked along my neck and bit my ear before planting her lips on mine.

Pressing her harder into the door, I lifted both thighs, wrapping them around my waist. Her sex lined up perfectly with mine as I swiveled my hips, just giving her the tip of my cock. Her legs tightened around my waist, desperately trying to force me into her completely. With a tilt of my hips, I gave her an inch or so more. Her head fell back with a thud against the door.

"Please." She licked her lips.

"You'll have it when I give it to you." I pressed another inch, dastardly slow, gripping her ass. I gritted my teeth, doing everything I could to hold back from impaling into the treasure between those toned thighs.

"You're killing me. Fuck me!" She growled then swooped to take my lips. Slowly, I pushed another inch and she gasped.

"No, you're torturing *me*, beauty. I want you to know what it feels like to have something you want right in front of you, but not get to keep it."

Her thighs tightened around me and her eyes closed in defeat.

"Don't do this," she begged.

Another inch earned me a deeper moan. "Please, Collier. I want…"

"I want another date. Another chance. Give it to me and I'll fuck you so hard you'll see stars, beauty."

"Yes, okay. Anything, just…"

Yes was all I needed. I pulled back my hips, gripped her ass, and hammered into her, making sure to crush her clit with my pelvic bone on every stroke. Between cries and moans, she said nonsensical words I couldn't grasp as I pounded into her, breathing life back into our souls again. I needed this. She needed it.

The tight coil of pleasure built low in my back, flitted up through my groin and chest. Pure nirvana was approaching fast but I wanted her with me. Always with me.

"Beauty, I'm gonna come. Fill you up, make you mine again," I whispered into her ear. Her teeth bit the side of my neck so hard she may have drawn blood. Didn't matter. Nothing mattered but her crooning into my neck, licking sucking the skin there. Her nails dug into my shoulders. All the while her pussy flooded with heat, squeezing and gripping my cock like a fist. Her body physically pulled the orgasm up from my balls, out my dick and into her waiting heat in long deep bursts of release.

"Fuck," I practically roared, not caring who heard me, hoping Tripp did.

Both of us were spent while I held her tight, still gripping her ass, fingers white with the effort to hold on. She pulled back and kissed my mouth, slowly unhooking her legs.

The room smelled of sex, sweat, and cinnamon. Perfect. She pulled her dress down and fixed her top. It was almost a sin to put those lovely knockers back in their hiding place. I yanked up the pants, never having moved from the spot around my ankles.

I nodded to a door across the room. "Toilet's over there." She nodded and made her way there. I sat down on the bed and waited for her to return.

When she came out, she looked refreshed, yet like a woman who had just had a thorough rogering. I couldn't help but grin.

London smiled widely, her cheeks pinking up as if she were shy. The woman was not shy, though I'd pretty much give anything to see that smile on her face every day, be the one man allowed to put it there.

"We'd better get back. We've been gone awhile."

"I'm pretty sure they all know what we were up to. Though your friend Tripp may have an issue."

She balked, which made me feel a little relief. "Why? Tripp and I are friends. I've told you that."

"Does *he* know that?" My voice sounded gruff.

Her eyes narrowed and she bit her lip. "As a matter of fact, he does. Now, let's go." She held onto the door handle.

"Wait." I grabbed her wrist and pulled her into my

arms. "That date you promised?"

She rolled her eyes. "Really, you just got laid. Can you give it a rest?"

"No, I won't. You promised."

"While you were fucking me!" she retorted. Her face showed irritation, but her eyes held a hint of wickedness. I could so easily fall in love with that face.

"Doesn't matter. I will use whatever superhuman powers I have at my reach. So next weekend?"

"Fine," she answered briskly.

"Fine," I finished in a huff, not sure why either of us was holding onto any annoyance, seeing the fabulous coupling we'd just had.

We made our way down the hall. The entire table stopped talking when we entered. Nathaniel clapped. "Cheers, mate! That was quite the entertainment. Did I tell you one of my issues with this apartment? The walls are very thin, brother mine?"

London's face turned bright red. Aspen and Oliver laughed their asses off. Hank looked embarrassed but coughed into his hands and adjusted his pants. Dean held a knowing smile. Emma's cheeks were tinged pink, probably matching my own. What caught my attention though were the daggers being thrown at me from across the room. Tripp looked at me, jaw tight, eyes narrowed. His hand was a tight fist on top of the table. Clearly, he had a difference of opinion on the status of his and London's *relationship*. I vowed to get to the bottom of it. If London and I were to be anything in the future, this skeleton in her closet needed to be buried.

CHAPTER TEN

Dinner progressed after a little more ribbing from our friends. I tried valiantly to blow it off. Collier looked flat out like the cat that ate the canary. He spent the rest of the evening sending erotic little messages with his eyes and lips from across the table. We'd just had sex, and he was staring at me like I was his next meal instead of the dish Nate and Emma were serving.

"Aren't you just the sweetest thing." I heard Tripp address Emma as she refilled his wine. She blushed and looked away, smiling. Tripp grabbed the hand not holding the wine bottle. "I don't think we've been properly introduced," he said in that low smooth voice of his.

Oh no. Not good. Something was already wiggy between Tripp and Collier. Now Tripp was using *that* voice on Collier's sister. I closed my eyes and waited for her reply, wishing silently that he wasn't doing what I think he was doing. It was hard to tell where Tripp's feelings were when Mr. Sexy Englishman was throwing erotic, lusty emotions across the table that were so powerful they stole my breath. It skewed my empathic radar, and made it impossible to focus on anything other than the pulsating desire practically ripping off my skin.

As I focused on Tripp and Emma's conversation, Nate interrupted Collier, effectively breaking the tether between us.

As I turned to focus more closely on Tripp, he was responding to something Emma said about not knowing anyone in the States. "Sweetheart, you just need to get out, have a little fun. I'll take you on a trip." He waggled his eyebrows and Emma beamed. Her elegant features lit with joy; clearly, she appreciated his advance. "Let's exchange numbers and I'll take you out this week. Show you a bit of the city. Would you like that?" He kissed her hand. Smooth Tripp, real smooth.

I rolled my eyes and bumped his elbow, throwing off his mack on Collier's sister.

A noise that sounded an awful lot like a growl made Tripp and Emma look across the table. Collier's brown eyes were so dark they were practically black. Anger pumped off him with a passion, turning his aura a muddied red. Emma pulled her hand away, quick as a snap of the finger.

"We'll connect a little later," she offered and continued her merry way, filling wineglasses until the bottle was empty and then leaving to retrieve another.

Collier took a deep breath and focused on finishing the food on his plate. A frown marred his five o'clock shadow and his lips moved as he stared at his plate. I think I caught the word "bastard" and "sucker" but I couldn't be sure. It would be easy enough to figure out what he was saying and who it was directed at.

Allowing Collier to brood, I looked around the room at the different folks deep in conversations. The white walls of Nate's house served as a perfect background to evaluate each person's mood and aura. Of course, it was a cinch if their emotions were spilling off them strong enough I didn't have to focus, like Collier and his present angry state.

My scan first settled on my sister, Aspen, and her fiancé Hank. Their auras matched, a luscious pale pink, indicative of a revived romantic relationship filled with love and affection. Hers had the telltale flicker of white stars or sprinkles of light along the edges. Those effervescent glimmers signified she was pregnant. Those little bursts of light reminded me of the lightning bugs we used to chase across the large grounds of our parents' estate, beautiful light that was almost impossible to grasp, though we spent countless hours trying. This time my dear sister had caught her light source, and it had something to do with the man currently cupping her cheek reverently.

Dean was laughing at something Hank said about the upcoming wedding, his blue aura consistently gleaming. Out of the entire group, Dean was the most centered and cool-headed. It was interesting to see him and Oliver react to one another because Ollie was so eccentric, boisterous, and downright jolly. His aura shined silver like a fine metallic sterling. He was in his full mama-bear state, sitting close to Aspen while touching Dean. He was a nurturer by nature, and this baby gave him an opportunity to experience life being brought into the world, something his own relationship choices would likely not offer him.

Parenthood was an option if they had a surrogate. As far as I knew, they weren't planning a family, but I'm certain Aspen having one was going to give Oliver the baby bug. Hopefully, he'd get his fill through her child.

"So, Aspen, have you and Hank thought of any baby names yet?" Emma sat down between Collier and Dean.

Hank grinned and Aspen perked up excitedly. "Not really. The only thing we've been able to agree on is that the name will start with the letter H."

"Why's that?" Emma took a sip of her wine.

"Hank's father, brother, and two nephews all have H names. We want to continue that with our child."

"What if it's not a boy?" I asked.

Aspen shrugged. "Doesn't matter. Hank and I like tradition. Though Hank would be fine with a Hank Jr. of course." She rolled her eyes as he slid his arm around her shoulder lovingly, a huge smile planted on his rugged face.

"H for healthy is all I'm concerned about, angel," he said, kissing her temple. She nuzzled into his kiss.

"Is there something we should be worried about?" I asked, immediately concerned. Oliver perked up and grabbed Aspen's hand.

"Not a one. Our little lemon is just fine!" Hank added proudly.

"Lemon?" I asked.

My sister grinned. "He's referring to the baby's size. According to the growth chart, the baby at fourteen weeks is the size of a lemon. It's endless entertainment for Hank. He actually tells me each morning how much the baby has grown, what new thing with my body I should expect to be feeling. And weekly, he humors me with what size the baby is compared to food." She shakes her head and grins.

"Those daily e-mails are perfect. Just what you need to keep you up to date. A man doesn't need to be told what's happening with his baby. He should already know." Hank's chest puffed up a bit as he placed a protective hand over Aspen's stomach.

"Let me get this straight, mate. You get e-mails telling you about your wife's pregnancy every day?" Nate asked while he leaned against Emma's chair from behind.

"That's right. My baby, my fiancée, my family. Not going to be blindsided by nothin'. And I'm completely fascinated by the entire process. Her body is incredible and sexy as hell!" He nuzzled my sister's neck and kissed the ball of her shoulder.

"You're whipped!" Nate pointed at Hank, and everyone sitting at the table laughed.

Hank shrugged and pulled Aspen closer to him. "Don't care," Hank answered with all the confidence in the world. Truly, the macho thing did come naturally to Hank, especially considering his old-fashioned upbringing. When it came to anything related to my sister, he was all in.

"Well, I think it's fantastic. A man should want to know about his child. So many children don't have a loving father. Hank, I think you're better than most men," I added with meaning. I truly was proud of the relationship Aspen had with Hank. He seemed to care only for her and their happiness.

"Now what about the wedding? That's in two or three weeks?" Nate asked and sat in his chair.

"Honestly, I'm not doing much," Aspen responded. "The wedding planner and Hank's family are taking care of most of the arrangements. With *Bright Magazine* releasing in January, the baby due in May, and Hank's business expansion to New York"—she sighed heavily—"we're crammed with activity. Not to mention how crazy we are for getting married the week before Thanksgiving during winter in Texas."

"Angel, we're lucky that we're having an unusually warm winter this year. 'Sides, we'll be doing all of it in the heated tents. It's going to be fine. Come rain, snow, or shine, I'm marrying you in a couple weeks." Hank smiled so wide his grin almost looked manic.

I remember that kind of love. I had that with James. It's times like these, when something life changing occurs, that I miss his presence the most. He would have been delighted to see Aspen so happy. He always thought she took life too seriously and lived to work, not worked to live. Yes, James would have approved wholeheartedly of Hank and Aspen. Hank was the opposite of Aspen in all the ways that didn't matter. The things they had in common, their core values, their love of good food, books, work ethic and deep friendships were a perfect foundation for a happy long life.

"Y'all are coming out to Texas, right? We've got room in Aspen's jet for a whole basketball team."

I waited, holding my breath while Collier looked at me, held my eyes, and responded to Hank's question. "Wouldn't miss it for the world."

I closed my eyes, knowing that no matter what I did to avoid him this week, including bailing on our date, he was going to find me and I was going to cave. It was too hard not to when his arms and warmth surrounded me.

A memory of a different time seeped into my subconscious. The voices around the table slipped away until I could hear only one voice, the one with the power to break me.

"Come on, you know you want to!"

"I do not! Stop bugging me, James, I swear to God I'll get my brother, Rio, to come kick your ass!"

"That snooty rich boy wouldn't want to get his hands dirty.

He's never been in a fight in his life!" James jumped over the bush I'd just launched myself around on my way to my car. His hand grabbed mine. I was struck with the feeling of warmth, tenderness and something I didn't want to name. "Hey, London. Please, just… please." His voice came out in a rush.

I twirled, rocking his hand loose. "What!"

James put a hand to his neck and his body swayed as he looked left and right. "I like you, okay. I thought maybe you might like me, too." His tone was sweet yet held a deep timbre. His seventeen-year-old body was slowly catching up to the voice that matched a grown man.

Taking a nervous breath, I pulled my books to my chest and twirled a lock of hair around my finger. "I do…like you," I whispered.

He leaned close and swept the black bangs from my eyes. "You do?" He smiled.

I nodded.

He whooped and hollered and gave the air a fist pump. "All right! I mean, that's cool." We both laughed. "So then, you'll go out with me? On a real date?" His eyes were pleading, his thumbs loosely clutching the belt loops of his Calvin Klein's as he waited for my answer.

I couldn't believe James Kelley was asking me out on an official date. This whole time I crushed on him but thought we were just friends. Then he surprises me with this. I can't wait to go home and call Aspen. "Yes, I will James." His eyes sparked with excitement. "I'll go with you anywhere."

"Bridge honey, earth to Bridge? Damn, she's doing it again." I heard Tripp snap in front of my face. I shook off the memory and stared into the nervous eyes of my best friend.

"Sorry. What did you say?"

Tripp took a breath and shook his head, smiling. Collier stood arms crossed, one over the other along his broad chest. He had his head tilted to the side, assessing me. A shock of dirty blond hair fell over his forehead. I wanted to stand and push that lock back in place, then nibble on his perfect lips again.

"Bridge, we lost you there. Where'd you go?" His eyes met mine, and I threw some daggers I didn't think he expected. His neck shot back in surprise. "Um, sorry, never mind. You ready to go home?"

"I'd be happy to give you a lift," Collier offered.

"No, no, that's okay. Tripp and I live together. Makes sense to go together. I'll just get my coat." Tripp and I both stood. He put his hands in his pockets and had a weird stare off with Collier. It was the strangest thing. I'd seen him do it once before with Andrew, the crazy stalker, but never with one of my clients or any of the other men I'd been with intimately. Just didn't add up.

Collier followed me to the coat closet and helped me pull on the heavy wool. He pulled my thick mane of hair out of my coat and started buttoning me in. The sweet gesture melted my heart and had me smiling.

"Next weekend, you and me. Plan for a casual evening. Nothing pretentious, I promise." The lovely undertones of his British accent when he spoke made me giddy. His eyes twinkled as I took in his ruffled hair, dark eyes, and his full lips as he licked them.

He was doing his own assessment. He leaned close as if to hug me and then planted his hands on each bicep pulling me against his chest. The thrill of his touch skated along my nerves. "I can still smell you all over me…it's making me ache for you."

Without warning, I cupped the back of his neck, tangled my fingers into the hair at his nape, and pulled his lips to mine. He tasted of rich wine and hot-blooded male. I slid my tongue against his and he moaned into my mouth, giving back as much, if not more than I gave initially. Quickly, he pinned me against the hallway wall, a knee between my thighs and a hand on my ass. He was everything I wanted in that moment and more.

★ ★ ★

Her lips were soft and sweet as I tugged on the bit of flesh, then soothed it with my tongue. She groaned the moment my thigh pressed against her center. Christ on a cross, she was beautiful. Her breath was heavy against my lips. I pulled back to look into her eyes. Every second with her seemed weighted, filled with desires unspoken. We didn't have to speak. Her body told me everything I needed to know.

When I squeezed her arse, she mewled like a baby kitten. Hearing that sound for the rest of my life wouldn't be long enough. I was lost in a haze of lust. I pressed my erection directly against her center as I hiked one thigh over my hip, palming her arse, mimicking the position we were in earlier.

In her. Needed…*press*…to get in…*press*…her.

London moaned and moved to hike her other leg up before a booming voice broke the spell.

"Damn, Bridge! Can't leave you two alone for a fucking second!" Tripp's voice grated and echoed off the walls of the long hallway. I groaned and pulled away from my beauty.

She leaned her forehead against mine and smiled, and then started to giggle. "What's so funny?" I asked, annoyed by the interruption yet loving the smile across her gorgeous face.

"It's like he's the hall monitor."

I chuckled and pulled her skirt down. Without a second thought, I gave her sweet arse a loving pat. I planned on reacquainting myself with that bum very soon.

"You guys finished?" Tripp stood hands in his pockets, a scowl on his face. He'd be a good-looking bloke if he didn't have such a sour expression plastered to his mug.

Waggling my eyebrows, I responded, "Not even close." Then I smiled wickedly at London.

She nudged me playfully in the shoulder as she pulled herself from my embrace. That's one thing about Americans I never understood. They sure touched an awful lot to make a point. They couldn't just say something. They had to poke and prod to express themselves. Quite uncivilized, but as long as it was London doing the touching, I'd be happy with about anything.

Tripp rolled his eyes as London passed. He stopped me midstride as I made to follow. "You." He pointed to my chest. "Don't fucking make her cry again. She's more fragile than she lets on. You got me?" He pointed his finger on my chest in some macho move made to frighten me. Instead, my fighter instincts flared, and I grabbed the offending digit, twisted it and his hand, and then pressed it back into his chest. He gasped, and then gritted his teeth in pain.

"You're sending very mixed signals, mate." The words spilled through my clenched teeth. I made a show of putting my face in his direct line of sight, close enough that he could feel my breath on his face. "One minute you're all over her. The next you're suggesting a bloke make a go of it. What's your story?" I tipped my chin for effect. "I've made it perfectly clear I intend to date Ms. Kelley exclusively. How about you? Hmm?"

"She doesn't date." He pushed my arm back with his elbow, and I let go of his finger. He shook it, and then cupped the other hand over it protectively.

"Fancy that. She's going on another date with me next weekend. Please, stay out of it. You seem to have a very close relationship. If you read people better, you'd understand my only intentions are to make her happy."

"Is that what you call it? Fucking her against a wall during a friendly dinner party. Making her happy?"

"Didn't hear her complaining. As a matter of fact, she was very happy as I recall."

I felt the air shift as Tripp pulled his hand back, preparing to hit me. "Tripp! What the hell do you think you're doing?" London's voice was shrill. I hoped the tone was never directed at me.

Tripp took a deep breath as London put her hand on his bicep. He closed his eyes and clenched his jaw. For the life of me, I couldn't figure out what this fella's problem was. One minute he was happy she'd met someone. The next he's warning me off. It was a downright clusterfuck.

"Just Bond and I having a little chat is all."

"Didn't look that way to me." She pulled Tripp's arm, and I clenched my fist at her easy familiarity with the man's body. I wanted to be the only man she put those delicate hands on.

"Just a little misunderstanding. I believe we understand

each other better, yeah?" I clapped Tripp on the shoulder. His gaze shot to mine briefly before he nodded and shrugged off my touch.

"Let's go home," London urged him. "Collier, I'll connect with you this week. Just text me your plans. I'll be with Dylan all week."

The name Dylan sent chills up my spine. I knew she had a client and suspected she was doing more with that client then just work.

I tugged her hand and brought her body fast against mine. My other hand slid against her lower back anchoring her to me. "Are you still living with your client?" I could see Tripp grin out the corner of my eye. I hated it, knowing my answer.

Her eyes clouded. She pulled me to her in a tight hug. Her lips grazed my ear. "I haven't been with another man since we were together at your place. And I promise not to be with anyone intimately, going further."

I gripped her tightly. "And since the night we met?"

She closed her eyes and bit her lip. That was not the answer I wanted. She shook her head and seemed to shrink right in front of me. Sadness and a sense of unease filled the air.

"I told you I wasn't the right girl for you," she whispered.

"You're the perfect girl for me." I pulled her into a quick but hard kiss. She returned it willingly. For now, it was enough. "Next weekend. Promise me you won't run."

Her face lit in a huge smile. "I promise." I may have been so hopped up on endorphins, but I believed her. Deep inside, she wanted this as much as I did. Had to. There wasn't another option. I intended to make her mine.

After making sure the rest of the guests left, I stayed to help Nathaniel and Emma clean up.

"So shagging London in my guest bedroom during a dinner party? You're a filthy scoundrel, big brother. I'd have never thought you had it in you," Nathaniel said while stacking dishes into the dishwasher.

"You haven't taken a woman in worse places?" I countered.

"Oh, boy talk. I'm in. Where was the dirtiest place you've shagged a girl?" Emma joined in. Both Nathaniel and I looked over at our baby sister. One or both of us must have shown a shocked expression because she continued, "I'm a married woman. Hello, I've been shagging Evan for years, remember."

We both grunted and grumbled. "Cocksucker," slipped through my lips and Emma laughed. That was the second time this evening that expletive had made an appearance.

"Seriously, I want to know the craziest places you've bonked a girl." Both of us stayed silent and continued to pack up the leftovers and put away the unused stemware. "Come on…no? Neither of you? Fine, I'll go first."

Not wanting to hear anything pertaining to our baby sister having sex, Nathaniel and I both said, "No!" at the same time Emma said, "Mum and Dad's bed."

"No way. You and Evan shagged in Mum and Dad's bed! That's just nasty. I can't believe you." I laughed. Nathaniel made gagging and unpleasant noises.

"That's pretty bold, Em." We both chuckled. Her cheeks pinked.

"I'd have to say for me it was the toilet at a pub. Those stalls are tiny and filthy. When you're pissed and horny, it doesn't matter though," I answered, sipping the remainder of my wine and adding the glass to the sink next to the others awaiting a good washing.

"That is gross, Colly." Her pretty face scrunched in a grimace. "How about you, Nate? Come on. We shared." She pouted.

He sighed and took a moment to think about it.

"On a bakery floor."

"That's lame," Emma said.

"Yeah, bollocks. Pick a new one."

"What? You guys have no idea what falls on the floor of a bakery. It's sticky, gritty, and slimy all at the same time. Imagine a beautiful bird riding you, yet all you can think about is the disgusting muck scraping along your bare back and arse. It's quite possibly the single most revolting experience of my life. Couldn't look at the girl the same again. Had to break it off."

Em and I looked at our brother and cracked up laughing.

"What? It was horrible."

I shook my head and grabbed Em around the shoulders. "Come on, baby girl, let's go home. Your brother has gone barmy. Thanks for tonight. Cheers!" I threw over my shoulder.

We could hear Nathaniel going on and on about how he had to scrape egg and flour off the hair of his legs and that he could still feel the sugar granules piercing his shoulder blades against the tile floor.

"He needs a good woman." I hugged my sister to my side as we made our way into the elevator and down to the garage.

"I think you're right. If only he'd allow himself more

than one date, we'd be getting somewhere."

Pulling open the car door, Emma slid into my beloved Porsche. She had a point. It was rare that Nathaniel would have a second date with a prospective love interest. Lately, we'd both been pulling the one-night stand routine. Far longer than I wanted to admit.

That is until London came along.

Her face was the only one I'd seen for the past three weeks. Man, I was looking forward to our date. I'd have to get Jane to assist since she picked a great place last time. This time though, I wanted to show London I'm a regular guy who just wants to take a pretty girl out for the night on the town.

CHAPTER ELEVEN

"Wake up, my love. Today's the day." His voice was chipper this morning, and then it dawned on me. Today's the day. My smile was huge as I flung out of bed. But he wasn't there.

Slowly, I searched through the apartment, checking door after door. All empty. Gone. He was gone. Nervousness twitched in my gut.

"London," a voice called teasingly from outside the apartment.

I laughed and hurled myself out the door, all smiles. I looked left and right down the long hallway. Nothing. Where is he? I strained to hear more of his voice.

"London…I need you." I heard him call from somewhere to the right, his voice now pained, gritty. "My love, please…" tapered off into nothing, sending shivers skittering through my limbs. I pounded down the hall in my bare feet until I reached the heavy metal doors. Bright white light stung my eyes, blinding me as I pushed the doors open.

Rain pelted my face, wetting my hair and clothes. Cold, so cold. I shivered bone-deep, standing on a street I couldn't recognize, wearing only a tank top and bed shorts.

"Where are you?" I screamed, trying to get my vision back, blinking furiously at the spots of rainbow light.

"Here. I'm here!" I moved on pure instinct. Gravel and rocks dug into the tender patch of skin at the arches of my feet. My hands were straight out in front of me until they hit cold metal. I slid wet fingers along the surface as if reading Braille until I felt the handle.

Slowly, the lights blinding me faded away and I gripped the car door handle and pulled it back.

Blood. Blood was everywhere. His head, chest, and abdomen are coated with the thick burgundy substance.

"Don't forget me, love. Never forget me," James said. Blood oozed from his mouth in a sickening river of red.

Gut-wrenching screams ripped from my lungs as James took his last breath. I covered my eyes with bloody hands. James's blood was all over me, soaking the white tank a deep crimson. The coppery smell gagged me. The sour taste filled my mouth. When I looked up it was no longer James sitting there coated in death, it was Collier. My sweet, sexy Englishman's chocolate eyes were devoid of light. Gone. They both were gone.

James.
Collier.
Dead.

"Wake up, God dammit! Baby, wake up!" Tripp's voice pierced my mind and I woke with a start. A scream still clogged in my throat screeched out into the light of day. "London, oh thank God! Are you okay?" Tripp's arms were around me, holding tight. Tears poured down my cheeks and fell to his chest.

"Dead, they were dead."

"Who Bridge, who was dead?"

"James…and…and…" Another bout of deep sobs tore from my lungs as I gripped his back, hiding in the comfort of his chest. The sickening images from the dream were still fresh.

"It's okay, I'm here," he spoke in a calm voice, one you'd use with a frightened child. Right now, I felt like one.

Fear's evil claws closed around my heart and squeezed tight, choking off my sanity.

"C-c-collier…dead. It was James and then…and then… it was Collier. Oh God, it was awful," I cried into Tripp's chest. "He left me, Tripp. He left me just like James."

"Bridge baby, it was just a dream. Collier is—" He gritted his teeth and pulled me back to look into my eyes. He swiped away the tears that wouldn't stop and took a deep breath. "Collier is not James. He's very much alive." I had a feeling he wanted to say something else, but he didn't.

"It was so real, it was my wedding day, and James was waking me up like he did that day. I actually remembered how I felt when he woke me. Like everything in the world was just right…until it wasn't anymore." I sniffed and wiped my dripping nose with the back of my arm. Tripp grimaced and pulled a tissue out of the box on the end table and handed it to me. "Thanks." I blew my nose and took a deep breath, trying to expel the images scratching to the surface. "It was… God, Tripp. It was so real."

Tripp pulled me into the warmth of his embrace, cradling my head. "So, Bond has gotten to you then? He's under your skin." He didn't say what I knew he was trying to say, and I was thankful. I was nowhere near ready to think things were any different with Collier than they were with any other man. If I wanted to be with Collier, I couldn't be with other men. Knowing what I knew of Collier and his third degree last night, he would not share.

No, I'd see this through until we'd worked each other out of our systems. It was bound to happen. This thing with Collier was unique in the sense that I wanted to see more of him and often, but it wouldn't last. It never did. Eventually

I'd tire of him.

But why the dream? The only man I'd ever dreamt about was James. In four years, I have only ever dreamed of James. and now I've had a fantasy and a nightmare about Collier.

"So you're dating Bond officially?" Tripp stood up to pull my robe off the door hanger. I wasn't naked, but goose bumps were still prevalent on my arms and legs, giving physical proof of how frightened I'd been.

I nodded and slipped on the robe he handed me, not really sure what to say as I pulled my knees into my chest. This was new for me. Dating. I hadn't officially dated anyone since my husband died. If you'd ask me three weeks ago, prior to meeting my sexy Englishman, I'd say I was the queen of hookups. Even those had only been in the past couple of years.

It was the perfect answer to my ongoing problem. Burying my secrets in another man's flesh was easy when you didn't plan to keep them around. It also took away the constant thoughts of James. I could fuck my way into sweet oblivion and find a small respite from the grief, the pain, the wide open hole where my soul once lived—the soul that died right along with the only man I'll ever truly love.

Tripp dropped on the bed and spread his arms wide. I snuggled right into the crook of his arm, my head resting on his bare chest. At least he had on pajama pants this time. A naked Tripp hugging me led to groping more often than not. Though I think he's gotten the hint that he can't be as familiar with me as he once was. I'm just not in that place anymore.

"This is weird, Bridge."

I placed my hands over his chest and rested my chin on top. "What is?"

"You, dating. Like, really dating someone."

Tilting my head to the side, I tried to gauge his mood. "Yeah, kind of. What was going on with you last night? You were acting like a jealous boyfriend." I kissed his chest right above his heart. One of his large hands came up and ruffled the shaggy hair. He needed a trim.

"Truth?" he asked.

"Truth," I said and nodded, waiting for him to continue. He obviously had something on his mind. He'd been acting strange the last couple weeks, but last night, his anger and irritation with Collier took the cake.

"I'm not sure I'm capable of letting you be with another man." He threw a hand over his eyes as the words smacked me up the side of the head like a frying pan.

"Tripp, I'm not sure I understand? I've been with more men than I'd like to take credit for. You know that." My best friend looked at me with those sparkling eyes, sorrow and pain etched into deep lines in his normally perfect face. I hugged him tight, trying to put all the love I had for him into that one embrace. "Tell me what's going on?"

"Bridge." His voice was dry, cracked, sounding like sandpaper along a prickly wooden surface. "You're all I have."

I sat up, tears pooling as understanding dawned bright and clear as a new day. "Tripp Devereaux, I love you more than anyone. No man I'm dating or not dating is ever going to change that." He gripped my hand and kissed my palm. "Truth!" I let one tear fall. He kissed it away from my cheek.

"Still doesn't keep me from being afraid. What happens

when you finally take that leap? Can you promise you'll never leave me?"

Tripp's biggest fear, live and in living color. He lost his whole family when he came out about being bisexual, not that his family was anything to brag about. His mother constantly abused him, mentally and physically, until the day he tried to take his own life. He also had a brother he left to drown in a life filled with sex and drugs. The guilt over leaving his brother in that house was a whole different ball of hell he constantly carried around.

It took all I had not to scream at him that I would never, was never, going to leave him. But I couldn't say that. James said it to me and he left…forever. "We never know what our future will bring, but I do know that wherever I am, whatever I'm doing, you will always be one of the most important people in my life." I forced him to sit up and I crawled into his lap, hugging him. "You're my family. No man can take that away from us. If he even tries, he's not worth my time. Now *that* I promise you!"

We spent long moments just listening to one another breathe, calming the rapid beating of our hearts. Slowly, I tunneled my fingers through his hair.

"You need a trim. You want me to cut it today?" He nodded against my chest. I waited a couple more minutes until he took a deep breath. "You gonna continue to give Collier a hard time?"

The smile that lit his face was priceless. It spoke of everything I loved about my best friend. His boyish charm, his roguish features, his sad eyes. "Yes, yes, I am. If he's got my best girl on his radar, I'm going to rile him every chance I get."

I slumped into his chest, defeated.

He laughed. "Hey, it's my job as your heart's protector to make sure he's good enough for my girl."

"You are not my protector."

"Oh yes, I am. Just like you're always flicking at the little bimbo cling-ons that try to stick to me, I'll be keeping an eye on Mr. Bond."

"He really hates that you call him that," I mused.

Those eyes lit up again. "I know." He waggled his eyebrows.

★ ★ ★

To: London Kelley
From: Collier Stone
What are you doing right now?

Okay, so I've resorted to the wanker's way out of calling London. Texting is impersonal but it gets the job done. She can avoid a call or choose not to check her messages. With a text, you know from the little icon that she's seen it. Several minutes go by and the icon still says "Sent" instead of "Seen." Curse the blasted thing. Jane comes in to bring me my afternoon tea and biscuits or as the Yanks say, cookies. I figure eventually the American terms will filter into my regular speech but after five years, I've not lost my accent, though I definitely find it easier to understand Americans after having lived here for so long.

In the beginning, things I would say would bring down the house. I recall addressing our staff at a Christmas party and I said, "Blow me! You all look terrific this evening." The entire audience, including each staff member's plus one, howled with laughter. I didn't get the joke. In England, "blow me" is a common term for being surprised or blown away by something. Yanks think it's an offer of sexual service. Over time, I've gotten used to items that put me arse over tit with the Americans and have worked hard to learn more about their culture and colloquialisms.

"What type of *cookie* is this?" I asked Jane. She smiled, knowing I was making the effort to use her term.

"Very good." She smiled sweetly. "These are shortbread Girl Scout cookies. I figured they'd go well with the tea."

I took a bite and smiled, letting the dark tones of the Earl Gray flutter over my taste buds. "It does. Very well, thank you. Might I chat privately with you about a personal matter, Jane?"

She sat down abruptly. Her pristine gray suit was a bit big on her lengthy frame, but she's not the type to worry about looking attractive over smart. Jane is by far one of my most trusted employees at Stone, Walker, & Associates. She's been with me the entire five years since we opened in the states. If you looked up the word smart in the dictionary, it would have a picture of Jane.

"You recall that dinner you set up?"

"For you and Ms. Kelley? That would be London Kelley, sister to client Aspen Bright-Reynolds of Air Bright Enterprises."

"Bloody hell. That's fantastic! How did you know all that?"

Her pink lips tipped into a soft smile. Jane's face was plain but not unattractive. She'd be quite a fine bird if she smiled more often. The sweep of thick hair was pulled back in an ever-present bun. I don't think during her entire sojourn here I've ever seen her hair down. There has to be a lot of it. Made me wonder what she looked like in a casual setting.

"Mr. Stone."

I rolled my eyes. I'd asked her to call me Collier for five years and to this day, she still refused.

"When my boss suddenly asks me to make reservations for a date, something he has never asked me to do, I make a point to glean as much information as possible. Would you like to know more?"

More about London Kelley? Hell yes! I wanted to scream. Instead, I played it cool. "By all means, share."

"London Abigail Bright-Reynolds was born on February fourteenth and will turn twenty-seven next year."

"Wow. And her birthday is Valentine's Day? Fits the woman." Completely afraid of love. How ironic.

Jane smiles and continues. "She married James Kelley at the ripe age of eighteen and was married for four years before being widowed."

Jane knew her stuff.

"Ms. Kelley lives with one Tripp Devereaux but the only information I could find about him was that he's worked in modeling for AIR Bright Enterprises and has spent the last few years working in restaurants. He currently works in that overly priced French restaurant next to Armani on Fifth called Magnifique."

She was about to continue when I cut her off. "That's all. I prefer to find out the rest the old-fashioned way. But London is the reason I wanted to chat with you. Was hoping you could help me again. I want to take Ms. Kelley on another date. Something a bit more casual. What do Yanks find entertaining?"

"You act like we're the foreigners. We're not that different from you British folks. Have you considered something like dinner and a movie?"

I jumped up and pulled on Jane's hands. Her eyes widened with concern as I yanked her into a full-bodied hug. "Smashing, Jane! You're brilliant!" I hugged her tight, but she kept her arms at her sides, clearly uncomfortable. I didn't care. My most beloved personal assistant was the bees' knees and I wanted to show it. Quickly before she could escape, I kissed one side of her face, then the other, and let her go. A beautiful pink blush rose on her cheeks as she smiled shyly.

"I'm glad I could be of service. A bit more tea, Mr. Stone?"

"Another would be lovely. Thank you."

As Jane left, I pulled up Google to find out what shows were playing on the big screen. As I searched, my phone pinged. Finally!

To: Collier Stone
From: London Kelley
Fighting with a boutique on a piece of furniture they are trying to overcharge me for. What are you doing?
To: London Kelley
From: Collier Stone
Planning our date.
To: Collier Stone
From: London Kelley
Really. Give me a hint?
To: London Kelley

From: Collier Stone

Nope. Mum's the word. May I be so forward as to suggest you pack a bag for the evening?

Nerves scuttled up my spine and a fine sheen of sweat broke across my forehead as I waited her reply. Suddenly it was very hot in here. Stifling really. I undid the noose they call a tie and a couple of the buttons on my dress shirt. Would she find me too bold? Was asking her to stay the night inappropriate? Shite. I'd have to get rid of Emma.

I pressed the button for Emma's desk. She answered on the first ring. "Hello, brother mine."

"Hey, Em, can you plan to stay at Nathaniel's this weekend?"

"Hmmm depends…" she responded coyly.

"On what?" Fury laced my tone.

"Who's coming over? Is it the hot woman you manhandled at Nate's party?"

"Yes. I mean, I didn't manhandle her." I sighed. "Can you please stay with him? I want some time alone with London."

After a beat, she replied, "You really like her."

I took a deep breath and laid it out there. "I do, Em. More than I want to."

"I'll make myself scarce this weekend. Love you. Bye."

My phone pinged again.

To: Collier Stone
From: London Kelley
I like forward. Bag will be packed. Where are you taking me?
To: London Kelley

From: Collier Stone

Nowhere you'd expect. And we will be staying at my place. My sister will be at Nathaniel's.

To: Collier Stone
From: London Kelley

Hmmm I'll bet I can get it out of you. That's nice of your sister to give you space. I'd jump you with your sister there or not.

Criminy! Talk about forward. London takes the term to a whole new place—one that quickly worked its magic down south. My willy was hard as steel at the thought of shagging her while my sister slept in the other room. Almost sounded indecent even though we were grown adults.

To: London Kelley
From: Collier Stone

Christ, woman. Keep that up and I'll be taking you in the car when I pick you up.

There. Now I've played her game, settling the score. Too quickly, my cell phone pinged again. The woman was wicked fast with her texts.

To: Collier Stone
From: London Kelley

Promises, promises.

That was it. She was the perfect woman. No one in the world could take me from zero to a hundred on the lust-o-meter in the middle of the blessed day while at work. My cock was painfully hard just thinking about taking her in the car. And the bed.

Somehow, I had to make good on this date. London was quickly becoming an obsession. Thoughts of her filled every recess of my mind at work, at home, in the shower, eating dinner, sitting in front of the TV, poring over legal documents. If I didn't get her to commit to being mine for whatever length of time this was between us, I'd never be rid of the righteous need to have her constantly. As it stood, I was on the sheer edge of jumping in my Porsche, finding her, and taking her on the steps of wherever she was. Public be damned.

Just focus on this weekend. A few more days and she'd be by my side, all around me. I couldn't wait. I decided one last text was in order.

To: London Kelley
From: Collier Stone
I always keep my promises, beauty. Always. Friday night. 6:00 p.m.

CHAPTER TWELVE

Tonight was the night. I'd spent all week staying exceptionally busy. It had been easy. Tripp was clingy and Dylan was barely speaking to me. Even though I'd made it clear to my client that our personal relationship wasn't happening under the sheets anymore, he had taken offense.

We had the discussion last week about not having a physical relationship and he didn't understand. He felt as if he'd done something wrong. I could have told him that I'd met someone else and that someone else didn't take too kindly to sharing, but frankly, it wasn't his business.

And telling him would kill all the progress Dylan had made in learning to let loose, and be freer with his feelings. I'd simply told him I was no longer interested in a physical relationship and would not have sex with him. He spent a full week ignoring me, making it incredibly uncomfortable to share a living space. Several times, I thought about just staying home. Unfortunately Tripp's clingy behavior put a kibosh on that. He needed time to work through his own issues about my…whatever this was…with Collier.

"Check this out!" I laid a flyer for a new club opening up in front of Dylan.

"Looks fun. Do you want to go?" Dylan eyes shone with a new happiness. I hadn't seen it in the better part of two weeks.

I shook my head. "Nope. This is the part about

changing your life. You need to call some buddies, take these tickets"—I laid four VIP passes next to the flyer—"and dress up. I'll pick what you wear. And go to this club. Your next task is to troll for women…alone. Without me. I'll be leaving for the weekend. When I come back, I want to see at least a handful of phone numbers of the women you picked up."

"London, I don't know. I feel a little better about hitting on a woman, but several? I'm not sure I can." He shrugged and wiped a hand over his face.

Rolling my eyes, I plopped into the kitchen chair next to him and placed my hand over his. "Dylan, you are a good-looking guy. You're nice. You're secure financially. And you respect women. There's no reason you can't go to a club and pick up several women. Start building your own list of hotties, if you will. The goal is to change your life, not just your home. You can do this. I believe in you."

Dylan picked up the tickets and spread them out like a wad of cash. "You think so, eh?"

"I do. It's what you need. What friends can you invite?"

"My brother and maybe one other guy would be interested. I've spent the better part of the last few years building my career and working my ass off, not keeping in touch with old friends or making new ones." He seemed a bit sad to admit his lack of friends. That needed to change.

"That's why it's time for a change. You need to enjoy everything you've put into your life so far. Part of that is being young. Partying a little, hanging out with other guys, having hot no-strings sex with several women. Maybe along the line you'll find one you want to spend more time on. Let go a little. This is your last weekend before the renovation. Have you booked your hotel?"

"Nah. I'll stay with my brother and his girlfriend. He thinks we need more time to get to know each other as adults."

I smacked his bicep. "Exactly! He's right. But don't let him bring his girlfriend out. She'll deter other women. He can be your wing man." Then a great idea hit me hard. It was perfect. A win-win if I did say so myself. I would help my client and my best friend. "Hold up, I need to make a call."

Dylan handed me the house phone and I dialed home. Tripp answered after a couple rings.

"Hey, Bridge. What's cookin', hot stuff?"

God, I loved him. "I need a favor."

"Anything for you."

My smile must have been infectious. Dylan watched me intently, a big smile of his own plastered across his scruffy face. "This Friday, I need you to meet up with my client Dylan and check out that new club, Roxy's."

"Roxy's?" Tripp paused. "That's right. You did the redesign of that for Roxanne Thibodaux when she took over that building."

"Yup, and it's incredible inside. But what I need is help from you with Dylan. He needs to learn the art of picking up women...lots of women. Can you do that?" I grinned and winked at Dylan.

His face had turned red, and he scratched the back of his neck nervously.

"Does Oprah have more money than God?" Tripp snorted into the line.

"Excellent. I'll owe you one. Hey, we're meeting up for lunch with Pen and Oliver right?"

"Yeah, Oliver texted that we're set for one at The Place. We need to go over some wedding shit. We leave in two weeks, which means you're going to have to do the renovation in a little over a week, and then have the reveal on Friday. We fly out Saturday with your family."

"Okay, yeah. We'll talk later. See you at lunch."

My shoulders slumped. Being pulled in so many directions was exhausting. Aspen's wedding was less than three weeks away. I needed Dylan out of his funk and back on schedule, which Tripp would help with, thankfully.

Tripp was a ladies' man. Yes, he batted for both teams, but the ladies literally fell at the man's feet. He had an air of confidence that attracted both sexes. If anyone could help Dylan with the art of picking up a lady, it was Tripp. It would also help him get past his own insecurities over Collier.

The next issue was the reveal. Usually I didn't plan with such a tight window of time, but the wedding deadline had me pushing the limits with my contractors.

Actually, that gave me an idea. I wondered if Hank's company could spare a couple men for the project? That would help ensure my deadlines.

I pulled Hank's company's number on my cell phone.

"Jensen Construction, Cami speaking," a small sweet voice spoke through the receiver.

Cami? Who the hell was that? "I'm sorry. I was expecting Rosie?"

"Yes, Rosie's still here. She's the office administrator. I'm the new receptionist. Just started today actually," the woman's voice held a twinge of nervousness.

"This is London Kelley. I need to speak with Hank. Can you put him on?"

"Actually, he's busy at the moment. Is there something I can help you with?"

I wanted to come back with a smart retort that there was *not* anything she could help me with, but something in what she didn't say gave me pause.

"I'm his soon to be sister-in-law. Whatever he's doing, he'll take my call."

"I'm sorry, Ms. Kelley. Hank is in his office with his fiancée and said not to bother him no matter what." She was clearly concerned that I was about to be angry. I was for a moment. If Aspen was there, I knew exactly what they're doing. Those two can't keep their hands off one another.

"Beautiful blonde, suit, pregnant?"

"She's pregnant? Oh, that's amazing. She doesn't look it at all. Yes, she's incredibly gorgeous," Cami offered happily. Probably not something a receptionist should share with just anyone, but the more she spoke, the more I wanted to get to know her.

"That's my sister. Tell you what, take a message. Tell Hank I need to talk to him when he finishes with Aspen. Tell my sister I'll see her at one, as planned. Got it?"

The woman was quiet, and then finally responded. "I have a message for Mr. Jensen to call London Kelley and the message is urgent. I have a message for Ms. Reynolds that you will meet her at one, as planned."

"You're good. How do you like the job so far?"

"Thank you. I love it. Everyone is so nice and Mr. Jensen is a gentleman. Asked me if I'd like a cup of coffee and had a muffin on my desk as a welcome when I started this morning. Meeting Oliver and getting this job is my dream come true," she whispered.

Oliver. Of course. Ollie would find a sweet little thing who only wants to work. He's the only other person I know who seems to have a keen sense about people. He can fetter out the bullshit people try to sell regularly.

"I look forward to meeting you, Cami. I think you'll enjoy working for Hank. Plus, he's good eye candy, isn't he? But hands off. My sister looks like an angel but brings out the claws when it comes to her man." I laughed.

"Oh my. I'd never!"

"Relax. I'm just kidding. It was great talking to you, Cami. I look forward to meeting you in person someday."

"Me, too, Ms. Kelley. I'll give Mr. Jensen and Ms. Reynolds your messages. Good-bye."

She hung up and I got ready to meet with the contractors for the day. Hank called thirty minutes later and agreed to release a couple guys for the week to help finish the renovation more quickly. He said his guys would be happy for the extra weekend work; if they did well, I'd move some of my business to Jensen Construction. Having close connections to a builder is a decorator's dream come true.

The renovation was planned and all the furniture would show up in a few days, along with the special art piece and the new entertainment center. Flat-screen, surround sound, six-disc changer, the works was being put in. A jetted tub and shower would be installed, big enough for a several bodies. Not that Dylan was going to go man-whore-style like Tripp would. Having the option to have some acrobatic sex was a good thing for a bachelor.

The plan with Dylan was to give him a bachelor pad that was sexy enough to awe the ladies yet not make his family balk. I'd purchased a set of dark gray leather couches that fit his lifestyle and age. My client loved fast cars and that was the one thing he splurged on, until my contract of course.

An artist I knew designed a glass-top table that had a square see-through stand that highlighted different car ornaments within it, such as the leaping jaguar, a BMW license plate, and several other choice trinkets, including the steering wheel from a winning Indy 500 race car and a checkered flag. I'd seen the table's design and decided it was tasteful and would be a real showpiece. I couldn't wait for Dylan to see the final product.

His bedroom was going to be a three-hundred and sixty-degree job. Everything in it needed to go. Currently, he had a treadmill and weight bench, white walls, and a boring bed and nightstand. The picture of a race car framed over the bed did not say, "Hey, hottie, want to stay the night?" It said, "I'm still sixteen and I don't know how to be an adult."

I'd ordered him a huge new bed that sat atop a low cappuccino-colored platform, a very minimal Asian-inspired design. A large tapestry in rich colors and shapes would hang behind the bed. Very gender-neutral. The back wall would be painted a rich mocha to add warmth and would be a nice backdrop for the hanging. The workout equipment would be moved to an in-home gym, complete with all new equipment, flat-screens, and a sound system. He had two more bedrooms in the apartment. One would be a game room and the other his guest room.

The plans were in place, including the weekend, which included a night out with the boys for Dylan and a night for me with Collier.

Shivers of excitement filled the space around me.

Collier and I had only spent one full night together, but oh, what a night. A repeat was definitely in order. Now that we'd cleared the air, I looked forward to spending time with him.

Anticipation ran high for the physical aspects of our time together. Being with Collier the other night, letting go, him taking me against the wall, pushed every button I had. I wanted, *needed* to be with him again. When our bodies connected, a fire ignited. One so bright it was impossible to ignore. For now, I was willingly going in, planning to get burned.

★ ★ ★

The earth fell beneath my feet as I took in her form. Thick black hair tumbled in curls around her shoulders. An aqua-blue cashmere sweater, the pristine blue hues mimicking the Caribbean ocean, set off her eyes and molded to her breasts like a second skin. Her hips were encased in a dark gray, almost black, pencil skirt that ended just above her knees. Tall suede come-shag-me boots covered an incredible set of gams. London was mouthwateringly stunning, and it took everything I had not to push her into the wall behind her door and take her. Right here. Right now.

"Hey, Colly." She used the childhood nickname my family had given me. I grimaced. "What? You don't like being called Colly?" she asked with a wicked grin.

I slid a hand around her neck and caressed her cheek. "I prefer other names." I stepped closer, crowding her, letting our bodies barely graze. The familiar crackle and sizzle filled the air surrounding us and the rest of the world faded away into nothing but London. Her lips, her eyes, just…her.

Slowly, I dragged my lips along the cheek I wasn't holding, pressing our chests together.

She gasped. "And what would those names be?" Her vibrations sluiced down my chest, hardening my cock.

With my thumb, I tilted her neck up and to the side, so I could nuzzle the silky skin. Christ, she smelled amazing. Cinnamon and spice and everything nice. I wanted to drown in it. Sink my teeth into it. Mark her perfect skin so that everyone knew where I'd been. Where I'd always want to be. What would be mine for as long as she'd have me.

She inhaled slowly while I licked the tender patch that made her knees shake. I gripped her hip, digging my fingers into her willing flesh. Her heart beat and her breasts mashed against my chest as she tried to press closer.

Nibbling the delicate skin of her ear, I reminded her of the words that haunted my fantasies, "Lover."

She groaned.

I trailed my tongue around the edge of her ear. "Oh-God-Fuck-Me," I whispered the words she used the last time we were together. I kissed and licked a trail down the sweet column of her neck until I reached her clavicle.

"Sexy Englishman," she said on a trembling exhale.

I hummed deep in my throat, kissing my way back up her neck until I reached her lips. They were slightly parted as I slid just the tip of my tongue around the swollen flesh.

"Collier…" she breathed against my mouth. Her hands held me around my neck, trying to bring me toward her.

I pulled back and her eyes shot open. Confusion, mixed with desire and lust, swirled in her gaze.

"Later, beauty. By the end of the night, you'll be begging to be shagged."

Those eyes of hers squinted at the confirmation I was going to make her wait and shite, it was hard. Sod all. I had to have just a taste. "But here's something to hold onto…" I slanted my lips over hers and pressed her deep into my body. Every part of me felt like it was touching every part of her. Pure bliss.

She sighed into the kiss and I took that opportunity to lick into her mouth and let our tongues dance, mingling and twirling in endless loops.

Mint and tea burst over my taste buds, reminding me of London…the woman and my home. Time ebbed and moved languorously until I knew if I didn't pull away, we wouldn't make it out. She deserved more than a quick bonk against another wall. Wooing *then* fucking was on the menu for tonight. I planned on courting this woman to within an inch of her life.

She didn't date? I planned on being the first and possibly the last if what I was starting to feel for this woman was accurate. Only time would tell, but in order to do that, I had to forcefully pull away from heaven.

Her lips chased mine and her finger nails dug into my shoulders. She tugged on my bottom lip with her teeth. "You know, dates are overrated." She pulled away and the look in her eye almost broke my control. Almost.

"That's because you haven't been on any worth rating. Time to go."

London smiled and bit her lip, finally untangling her luscious limbs from her death grip on mine. She shook her head and pulled on the handle of her small carry-on sized suitcase. "You know, you surprise me. Not many men would push me away when they want me. And believe me"—her hand came out and cupped my rock solid erection through my jeans. I groaned and tipped my head back offering my neck as she slid her hand up and down the hard length between my thighs—"I know when a man wants me." I brought my head down and gazed into the depths of her clear-blue eyes. "Maybe by the end of the night, you'll be begging *me* to get fucked." Her voice rose on the K, punctuating her point nicely, bringing me to boiling hot for her, instead of the other way around.

I had no chance of surviving this woman. Everything I ever knew or thought I knew about how women acted and reacted flew out the window. London Kelley was the exception to all rules.

Finally, she removed her hand after one last teasing squeeze of my rigid cock. Christ, the woman would test the reserve of a celibate monk.

"All right, lover." Her eyebrows rose into pristine triangles. "I'm all yours."

"Not now, but you will be." I grinned and grabbed the handle of her bag in one hand and her hand in the other.

After the twenty-minute drive in an easy, comfortable silence, I pulled up to Ma Limbardi's. It was a hole in the wall pizzeria that specialized in thin-crust, melt in your mouth bites of nirvana. All ingredients were fresh, produce bought daily and Ma's sauce was to die for.

"A pizza parlor?" London smiled as I placed a hand to her lower back and led her into the brick building.

A young girl with dark skin, hair, and eyes welcomed us. Her name tag said "Jo" which I'd bet a few quid was short for Josephine. Her Italian heritage was prevalent in her coloring and her small stature. When I gave her my name, her eyes widened and she led us through the throng of patrons, past the bustling kitchen where you could hear a woman shouting in Italian and a male shouting back, then to a door leading to a small patio alcove.

A brick oven sat in one corner. The fire within was bright and crackling. Two heat lamps warmed the outside area, even in the late Fall in New York City. Twinkling lanterns lit and lined the perfect square. In the center was a lone table, complete with a red-and-white checkered tablecloth.

"Collier, this is…it's magnificent!"

"Simple elegance." I smiled and held out her chair. She sat and looked up into the sky. We were surrounded by skyscrapers but the windows didn't face our little space in the universe. We had a clear view of the stars above, glittering the night sky with light.

"It's amazing," she whispered.

"Stunning," I said, but I was looking at her, watching her, soaking up her beauty. Her gaze came down and she noticed I wasn't talking about the sky. A rosy hue flooded her cheeks. "You're lovely when you blush."

London rolled her eyes and leaned her head on her hand, elbow on the table. The candlelight from the centerpiece bounced off her eyes, accentuating their unique color. In that moment, I knew, I just knew she was going to break me, ruin me for other women. She licked her lips and was about to say something when we were interrupted by the waiter.

"Tonight, you will start with *vino*, yes?" said the older waiter with a thick Italian accent, a round belly, and a jolly smile.

"Yes, thank you," I agreed.

"This is Villa Sandi Prosecco from my hometown in Italy. It is *magnifico* with my wife's pies. You will try, yes?" His accent was heavy but easy to understand. Then again, I wasn't one to throw stones. Even my own staff had trouble with my English accent.

"I am Anthony." He pronounced it *An-toe-knee*. "And I will be providing you *eccellente* service. You need. I get for you, yes?"

"Yes," we both said and smiled.

"Tonight, you will be choosing your own *guarnizione* …eh, you say, toppings."

"That's what I had planned. Do you have a list?"

"No, no, no, no, no." The man shook his head. "You tell me what you like to taste, I make for you. And I make even better. We add a little of this, a little of that…" He pinched his fingers together and kissed it, pulling it away with a flourish. "*Perfetto!* Yes?"

London looked at me, eyes bright, lips smiling. We both shrugged and nodded.

"*Signora*, what you normally like on *schifoso*, eh? How you say, lousy pizza?"

London's head fell back as she laughed. "Pepperoni, cheese, veggies, but no onions!" She crinkled her nose and grimaced.

"*Si, si.* And *signore*? For you?"

"Same. Surprise me. But no onions." I nodded to the pretty woman across the table and blew a kiss.

"Good." Anthony winked. "I make for you best pie ever. Yes?"

We both said, "Si," in unison, and then laughed.

The waiter, who I'm pretty sure was the owner, waddled away, his round belly leading him.

I lifted my glass of wine in cheers, and London clinked our glasses. "To the best pizza ever."

"To the best date, ever." London surprised me with her words. We both sipped. The berry and plum notes burst in my mouth. London nodded. "Amazing wine. So light and fruity."

"Tell me more about you." I was dying to glean more information from the sexy enigma.

"Well, you already know the deep dark part about why I'm a widow. What else do you want to know?"

"Tell me about your job. I want to understand why you feel you need to move in with your clients. Why that unconventional approach?"

She sipped her wine and clasped her hands together, leaning her chin on them. "Some would say I'm not only a designer but a life coach."

"How so?"

"When I move in with each client—"

I tried not to stiffen, but she noticed my change in body language instantly.

"Relax. I stay with them, but that doesn't mean I sleep with all of them."

My shoulders sagged.

"Doesn't mean I don't either."

The tension was back.

"You are wound so tight!" She laughed. "I think we'll have to do something about that, though we could have done something about that before, had someone let go of his gentlemanly side," she teased.

"Sorry, love. A gentleman doesn't just take… Well, he does, but usually after he's given his woman a nice meal and an evening."

She giggled. London Kelley giggling was utterly priceless. I'd strive to make that sound come from those berry-red lips again.

"So finish. Explain how you are a life coach and designer. The two don't really go together per se."

"Not conventionally. Basically, I spend a month learning about the person, getting to know their likes, dislikes, the things that make them who they are. We discussed this on our last date."

I smiled over my glass, taking a long pull from the fruity wine.

"Let me put it into real life. For example, the Maxwell reveal you went to."

I nodded so she'd continue uninterrupted.

"I had to help him open his life to a woman. He was in an endless cycle of one-nighters in between the one woman he wanted, Michele." Sounded familiar.

"His girlfriend?"

"She wasn't then. She was the one woman he rotated between his flights of fancy. So I made his apartment something that would open him up to the idea of having a woman stay there."

"Did you sleep with him?"

"Yes," she said without hesitation.

Jealousy rippled through me and spun me like a race car circling round and round an endless track.

"Why?" I choked down the scathing tone, drowning my irritation in several gulps of sweet wine. Her eyes narrowed and she watched me carefully.

"Because I wanted to. Because I could. Because he was willing. I don't really need a reason." Her answer was so flat and unfeeling. It tightened my chest like a straitjacket. "It wasn't until I got to know him that I realized what he needed. Sometimes part of that process is enjoying a few tumbles in the sack."

God, she was so callous and flippant about it, about opening up her body. I wondered if that was how she saw me and this thing between us? She took a sip of her wine and then set her glass down. Her eyes bored into mine.

"I made sure he asked Michele out and brought her home. He'd never actually brought her to his home before, preferring the distance. Once he brought her there, worshipped her in a place that was perfect for sharing with someone you care about, we were done." She shrugged and tilted her head to assess me. The designing was actually her tool to do the higher valued work. The coaching secured the best possible end result. A well-rounded happy client.

I took several deep breaths, trying to contain my jealousy over her admitting to sleeping with Maxwell. "Excuse me, I'll be right back. I need a moment." Instead of ranting and raving, I rushed through the restaurant and made my way to the loo. Once inside, I laid my head against the cool wooden door. Fuck. *Get your shite under control, Collier. She's not with that man anymore. She's with you. You've had many one-night stands of your own. Look at things from her perspective. She's a beautiful, single widow who's been hurt by love. Who wouldn't want to bury their sorrows in willing flesh? You're guilty of the same thing.*

Deep breath in. Deep breath out. Time to start fresh.

CHAPTER THIRTEEN

Shit. Shit. Shit.

My honesty was going to be the end of me. At the very least, the finale of whatever this was with Collier.

His body language was off the charts jealous when I admitted to sleeping with some of my clients. Jesus, what if he asked me if I'm sleeping with my current client? With Dylan? It's not as if I haven't dropped hints that I'd had sex recently, prior to our first night together. I was honest with him when I said I wouldn't sleep with anyone else, effectively committing my body to only him. For the time being anyway.

I felt him before I saw him. He was apparently struggling, trying not to go off half-cocked.

I stood to greet him. His eyes were cloudy and tension pumped off his long, muscular form, tugging at my heart. Before he could sit, I clasped his hand. Nervous energy jolted me as I laced our fingers together. The moment our palms touched, a wave of heat spilled through every neuron and sizzled, popped, and crackled like Rice Krispies. It was too much, that single touch. It floored me with its magnetic pull, surprising and disastrous at the same time. Being with Collier, touching him, connecting our bodies was jolting, shocking, abrasive, and eruptive like a volcano, bursting at the seams after years of dormancy.

"You feel it, too?" I whispered as he tugged me close.

Our noses touched lightly.

"Anyone within a mile could feel this." He held me tight as I brought my lips to his. "It's magical," he breathed into my mouth as I kissed him.

Sparks flew and that volcano within exploded into a burning ball of fire, consuming everything in its path. My shoulder blades, the sensitive skin of my lower back, even my ass. I felt the ultimate heat. When he bunched my skirt a bit and pressed his erection hard against my center, scalding white-hot pressure forced a need so strong through me that I practically crawled inside of him. His mouth, his chest, against his manhood. I wanted nothing but to take him into my body.

"*Mi scusi.*" Our Italian friend fumbled in, carrying a tray of dough-filled platters. Collier and I broke apart panting, both unable to pull much-needed air into our lungs. Jesus, the man is a freight train, powering through every wall I place around my heart and mind. He seemed determined to make me insane with lust. He was right earlier. I would beg to be taken by the end of the night. Hell, I'll be begging in about five minutes if our host leaves.

After taking a deep breath and adjusting his brown corduroy blazer, Collier pulled my chair out and I sat. He settled next to me. "Later," is the only word he issued as we sat in silence, staring, practically undressing one another with our eyes.

"Come here, lovebirds," Anthony said with a laugh. A big beefy hand motioned for us to come to the brick oven. I hadn't realized it was a functioning brick oven. I thought it was for warmth and decoration. The Italian held a huge wooden spatula with a pizza a foot in diameter on top. "Signora, you place the pizza over to the right under the heat, there. Signore." He handed Collier his pizza. They were identical. "Place it there." We shuffled our pizzas into the oven. My spatula got stuck, and Collier put his hands over mine and lightly yanked it free. His touch burned hotter than the heat pouring off the oven. I closed my eyes as he kissed my temple.

"My beauty," he whispered into my hair and then pulled away.

"Now, when the smells call to me, I will be back to dish out pieces of eternal amore, for it was made by my wife. She puts all her amore…you say love…into every pie. It will be *fantastico*! I am so excited for you!" He said the word "excited," but it sounded like it had a couple more "d's" than were needed.

His excitement was palpable, and the love for his life, the food, and our presence spoke volumes about the type of establishment he ran. I was honored to be here, experiencing it with a man like Collier.

"You are a truly kind soul, Mr. Anthony," I told him.

"Such sweet words from a *bella donna*, yes?" he asked Collier.

"Si, she is a very lovely woman, Anthony. Molto bella." Very beautiful, he added to our server.

"Si, si. I leave you to it. Do not kiss too much. You may not want to stay to eat my food!" he warned, and we both laughed and sat back down. "It will be good tomorrow, but it will be magnifico tonight! Yes?" We nodded, and Collier refilled our wine and then set a bruschetta on my plate. Apparently, our host was fast. I hadn't even seen him bring it. Must have been when Collier and I were fumbling with our pizzas.

"So, what else is there to know about London Kelley?" Collier asked, taking a bite of the appetizer.

My face fell. I wasn't sure what else he could handle. Never in my life had I been sorry for the decisions I'd made until right now, with this man who was far too good for me. "I'm not sure what else to say?"

"Tell me about Tripp?"

Fuck! Not the person I wanted to talk about. Somehow, I just knew that if I told him Tripp and I had been together physically, his face would turn bright red and steam might blow out his ears like those old Bugs Bunny and Yosemite Sam cartoons. I stalled, trying to roll over what I could tell him by taking a bite of the bruschetta. The chopped tomatoes, fresh parsley, and garlic were a dream. Thank God, both Collier and I were eating it. We'd be fire-breathing together, cancelling out the garlic breath.

"Tripp and I have been best friends since just after James passed. I was in grief counseling. He was in Narcotics Anonymous. We ran into one another in the hallway and we just clicked. I needed someone who didn't know me or James to help me get past my grief; he needed someone to care about that would care about him in return."

Collier's brown eyes sparkled with compassion and sympathy. "Tripp is a recovering addict then?"

I nodded. "He's been clean awhile. Now and again, it still crops up. He fights it though. Sometimes I help."

"Were you two ever an item?" He asked the one question I really didn't want to answer. Didn't think he could handle me answering. In the end, this was me. My life. If he wanted to be a part of it, he'd have to understand who I was and who was important to me.

"You could say that," I answered vaguely. "We suffered through a lot together. There was a natural progression of that relationship, but we're better as friends. We have a very toxic relationship emotionally when physical aspects are in play."

Collier's jaw tightened. He gazed to where the pizzas were cooking. I could feel jealousy like a vile acid, eating away at our good evening once more.

"You're not together now. At all?" he asked.

I could tell a great deal hinged on how I answered this question.

"Collier, I wouldn't be with you if I was with Tripp."

"But you live with him," he countered. The words were accusatory. It took amazing effort to swallow my pride and answer calmly.

"We do. And we sleep in our own beds in our own rooms. I will say this to you once, and that will have to be the end of it. Tripp and I love each other very much." Collier stiffened from the tip of his wheat-colored hair to the bottom of his leather boots. "Let me finish. We are not *in love* with each other, nor have we ever been. We've had a mutually enjoyable physical relationship in the past. It ruined our friendship. So we choose to meet our physical needs with other partners. We are friends and will always be friends. Do you understand?"

Collier gritted his teeth and took several deep breaths.

I waited calmly. Slowly, I could feel the jealousy in him being capped, and the space around him filling with understanding and acceptance.

I smiled. When he opened his eyes, he looked at me

and grabbed my hand.

"If you say it's over between you and Tripp, I believe you. However, the bloke has a huge protective streak when it comes to you, leading a fella to believe he may feel more toward you than he admits."

"I'm all he has. His family disowned him years ago for being bisexual. Didn't matter though. His mother was a tyrant who hurt him mentally and physically. He escaped and turned to a life of drugs to bury and numb the pain."

Collier nodded and rubbed his bottom lip with the tip of his index finger.

"After he OD'd, he finally got help. Now he works his ass off to stay clean and has built a healthy life for himself. He does some modeling for Aspen and keeps me straight. Kind of like Ollie, Aspen's assistant, only I don't need him full-time."

"For you, I will work to mend the tiff we had last weekend. If he's an important part of your life, I'll make him one in mine."

I stared at his handsome face and shook my head. "That's probably one of the nicest things anyone's ever said to me. And very mature of you." I grinned.

"I try." He waggled his eyebrows.

Anthony came back and delivered gooey, cheesy pizza that was everything he claimed and more. The mix of mozzarella, herbs and spices, veggies, fresh roasted garlic and the dollops of ricotta had me stuffing my face in the most unladylike fashion possible. I could not get the food in fast enough.

"Sod all, I love seeing a woman actually eat her food."

I smiled around a huge bite of cheesy goodness at his

compliment.

"It's so good. I can't stop! Mmm, taste this bite. It's the perfect bite of pepperoni, olive, artichoke, spinach, and ricotta. Oh God…here, taste." I held out my fingers with the bite. Collier grinned wickedly, grasped my wrist, and brought his lips to the morsel. Instead of taking the bite he turned my hand sideways and nipped at the tender skin where my wrist met my hand, then kissed his away up and over my thumb.

His eyes were dark as he finally took the bite into his mouth. He dragged the piece through my fingers licking and sucking the tips of them, sending jolts of pleasure straight to where I wanted the rest of him most.

My breath picked up and he held my hand as he chewed, swallowed and then smiled. "Tastes almost as good as you," he said boldly.

I closed my eyes as he kissed my palm once more, this time swirling his tongue around the sensitive tissue. Hot tension shot through me, rebuilding the fire he started earlier.

We finished dinner in a haze of lust, torturing each other with small touches and stolen kisses over tiramisu for dessert.

Collier held my hand as he drove through New York City. It was a lovely night—crisp, cold, and perfect for snuggling. I was a bit surprised when Collier passed his apartment building and headed out toward my own home.

"Where are we going?"

"You'll see." he smiled.

After another ten minutes, he pulled into an old-fashioned movie house, complete with the giant bulbs that lit the sign. The theatre boasted the classics. He led me to the ticket counter. "Which movie? They all start in twenty minutes," asked a man with a bad Tom Selleck mustache.

"Lady's choice." Collier snuggled his warm body against mine, helping to prevent the night chill.

I scanned the titles and then landed on the perfect one. "*Pretty Woman*."

Collier laughed and hugged me close as he paid the man.

We settled in the very last row at the top. I had a feng shui thing about sitting with open doors behind me though I wasn't going to admit that to the sexy Englishman. He'd think I was ludicrous. I didn't need to give him another reason to think I was crazy.

The theatre was close to empty, with only a handful of couples spaced out throughout the small theatre. The room turned pitch dark as the screen illuminated. The telltale music of Natalie Cole singing "Wild Women Do" roared through the sound system. The song gave me a wicked idea.

I looked around. All the couples were either paying rapt attention or sucking face. We were far enough from everyone and in a very dark corner. Time to up the ante. He had me at a level ten on the lust-o-meter all night. Turnabout was fair play.

★ ★ ★

London's hand slid from my knee and up the meaty muscular part of my thigh as I watched Julia Roberts bend over Richard Gere's Lotus Esprit to ask if he wanted a date. Damn, she had a mighty fine arse. Any man in his right mind would take a date with the hot American, though the hot American whose hand was currently doing indecent things next to me would put the flame-haired girl next door actress to shame in the looks department.

Her small hand covered my prick, which had been in a semihard state all evening. Now it was at full attention. "Christ, beauty, you'll kill a man with moves like those," I whispered into her ear, and then nibbled the skin there.

She leaned her head to the side, giving me lovely access to the open patch of London-skin I wanted at her neck. Her hand became very bold, unbuttoning my jeans and pulling down the zipper. My dick sprung free, chilled by the cooler air of the theatre. It immediately warmed when her little hand clasped it.

"Commando? I'm impressed," she whispered into my neck before nibbling the edge of my chin.

"Only way to go wearing jeans, beauty." I moved closer toward her body, mashing her breasts against my chest. With a quick movement, I slid my hand under her sweater and palmed a full breast. My thumb swiped the hardening peak in tight circles. She moaned into my neck and tugged on my prick.

She moved in quick, kissing me hard. Her lips warm and moist as she dipped her little tongue in to tangle with mine. She tasted of the coffee she drank after dinner, filling my senses with her cinnamon scent. A pearl of pre-cum leaked out the tip of my cock and she used her thumb to swirl it around the wide crown.

I groaned, my gaze settling on the screen where Julia Roberts' character had just unzipped Geer's pants and was tugging them down. There was something immensely erotic about watching a couple have sex while enjoying your own play time.

London pulled away from my lips, breathing hard. She looked at the screen at the exact moment Julia kissed her way down Gere's abdomen and went to work. With a seductive glint, London had a hand around the base of my cock and her lips swallowing down the crown.

"Christ!" I groaned and she giggled. The sound muffled by my dick.

She lifted and looked around. The other patrons were lost in their own world, nowhere near paying attention to us. Thank God.

"Shhh, if you can't be quiet, you don't get to come, got it?" she threatened in a harsh whisper.

My balls tightened and my dick swelled in her hands. Instead of responding, I did what any warm-blooded man about to get sucked off in a movie theater would do. I nodded and kept my trap shut. If we got caught, I'd fight the indecent exposure charge gladly.

Her red swollen lips covered my cock as she licked and sucked the head. She alternated her hands at the base, circling, rubbing up and down in time with her suction. I didn't want to think about how she got to be so good at giving head. That would make me want to beat the hell out of any bastard who had received my beauty's affection.

Slowly, she trailed her tongue down one side of my cock then the other. I tunneled my hands into her hair, pulling back the curls so that I could see her take me in her mouth, over and over. Dizzying circles of wetness and heat, coupled by her firm sucking, the same way I sucked her tight pink nipples into my mouth, had me humming deep in my throat.

Her hand slipped down to cup and fondle my balls, and as she squeezed, I surged into her mouth, reaching that tight ring of her throat. The pressure was intense, mind-blowing.

She pulled back and I pushed her head back down on my cock, not letting her lips leave without a fight. She went wild, wrapping her lips around my cock and bucking into my leg. I grabbed her hair in a tight fist, instinctively knowing she wanted to be controlled. With my right hand, I reached over and around her bent-over arse. Fuck decency. I pulled up her skirt, baring her to the entire room. Her black thong cut between her cheeks like a roadmap for my fingers. Thank God, we were almost against a wall or someone would be getting a two for one show.

Only I could see the perfect firm globes of her arse as I slid my fingers along the seam backlit by the movie screens soft glow. She moaned around my prick and I tugged on her hair, forcing her to tease the tip of my dick before shoving her down the length again.

I could feel the wetness at my fingertips as I reached around her. When I knew I was hovering just over her sopping pussy, I tightened my grip and tipped her head back to look in my eyes.

"Suck me, beauty," I whispered and pushed her head onto my cock at the same time two of my fingers dipped into her heat. She cried out, the sound muffled around my prick. I thrust my hips into her mouth and my fingers deep into her slit. She rode my fingers and I rode her face. Both of us shivering and jittery with the powerful need to release into one another.

I yanked hard at her core, digging my fingers in to find that spot, the one that made her fucking scream. When I found it, her entire body, withered, then strung tight like a drum, sucked me firmly to the point of physical pain, ripping my orgasm from me.

I pumped into her, lights flashing behind my eyes as she rode out her own release.

God, she was beautiful, sucking my cock, coming around my fingers, swallowing my cum. With London, sex of any kind was a full-body experience. Once her hips slowed and she'd gotten every last inch of pleasure plucked from her perfect pussy, I pulled my hand from her and put the coated fingers to my lips. Her eyes widened as I licked and sucked her taste off, groaning at the sheer deliciousness that was this woman. Every fucking inch of her was decadent. With ease, she sucked the last drops from my softening dick and then placed a reverent kiss on the tip.

I cupped her face in both of my hands, overwhelmed with thoughts I couldn't express. Instead, I pulled her into a scorching-hot kiss, tasting our sexual essence. It lasted minutes, hours. Fuck, if I knew. The woman had me twisted and needing to be connected to her after giving me the best blow job of my entire life. In a movie theater, for Christ's sake.

"You make me want to worship at your feet," I whispered against her cheek.

"I must have been doing something wrong. I figured you'd want me to be the one worshiping at your feet with your cock in my mouth."

"The things you say you, wicked minx." She bit her lip and grinned as I gloried in her beauty, sated yet looking forward to more.

We both laughed and finally, the other patrons caught

on. A couple of "Get a room," and "Shut up already," came from somewhere in the darkened theatre.

"You want to blow this Popsicle stand?" I asked while buttoning up.

"Nope. Been there, done that, bought the T-shirt." She licked her lips and threw a sideways grin. "But I'd love for you to take me home and fuck me until morning where you will then, make me breakfast, including eggs and toast with that incredible jam. In that order, please."

"Anything for you, beauty. Anything for you."

CHAPTER FOURTEEN

Our drive home was interesting to say the least. Collier couldn't stop touching me. His hand was either on my knee, my thigh, or trailing into my hairline as he pulled me in for a kiss at random red lights. It became obvious really quickly that our movie madness was only a prelude to a night destined to be memorable.

"What are you thinking right now?" When Collier speaks, it's as if a British army was hammering my libido into overdrive. Even a woman in a committed relationship would have a fleeting thought about bedding my sexy Englishman when they heard him speak. Everything he says sounds like sex-laced cinnamon candy, tantalizing the senses in a wicked and surprisingly fiery way.

"About how much I love hearing your voice. I think you underestimate how delicious your accent is."

"Delicious, huh?" I nodded and closed my eyes preferring to let his words roll over my senses.

I took a deep breath. "Speak to me, lover," I whispered surprised I was feeling so brazen. My hands slid to my knees and started to pull up my skirt. I wanted to give my Englishman something to look forward to, drive him mad with lust the way his words were undoing me.

"Bloody brilliant." He grabbed my skirt with one hand and helped me scrunch it up higher. At this point, nothing but my lace panties peeked out of the expanse between my thighs.

"Words, Collier," I reminded him after a lengthy pause where I presumed he was staring at my bare legs and panties.

"Knickers."

I bit my lip and slid my hands a couple inches down my leg to caress the soft skin at my thigh and knee. The inner thigh was a weak point for Collier. He liked to brand me there. Oh did I look forward to wearing his mark by morning. The love bite would give me a physical reminder of our time tonight, just like he did the last time we were together.

"Smashing," he said and I moaned.

"Totty." My hands crept up to midthigh.

"Knockers," he whispered and stroked the tight bead of my nipple through my sweater. His fingers twisted and squeezed.

"Shag." He pinched my nipple and I cried out, desire wetting my panties and filling the air in the car with the distinct scent of sex and leather.

I spread my legs wide and slid my hands closer to the target. "Roger," he said the word as if it moved over his tongue like honey dripping down the bark of a tree.

"Collier," I breathed and gyrated my hips. His fingers trailed softly along the inside of my leg. The anticipation of his touch was brutal.

"Touch yourself, beauty," his voice grated on a moan.

My fingers slipped into my panties and found my clit hard and swollen. Waiting. Wanting him, not me.

"That's it. Touch it for me. Pretend it's me," he encouraged.

I did what he asked, completely lost in the need to find

release once again. He covered my hand as I manipulated myself and felt both our fingers slide over the slippery button. Shock waves of pleasure rolled through my body in a rush of stinging hot pokers. Excitement surrounded me as I moved closer to that blissful edge.

"Christ, you're gorgeous. Fuck me! I can't get enough of touching you." Our fingers danced together over my wanton flesh. His breath came in ragged, rushed bursts of air. The sounds of moving traffic, of him manipulating my sex, all merged into a meditative place where pleasure consumed every thought and noise.

Collier's fingers plunged into my heat and took the moisture he found there, rubbing it over my aching bundle of nerves. I could feel twinges of my orgasm as it approached. "Oh God, Collier, right there," I begged and pleaded for him as I rotated my hips toward his hand.

"Sod all. This, this little bit of heaven." He twirled his fingers around my clit in tight dizzying circles. I thrust my hips for his taking, my hands clasped the back of the headrest, arching my body towards his hand. "It's bloody perfect. And it's mine. I can't wait to put my lips on it and suck you until you scream." His words had me panting like a dog in heat.

Almost there. The edge of the cliff was right there, ready for me to jump off…

"Don't come." The command left his lips.

Wait. What?

My eyelids flung open to see his hand had left my sex and was pressing hard on his dick. He was pulling into his parking garage. He screeched his precious Porsche 911 into the parking stall and exited the car. His movements were tight and jerky. Everything happened so fast, I had barely grasped the fact that my orgasm was now a distant memory. *Bastard*. I planned on getting him back. After I got mine of course.

He flung open the car door then pulled me out. His lips were on mine, his tongue down my throat, before I could say a word. I gave back in spades, drinking from him, tasting him, and rubbing my needy body along his hard edges.

When he pulled away, I was stunned stupid. The man kissed me like he was forever saying good-bye and touched my body like he'd never get another chance.

After one last deep kiss, he pulled me through the garage to the elevator. Once inside, his hands were everywhere, pushing me against the wall, the handrail digging into my lower back. I didn't care, as long as he didn't stop touching me.

"It's unreal," he whispered as he licked the column of my neck. "Bloody undignified how much I want you. The things I want to do to this body." He sucked at the skin just behind my ear, sending shivers of lust spiraling and swirling deep in my center.

"Do it. Anything. Everything," I moaned. "Just don't stop." I licked into his mouth taking his tongue and making it mine. He gave it to me with greedy intent. His hands yanked and pulled at the sensitive skin of my ass, proving that this first time tonight was not going to be slow and easy.

I wanted him hard, fast and right fucking here in the white-walled elevator.

The elevator dinged and the doors opened. He pulled away and gripped me around the waist, practically dragging me to his apartment. Once inside, he backed me against the door, pushing up my sweater and ripping it over my head.

His mouth instantly went for my breasts. He plunged into the cup and encased a tight nipple with the welcome wet heat of his tongue. He flicked and nipped until I brazenly rubbed my lower half along the hard length pressed into my hip.

"Need to get in you." He bit down on my nipple. I cried out, my voice hoarse from the heavy breathing, sucking his length at the theatre, and the car fun we had earlier.

"Jesus, Collier, if you don't take me now I'm going to lose my ever loving mind!"

He pulled me and into a fireman's hold, practically running to the master bedroom, smacking my ass. "Fucking tight arse," he gritted through his teeth on a particularly hard smack.

Once in his room, he unceremoniously dropped me onto the bed. His chest puffed and heaved as if he'd run a marathon instead of from the effort of restraint. I shimmied out of my skirt, left only in the tall suede boots it would take too damn long to remove and the lace panties. Apparently, Collier agreed because the second the skirt came off, his jeans dropped to the floor.

In seconds, he had me spread wide, feet flat on the mattress at the end of the bed where he still stood. He yanked down my panties, only removing them from one leg but he didn't care. With his shirt still on, his eyes glazed with desire, he lined up his cock with my center and plunged into me hard.

A fuse lit. The moment our flesh connected, a storm of need, lust, and want roared between us. Moving in tandem, I pushed against his body. He pressed both palms on my inner thighs and moved my legs up and back toward my head, opening me wide for his taking. I'd never been taken with such ferocity. It was as though he wanted to brand me, burn me up and use me in a way that could never be matched or outdone.

"Look at me, beauty. See what you've done." Collier held my legs tight as he hammered into me, spinning his hips like a madman, skating over every single pleasure neuron I had. My body shook as he took and gave in equal parts.

"You've fucking ruined me for other women. " His eyes burned black as coal but were brighter than I'd ever seen them. He plunged deep. A long moan tore from my lungs. He grinned wickedly.

"That's right. I'm going to ruin you, too. Shag you so grand, another decent fuck won't do. Only my prick will fill you and make you feel this way." Passion tingled through the words he spoke. "Do you feel it, beauty? Do you feel how this is different?"

It was hard to respond. Shimmering waves of ecstasy rolled through me, stealing my breath and my words. "Oh God," I swore as my orgasm rippled through me.

"That's right, beauty. Give me your pleasure. It's mine now." He slammed into me, relentless in his pursuit. As the pleasure subsided, he ramped it up once more. "Oh no, you don't. I'm not done with you yet!" he yelled. He leaned over the bed and me to get at my tits.

Collier licked, nibbled, and used his teeth to bite on the tender peaks as he moved my knees up and over his shoulders. I was in a pretzel position as he fucked me long and hard. Collier placed those large hands over the sweat slicked skin of my shoulders cupping them and using them for leverage. His cock hammered into me, slight twinges of

AUDREY CARLAN

pain turning into pleasure as with the perfect tilt of my hips, he slid along that heavenly place inside, stroking it over and over until I almost blacked out.

"I want it all, beauty. Now. You don't come for *you*, you come for *me!*" he commanded, pulling my shoulders and slamming his cock home, mashing the pleasure center inside and outside of me. I screamed, tormented gloriously as rolling streams of nirvana swept me away into nothing but a ball of light, a cosmic energy where I could feel everything Collier felt.

It was no longer my pleasure, it was his. It catapulted me into the most painful and pleasurable experience of my life. A wall of pure love and lust tangled together as Collier plowed into me one last time. When he finally gave in, taking his release from my willing body, I too received that same release, once more but through his outpouring of emotions.

Minutes or hours later, we lay facing each other, snuggled into one another's warmth, giving and receiving this moment of peace for what it was. A change. A huge plateau had been crossed. I enjoyed sex, especially with men I cared for, like James and now Collier. But never had I felt anyone else's orgasm as if I was the one having it. Nothing could describe it nor compete with it ever again.

He was right. Collier Stone ruined me for other men. At this point, I could only hope I'd done the same for him. He said I had, but I wasn't sure I believed him.

Men had a habit of saying whatever shit comes to their minds during sex. I'd heard a great deal of that in my promiscuous past. With Collier, things felt different. I actually wanted to trust him, believe the words he'd said.

Now I just needed him to prove it.

Could he put up with me and my history with men? Aside from the fact that I was so damaged by the love I'd lost that I wasn't even sure it was possible to fall again.

Collier's words broke through my thoughts. "Fancy that shag, eh?" Collier grinned salaciously.

"I don't even know what to say." I shook my head and smiled, knowing a rosy hue crept over my heated cheeks and neck.

"I bonked you mute, did I? Well, Bob's your uncle." He fist pumped the air and I laughed. "In truth, what we did tonight"—he looked nervous and uncertain—"did I hurt you? I was a bit out of sorts."

Taking his hand, I curled it to my bare chest and kissed his knuckles. "That was by far, an experience I'll never forget. Never. I'll take it with me to the afterlife." I looked down, not able to meet his brown-sugar eyes. He tipped my chin with one long digit, forcing my gaze to his.

"Hey, for me too." He searched my eyes. I saw truth and honesty there. He didn't try to hide anything from me. I liked that...too much, if I was honest with myself. "I wasn't kidding when I said you ruined me for other women, London. Now that I've had you, the love we made tonight, I'll do anything to keep you in my life."

I closed my eyes and let his words wash a blissful serenity over me. He splayed his feelings open and I received them, letting them coat my heart with kindness and grace.

"Collier, the only thing I can commit to you is now. This moment." My voice trembled. "Maybe with the hope for more."

"For now, it's enough."

★ ★ ★

As I entered the bedroom, towel low around my waist, I caught site of my smiling puss in the mirror over the dresser. Pure, unfiltered happiness stared at me. It was a look I hadn't seen on my face in a really long time, probably since I first opened Stone, Walker, & Associates with Nathaniel five long years ago.

The sound of London humming as she soaped up for the second time lulled me into a sleepy haze, grinning like a loon. We definitely needed sleep. Between the movie theater and our need to immediately copulate the moment we got home and then again against the shower cube's wall a minute ago, had us both spent.

Tonight we'd had a breakthrough of sorts. She agreed to letting me hope for more. I meant what I said when I told her it was enough for now. The fact that she was here with me, made love with me all night, proved something to her as much as to me. It proved that this thing wasn't one-sided. It was real and over time, I'd get her to understand I wasn't asking for more than I was willing to give.

That moment when I had her pinned to the bed, her legs over my shoulders, my lips surrounding her flesh as I surged into her...epic. It was unlike any other love-making experience. Even with Claire, our mating had been a little humdrum and lukewarm. The fires burned scalding hot without hope of ever being extinguished with London. I craved her body, her taste, and her scent almost like I was genetically predisposed to fall for her.

And of course, I would fall for a woman afraid of love, hurt by it so badly she couldn't see what was before us on this plane. We were both very much alive and meant to share this human world together. I just needed to convince her of that.

I don't begrudge her the grief she feels. Quite the opposite. I want her to let her dead husband go, yet cherish his memory and their time together. It's part of her past. I want her to make room for me in her world, her future. I needed her to consider the possibility that she may love again. I may be the one to make that reality possible. Queen mother, I was bloody tired. After a night like this, sleep never sounded so good.

Thoughts of snuggling up to her were interrupted by a vibrating noise. London's phone lit and rattled against the wooden side table where she'd dropped her purse in our haste to be filled with each other.

I grabbed the phone and saw Tripp's annoyingly handsome mug on the screen. In the image his arms wrapped around London in what I would consider a more than friendly embrace. *Smarmy cocksucker.* The phone continued to ring as I glanced at the nightstand clock. Fucking two thirty in the morning. And he's calling her? Probably drunk dialing her. *Imbecile.*

Without a second thought, I answered the phone. Before I could say hello, Tripp started speaking.

"Bridge, baby, I need you." His voice sounded guttural, inhuman. Fear and anger split through my thoughts. My hands shook with the energy it took for me to not rip into him.

"It's Collier. What can I help you with, Tripp? It's two thirty in the fucking morning, mate. This better be good!" Apparently, my ability to stay calm went out the window, along with my sanity. He had no right to call her at this hour, knowing she was in my arms for Christ's sake. Friend or not, I will not have him interrupting our time together for his loser shite.

"I need her. Now. Please?" His voice trailed. I could hear a muffled sob through the line.

"Who is it?" London's blue eyes looked worried. I was glad she wasn't upset that I answered her phone. Even though I thought of us as an official couple, she might not agree, even after the monumental thing we discovered this evening.

"It's for you." I handed her the phone, unable to conceal the contempt in my voice. Her eyes narrowed as she gripped the towel around her body and reached for the phone.

Water ran in rivulets from her hair into the sexy crease between her breasts. Christ, she was wet and slick like Amphitrite, the Greek water goddess, and the mate of Poseidon in Greek mythology. Right now, I wanted nothing more than to be her mate. To rage the seas and cross oceans with her by my side for all of eternity. Instead, I had to listen to her take a call from her best friend, otherwise known as 'dick in a glass case': Break in case of emergency.

"Hello?" Her face instantly tightened as she slumped down on the edge of the bed. "Tripp, honey, what's the matter. What do you mean?" She listened a couple moments. "Don't you dare. I mean it. You will ruin everything. Fucking everything you've worked for." Anger made her spring into action. She immediately riffled through her suitcase and shoved on a pair of jeans, sans underwear.

That did not make me happy. I had to grit my teeth while watching her. She grabbed my T-shirt from the back of the chair and threw it over her head and screamed into the phone. At least it was my shirt. Again, she didn't take the time to encase her perfect breasts in an undergarment.

"What the fuck is going on?" I grabbed a clean pair of jeans, sliding them on. Whatever she was doing, she was most certainly preparing to go somewhere. Wherever she was going, I was going too. Non-negotiable. She threw up a hand to cut me off.

Rage fired through my entire body as I watched the woman I lo…what? The woman I what? Loved? I couldn't even think about that right now.

"I'll be right there. Don't you do it, Tripp. Don't. No. Yes, God, yes. I love you. More than anyone." Those three words put me at a screeching halt. All the air left my chest and I slumped onto the bed. I put my head in my hands. She loves him. *More than anyone.* Fuck!

She hung up the phone and slipped on some shoes. "I have to go. I'm sorry. I need to pick up Tripp."

"What do you mean? If he's drunk or whatever, he can take a cab for crying out loud!" I roared.

She swung her head back. "It's not like that. He's about to use. I have to go get him. Right now. I'm sorry. I don't know when I'll be back."

"You're fucking kidding, right? Tripp calls and you run off? London, stay. Just stay," I pleaded, wanting her to understand.

"I can't." She shook her head; there were tears in her beautiful blue eyes.

"Yes, you can. He can take care of himself. He's a big man. But this, me and you, right now…this is our time." I struggled to get the words out. I wanted and needed her to understand how serious I was about her not leaving right now. For him.

"You don't understand, Collier. He needs me. I have to go." She turned and walked through the flat to the door.

"This is bloody insane! We've just had a night of incredible shagging. I thought it meant something this time."

Tears welled in her eyes once more, and she walked over to me to cup both my cheeks in her small chilled hands. For a second, I thought I might actually convince her to stay. To not leave me for him. Just like Claire left me for that rich fucker.

"It has meant more than anything to me in a very long time." She kissed me hard and pulled away. "But I can't let my best friend down. He's in a world of hurt, and about to use drugs again. It's my job to pull him out. Do you understand?" Her gaze searched mine, pleading.

I shook my head. "No. No, I don't fucking understand. I'm exhausted and am being denied sleeping next to the one woman in the entire world I want to be with. Who I know, I can *feel*, wants to be with me. Yet, she's leaving me for another man."

"It's not like that—"

"Isn't it?" I cut her off.

Her hands trembled as she pulled her hair over her shoulder and twirled a fat lock of black hair. "I have to go."

"Stay." I tried one more time. It was now or nothing.

She shook her head.

"Then I'm coming with you." I gritted my teeth and grabbed my keys off the counter. I stood in jeans, bare feet, no shirt and I was ready to drop everything for her. To help another man.

"I'm sorry." A tear slipped down her cheek and she rushed to the door. "You can't be a part of this. It's not fair to Tripp."

"Tripp?" I grabbed her arm. "Are you fucking kidding me? I'm making a compromise here. Help pull his ass out of whatever shite he's pulling you into and you're telling me I can't go?"

"I can't do that to him. He's already hurting."

"He's hurting? You're hurting me, London!" I roared.

She looked at me, tears spilling down her cheek. Even now, I wanted to comfort her, pull her into my arms, and make her feel warm and safe. Loved. She wanted no part of it.

"I'm sorry," she said and I let her go.

When she left, the air in the flat stifled me with staleness, loss, and despair.

I ran to the balcony, took in a huge gulp of air, and looked down just as she looked up, then stepped into a taxi. The first woman I've had feelings for in years, and she walked out. Maybe forever. I didn't know. I wasn't sure I'd ever know.

London left to be with him. No, to *save* him. Was there a fucking difference?

Why did I have to fall for the one woman who not only was afraid to love me but also was in a codependent relationship with her very male best mate? Maybe it was time to stop trying. Just let the bloody bird go. Stop giving a flying fig. It would definitely lessen the pain, the hurt I'd undoubtedly go through if I continued down this path with an unstable woman.

Was she really unstable though? Definitely hurting. Still

grieving from the loss of her husband. And presently in a toxic relationship with an ex-addict that she used to shag. Not to mention she's the sister of one of Stone & Walker's biggest clients, *the* Aspen Reynolds, billionaire business tycoon.

What the hell was I thinking, getting mixed up in her shite? All for what? *For London.*

Christ! Even thinking her name sent warmth spilling through my fingers and toes, warming my body from the inside out. Shite, it's too late. Too fucking late. The bloody bird already owned me.

CHAPTER FIFTEEN

It had been two weeks since the "royal blowoff" as I'd taken to calling it. Two torturous weeks of knowing exactly why Collier was avoiding me. When I got the call from Tripp in the middle of the night, I jumped right into action. It had only ever been me and Tripp. Dropping everything in his moment of need came second nature to me. Answering to a man in my life had never been the slightest concern since James. They were all expendable. Collier was anything but expendable.

Looking back, I know I handled it poorly. So many different scenarios have run through my mind on countless loops over the past fourteen days. What I could have said to him. How I could have done a better job of explaining why it was so important that I be there for Tripp. Explaining that I wasn't tending to him as a lover but as a true friend. I would have done the same if Aspen or Rio had asked for help.

That's where Tripp was in my life. He'd been relegated to brother status. I love him, will always love him, but I'm not in love with him. Not the way I am with… Shit.

Am I in love with Collier? No, it's not possible. People only ever get one go at finding true love. I'd had mine with James. The one I'd lost. At this stage, I'd venture a guess that I'd lost both men who had become more than a friend or lover. James and now Collier.

I tried each day to reach out to Collier, but he hasn't returned any of my texts or voice mails. I only allowed myself one olive branch a day. Today I thought for sure he'd be at the airport in time to board the jet to Texas for Hank and Aspen's wedding, but I underestimated his desire to toss me out of his life for good.

He'd asked me to stay. Repeatedly. Instead, I beat feet it out so fast you'd have thought I was walking over hot coals. Figuratively, I was. Not only did I need to get to Tripp, I needed to get away from Collier. What we'd experienced blew my mind. And it was not just the physicality of our lovemaking. It was the mental connection, the shared pleasure that went beyond physical walls and a sexually gratifying experience. It was unearthly. Not something I dared to think I'd ever go through again.

No, that night was a huge clusterfuck from the moment I picked up the phone.

Prior to that, I'd quite possibly had the best date of my life. The only other one that compared was our first date a month ago. The connection we shared even then crackled and fizzed in the air around us. The night out for pizza and a classic movie, the risqué sex we shared in the dark movie theater were things they write books about. The stuff movies are created from.

Then to top it off, backbreaking sex followed by an intense round of lovemaking that moved the earth and me right along with it. Even after, we couldn't get enough of one another and had another go round in the shower... right before everything turned to shit.

Each moment with Collier seemed better than the last. We were building to something more. The very more I'd promised I'd try for. And then I ran off to go to Tripp.

Could it possibly be over? Did I screw it up so badly he couldn't stand the thought of speaking to me, of hearing my voice?

Chills and nausea formed a pit in my gut. I'd been nursing it for the better part of a week. Knowing what I did made me sick to my stomach. Losing the one man in years that had reached me on a level that inspired me, made me feel cherished. A man who worshiped my body and hugged my soul cutting right to the center of my being.

Recently I'd been going over all my past choices and had found I'm not very proud of the things I've done. Collier makes me want more for myself, for him. For us.

Considering possibilities with a man, any man, is not something I'd remotely contemplated since losing James. The feeling hit home, churned and twisted my thoughts, forcing me to face the facts. I might have lost him and I had no one to blame but myself.

It still broke me that he didn't arrive at the airport to board Aspen's jet.

At this point, I wasn't even sure he and his brother were attending the wedding, though I don't think Nate would flake on Hank. They'd become close friends over the past few months. And they were business men. When Aspen Bright-Reynolds invited you to her small country wedding, you pretty much dropped everything on your to-do list and got your ass to Texas.

Her account was huge to Stone, Walker, & Associates. I didn't doubt she was their biggest client, even knowing they catered to the rich and famous on legal matters across the globe. Still, my sister was worth billions, stacked on top of more billions, which were sitting on solid gold bricks. You just didn't screw over the hand that feeds you. If she left their company, they'd lose millions of dollars of legal representation for AIR Bright Enterprises. And if other big wigs saw Aspen move away from them, they might jump right on the bandwagon and follow the leader.

The only hope I held onto was that Collier would be at the wedding and I'd steal a chance to speak with him. Corner him somewhere. Get Oliver to help. Maybe Nate. Anyone.

Explaining what happened that night was important. Even if he didn't listen and still wanted nothing to do with me, not having a chance to explain was hell on my conscience.

"Bridge, we'll be landing soon." Tripp held my hand. I squeezed it in return and continued to stare out the window, lost in my own thoughts.

Tripp had been giving me space after that horrible night when I left Collier to tend to him. When I found Tripp at the party in a scuzzy broken-down warehouse, two barely dressed coked-out skanks were rubbing all over him. White powder still sprinkled the table in front of his spread legs. I'd lost it. I went straight psycho on his ass.

One girl had her hand down his pants, and the other was trying to get him to smoke crank or coke, God only knows what, out of a pipe she literally held at his lips. Her bare tits and the pipe were waving in front of my poor Tripp's face like a veritable feast of sin and sex.

I broke three fingers punching skank number one in the face, knocking the pipe out of her hands. Even now, the three fingers on my right hand were taped together.

The wedding planner freaked out as if I'd committed a cardinal sin by breaking my fingers, more concerned about perfect wedding photos than my health. Tripp had served as a nursemaid and personal calligrapher since I was unable to write well with just the use of my thumb and forefinger.

Finishing off Dylan's home reveal had been painstakingly difficult. The end result was incredible and Dylan couldn't be more pleased.

The same night Tripp went to an after party with Skank One and Skank Two, Dylan had a very successful night out on the town. Not only did he come home with six different girls' phone numbers, but also he actually brought home a woman he met at the bar.

They had a wonderful night partaking of each other's bodies. Come sunup, she went on her merry way. Dylan couldn't have been happier. Not only did he have a night of amazing guilt-free sex, but also he felt revived and attractive to the opposite sex with renewed interested in living life.

Now he knew there was more he needed to experience than just accounting and rolling in the dough. My job was done. Happy client. Mission accomplished.

Then why did I feel like rubbish? *Rubbish.* Collier would say rubbish. London says *garbage* or *trash*. Six weeks of knowing my sexy Englishman, and I had already picked up his lingo.

"Hey, London, you okay?" Aspen came over and sat down. Her baby bump was visible in the tight sweater and slacks she wore. Her eyes shone against the angora sweater matching her gray eyes. They reminded me of a crystal-clear diamond with edges that sparkled in the light. Her golden hair was pulled back into a smart ponytail. She must have done her own hair today. Ollie did not make a habit of simple hairdos. No, he'd have twisted, curled, and pulled magic out of his ass to make her look like she was the winning contestant in a hair contest.

Speaking of the devil, Oliver glided into the seat next to Aspen, across from me and Tripp. "Is the maid of honor unable to do her duties? You know I'm ready to jump right in with two shakes of a lamb's tail." His smile was laced with mischief. If he weren't my sister's best friend in the entire world, and one of my best friends by proxy, I'd consider an evil pinch to his thigh.

Oliver continued, "Wait until you see the lambs, London. They are so white and poufy!" His eyes lit and Aspen smiled, bumping his shoulder affectionately.

"I'm fine, sis. Yes, Ollie, I'm perfectly capable of handling my duties as my sister's right-hand woman, unlike some people who have to stand for sloppy seconds." I gave in to my desire to lighten my heartache for a bit.

Oliver looked panicked. "Oh my God. Aspen? Is that what I am? No better than a Sloppy Joe with soggy buns?"

"Really, London? You had to mess with him? With this wedding in two days, he's a complete mess. You'd think he was the one getting married." Aspen rolled her eyes and blew her long swooping bangs to the side.

"We are getting married. Remember? You, me, and the hunky cowboy. Oh, and my fireman." Ollie clapped and winked across the plane to where Dean and Hank were deep in conversation about which football team would make it to the Super Bowl this year. Of course, Hank was convinced the Cowboys were a sure thing, but Dean wasn't buying it.

"I heard that, buddy. You are not marrying my woman. Cut the crap."

"Oh, stuff it, big boy!" Ollie squealed. "How many times do I have to tell you she was mine first!" Point for Ollie. He was right. Hank harrumphed and continued chatting with Dean.

"Do you see what I'm dealing with? It's been nothing but bicker, bicker, bicker with these two. Ever since we announced the wedding and the baby, the two of them have been at each other's throats with the jokes and barbs."

"You realize that's how normal brothers act toward one another, right? We just don't communicate enough with Rio to have that type of relationship. Mostly because he's a stuck-up rich boy." I laughed.

"I guess you have a point. I never thought of it that way. Maybe they bonded in a way I wasn't aware of," Aspen answered as she watched them verbally throw arrows at one another. I thought it was cute.

Finally, Hank and Oliver understood the other's place in my sister's life. It was refreshing. Yes, it had to be annoying as hell for her, dealing with two very demonstrative personalities, but their arguing was harmless. A lot of things were going to change once that baby came. Hopefully they'd all change for the better. I couldn't wait to be an Aunt and spoil the baby rotten.

"Sixteen weeks, right?"

"Just over," Hank yelled. "My baby is awesome. Big as an avocado!" He held up his huge paw to mimic the size.

Aspen hooked her finger over her shoulder. "He's a nut."

"But he loves you."

Aspen's eyes glazed as she stared at her husband to be. "Yeah," she said, all light and airy, completely smitten with her man. Love and adoration poured from her as she watched him, completely forgetting the two of us had been deep in the middle of a conversation. I didn't blame her. If Collier were here, all my attention would be focused on him, too.

If Collier were here. But he wasn't. Because I pushed him away.

Just like every other man who remotely gave a shit about me. I never allowed anyone to get too close, preferring to sleep around instead of holding onto a meaningful relationship, even if they pursued me. Collier was the only exception in the last four years.

How the hell was I going to fix this?

The situation seemed hopeless but I had to try. I wanted to be with Collier. I wanted the whole enchilada. A commitment to be together. Only him and me, with no end date, no worries about the future. Just a solid commitment to be a part of his life. It would take work, more on my part than on his, but he was worth the effort. God, was he worth the effort.

I scrolled through my phone and decided now was as good of time as any to send out my daily olive branch.

To: Collier Stone
From: London Kelley
Was surprised to not see you on the jet. I hope you'll be at the wedding. Please talk to me. I miss you.

I considered removing the 'miss you' part. I didn't want

him to know just how badly I had, but damn it. If I was going to win him back, get him to give me another chance at this thing between us, I had to lay my cards on the table. Quickly, I hit send and shoved the phone back into my purse.

"Was that Collier?" Aspen asked.

I shook my head. "No, he hasn't contacted me in two weeks. We had a falling out," I admitted. I didn't want my sister worried during her wedding weekend so I kept it to myself.

"They had a fight over my bullshit." Tripp shook his head, and then proceeded to hang it low in shame. I rubbed his arm to sooth the hurt. That didn't help since three of my fingers were broken due to the crap he'd gotten himself into that night. Still, he didn't mean to cause trouble between Collier and me. He lifted my hand and kissed each broken finger, his eyes focused down.

"So you didn't know then?" Aspen asked.

"Know what?"

Aspen bit her lip and sat up straight. She gripped my hand. I did not like the body language or the sympathy pumping off her. "His dad had a heart attack two weeks ago. Nate, Collier, and Emma took the first flight out to be with him."

My eyes must have been as wide as a house. My heart broke into tiny fractured pieces. Tears filled my eyes. "No, I didn't know. I should have been there for him."

"So, it is serious between you two?"

I nodded, not able to speak through the huge lump in my throat. Tripp handed me a glass of water and I took a few sips. "Is his dad okay?"

Aspen smiled brightly. "He is. It was relatively mild but was a definite scare to the family. According to Hank, Nate said their mother was a wreck. The past two weeks, they've been settling their dad at home and getting him on an eating and exercise plan. They're also trying to talk him into early retirement. He's only in his late fifties."

Knowing Collier had been gone the last two weeks helped relieve my fears that the thing between us could be resolved, once I had a chance to explain. But the fact that I wasn't there for him when he needed me? I felt gutted, and the knot in my belly tightened. My phone pinged from my purse and I scrambled to get it. Everyone I cared for, save one, was here. My heart expanded and warmth filled my chest as I read the words I'd been dying to see for two weeks.

To: London Kelley
From: Collier Stone

Beauty, I miss you more. It's been a rough fortnight. I'll be in Texas tomorrow. I'll be the one waiting...for you to come to me.

★ ★ ★

That thirteen-hour flight was the longest of my life. The past fortnight had been filled with heartache and nerves, for my stepfather, my overwrought mother, my baby sisters, and for London.

I missed that bird like I missed summer in Sussex. The thought of her cinnamon scent, her buttery soft arms folded around me did wonders to ease the ache I've suffered since our parting.

At first, I was ready to write her off. The bloody bird

brought men to her knees with her beauty. The sound of her New York accent sent rivers of pleasure down my spine, and her touch… Blimey, her touch was the balm to heal all wounds. She was the whole package, even if her edges were torn and stuck together, piss-poor, with tape and glue. She was a dear gift to receive, open, and cherish.

When I received that last text, finally admitting she missed me, that was all it took to break down every wall I'd tried to build around my heart. Those three little words, "I miss you," were all I needed. My beauty was strong and stubborn. The first week's messages and voice mails were a bit shoddy, trying to make light of what she did.

The second week's messages changed considerably. They were more pleading, carrying more desire for a reconciliation. This last text—her asking me to talk to her— laid her heart out for me to take. It was a huge step in the right direction. By the end of this trip, she'd be mine. Body, heart, and soul.

I think in her own way, she understands that there is no fighting what's between us. But we do have some things to work out.

Things like her job. At the risk of sounding like a brute, no woman of mine would be moving in with her male clients. Period.

I don't care if that's her unconventional way of connecting with them. She can spend her days learning about them and her nights warming my bed, giving herself time to be free to enjoy the people in her life. She also doesn't need to spend weekends there. That time needs to be spent with family, friends, and me.

If she wants to fix this between us, she will need to

make a couple concessions. When she's had time to spend with me and her friends during hours she'd normally be with a client, she'll appreciate her off time more fully. It will be more valuable and she'll not be so keen to give it away so freely.

The period for dithering is over. I needed to find my beauty. The anticipation of seeing her after not laying my eyes on her for so long has been quite unbearable.

I wished for her at night while I was in England. Having her by my side during the scare with my stepfather would have gone a long way to easing my burden. No more separation. It would be now or never. The next day or two would determine whether or not we'd be together and for good.

Nathaniel finally pulled up to a beautiful country home. White with dark shutters, it was lovely and reminded me of the sprawling lands back home on the outskirts of the country. I heard music in the distance.

When we exited the car, a man in a suit asked for the keys and notified Nathaniel he'd be moving the rental to an unseen parking location. The three of us walked up the wooden steps and were greeted by a lovely woman with long dark hair and eyes. Her smile brightened.

"Welcome, I'm Jess. Groom's sister-in-law. Thank you for coming. Go on back down the steps and you'll see the tents. A bar has been set up in the dining room if you'd like to wet your whistle," she added with a drawl that matched Hank's.

"You fancy a drink, mate?" Nathaniel asked.

"Oh, you're the British folks. Bride's sister will be so happy to know you're here. She told me to get her the moment the sexy Brits arrived!" She smiled.

I couldn't help but smile in return. "Please don't tell her just yet. I'd like to have a drink and then find her myself." I winked.

She nodded knowingly. "My lips are sealed. Now y'all go on back. The festivities will start within the hour. There's food set up near the bar to nibble on while you wait. When you see a handful of really stuffed shirts, you'll know you've reached the bar." She laughed.

We gave our thanks and made our way through the house. It was charming and lived in. Hank obviously appreciated comfort first and foremost in his home. I liked that. He was the real deal. What you saw is what you got with Hank Jensen.

Once we hit the kitchen, it was clear where the bar was. A line of primly dressed business executives held amber liquid tight in their grip and stood just off a room where a full bar had been set up. I could see the huge tent through the wall of windows. That was obviously where the service and reception would be held.

"Isn't it beautiful?" a deep voice to my left said.

I turned and was surprised to see Tripp Devereaux. It took everything I had not to deck the man. Instead, I gritted my teeth and scowled.

"I know I'm the last person you want to see, but I think we should talk."

"I've got nothing nice to say to you. Now is not the place for a friendly chat with an arsehole," I whispered close to his body. I distinctly picked up the scent of apples before I pulled a solid two feet away.

"Fair enough, but you're going to talk to me, or I'll

make a scene. Is that what you want?"

"Fine."

Tripp turned on his heel, expecting I'd follow. I took my time, shaking a few business associates hands on the way. Nathaniel handed me his gin and tonic as I passed him. "You'll need this more than me." He tipped his head toward a waiting Tripp. I had to give it to him. He didn't look flustered, or brassed off, even though I fully planned on taking his *friend* away from him in the very near future.

He led me down a hall to what must be Hank's study or office. Books lined both walls from floor to ceiling. A burgundy rug spread across the floor and beneath a desk. A couple high-backed chairs filled the space near a small lit fireplace. We sat in front of the fireplace and let its warmth bring feeling back to my cold hands.

"Well, now that you've got me here, what is it that you want to say?" I asked, not waiting to be addressed.

"I want to apologize," Tripp said firmly.

It wasn't at all what I expected to hear coming from his lips. Was it me or were we not both in love with the same woman? I crooked an eyebrow, not clearly following this line of conversation. "I'm afraid you have me at a disadvantage?"

His lips lifted into a crooked smile, showing his perfect teeth. He pushed his hands through his dark hair. "Look, I know you think there is more between London and me, and you have a right to know what it is."

I bristled and pumped my chest out instantly.

"Hey now." He put his arms out in a placating gesture. "What you don't know is that I led you to believe we were more than friends unintentionally. My relationship with Bridge is different."

God, that pet name annoyed me. *Her name is fucking London,* I wanted to scream, but held back.

"Continue," I answered calmly and took a sip of the cocktail. The bubbles from the tonic water soothed my scratchy throat, and the booze helped ease my frustration.

"Bridge is the most important *woman* to me. Hell, she's the most important *person* in the world to me. She's the only family I have. When I called two weeks ago, I really didn't intend to break up your night. I was completely hammered and about to make the worst decision of my life. Not only was I planning on having sex with two women who would have probably given me an STD, but also they were pushing me to get high with them—high as in snort and smoke crack cocaine. I'm an addict, Collier. I'd been clean for over four years now. But in that instant, I wanted it so badly. Partly, because of you."

"Me! Bollocks!" How dare he blame me for his relapse? His shenanigans?

Before I could call him on his shite, he continued. "Yes, you! I knew the night before Bridge met up with you that I'd lost a piece of her. It was only ever me and James who had any real effect on her. But somehow, I knew you had changed everything. When she talked about you, she had a light in her eyes. That sparkle was so bright it burned me to look at her. Her smile was so big she couldn't contain it. You did that for her." He propped his elbows on his knees and pushed his hands into his hair. "You gave her something I could never give her. You made her whole."

"So you decided because she didn't want you the way you wanted her, you'd go off half-cocked and call on her to save you?"

"In a way. Maybe subconsciously. I don't know. All I know is that I'm not in love with Bridge the way you think. I love her more than anyone and I would never deny her the happiness you clearly can give her."

"Damn right, I'll make her happy. I plan on fixing that dark place in her, filling it with love, not with meaningless sex. I'm in love with her, Tripp. Do you understand that?"

"Yeah, I do."

"And I think maybe if she wasn't so worried about you and your shite, she could love me too!"

"I understand." His voice cracked and he swallowed.

"Do you? Do you really? You're going to have to take a bit of a step back and let her go. Are you prepared to do that? For her? For her happiness?" My voice was so tight and restrained, it took extreme effort not to growl in anger. I wanted to tell him how incredibly selfish he'd been, how he was done using my girl as his own personal safe house.

"I'm prepared to do anything to make her happy. You're what makes her happy. But I'm not going anywhere. I'm not going to lose her in my life."

My eyes narrowed as the reality of what he said sunk in. He wasn't giving up on their friendship and wouldn't walk away. Any man would be a sodden fool if they walked away from my beauty, even as a best mate.

"You'll agree to give her some space? Allow her to find herself and what this thing between us could be?"

Tripp nodded solemnly. "It will be hard, but I can do anything for her. And though you think I'm a needy bastard, I plan on sticking around. That means you and I need to find a way to get past our issues. Got me?"

"Message received. But not now. Right now, I need

time to cool down. I have a woman to woo, one in which I haven't seen in a fortnight."

"I get it. Go get her. She's been waiting."

"And I for her. Thank you, Tripp. I don't know if we've worked through everything, but I think we've come to a solid understanding about the lovely woman in our lives. I'm not going anywhere."

"Neither am I," he challenged.

I smiled. "Touché. Come on, mate. I need another drink. Liquid courage and all that."

CHAPTER SIXTEEN

He appeared in front of me as if in a dream, standing at the end of the hall leaning his toned form against a sideboard. He looked calm and collected. His arms and legs were crossed casually. Layers of wheat-colored hair fell enticingly over his brow. Those perfect lips quirked up into a slow grin as he looked me up and down. The dark gray suit he wore perfectly set off his skin tone. He was the most beautiful thing I'd ever seen. There he was. The man I'd wanted to see for an eternity was there, in the flesh, waiting for me. Everything around me ceased to exist.

We spent long moments just staring at one another from down the hall, assessing the other. I felt nothing but love and acceptance spiral and plow into me like a breeze of fresh air from a window just opened. I lifted the length of the silver gown I wore. When I looked up, my target set on a sexy Englishman, his long arms opened wide, welcoming me from a distance. Bats straight from hell wouldn't keep me from my man. At a dead run, I plowed into his embrace, so hard I feared we might break the mirror on the wall behind him. I needn't have worried. Collier was strong enough to catch me.

Before anything was said, I covered his lips with mine. Holding his head captive, my hands caressed his cheeks and chin. I poured everything into the kiss: the hurt, the anger, the remorse, the lost time. All of it. He took it in, gobbled it up, and gave me back acceptance, gratitude, and desire. Every speck of my body that could touch him was pressed deeply against his. I slid my tongue into his mouth, over and over until I couldn't catch my breath. Winded, I pulled away and searched his golden-brown eyes.

"You waited for me?" His gaze searched mine. There was something strong and definitive behind the question.

"Yes. I don't want to be without you," I admitted.

"Christ, London, I just may be in love with you…" I placed my finger over his lips to shush the words I wasn't ready to hear. It was too much, too quickly. It had only been a couple months since we met and less since we last were intimate. There were things we needed to do and say before we went there now, if ever.

"There will be time for those words but right now, I'm scared." I felt the tension creep back into my body. His hands rubbed up and down my back, the silky fabric added a lovely caress to the movement of his strong hands.

"I know, beauty. And we have a lot of it. Time that is. But things between us are going to change. Considerably." His gaze warned me almost as much as his words did.

"What things?" I tipped my chin, prepared to defend my life and choices, even though I'd probably concede anything right now to keep this man a significant part of my world.

"For starters, no more spending the nights with clients." His eyebrow lifted as he gauged how the demand hit me.

Really, I had already started work on making that change, but he didn't know that. "Done! Next?"

"No working weekends?"

Now that was ridiculous. How the hell would I get my

work done in the six weeks' allotted time if I didn't work weekends? I was already booked into next year. There was no way I could change that now. "Not possible. Collier. I have a schedule to keep. This could affect my livelihood."

"Not if you're living with me, it won't," he said calmly, with no more emotion than if he asked about the weather or to 'please, pass the salt.'

"Okay, you went from weekends to me moving in with you? Are you insane?" Seriously, this man was two steps away from entering the loony bin if he thought I was ready for a leap that grand.

"Certifiable." He grinned, and then kissed my nose.

"Hopeless." He dragged his cheek along mine, sending shivers of desire to dance along my skin.

"Desperate." His tongue traced my lips and then dipped into my mouth. We kissed a few more moments, just enjoying the intimacy after so long.

"Seriously, you're not asking me to move in, are you? I'll work on the weekend thing, but I'm not ready—"

This time his finger covered my lips. "I know, my love. Take off two weekends a month as a start. You need time with me and your family."

"Okay," I conceded needing to give in somehow. "I'll work two weekends a month and I'll make sure the reveal is part of that timeline." He smiled wide and hugged me close. "God, you smell so good. Like fresh baked cinnamon pastries. I could just eat you up." He licked, kissed, and bit along the column of my neck and down to my shoulder. Forget the wedding—I just want to find a nice quiet room with a bed so we could properly have makeup sex.

"Anything else?"

"I want you staying with me at my flat as much as you're capable. Ideally, I'd also prefer it if Tripp moved out of your apartment."

Hold the phone. Huge warning bells clanged. Sirens blared and big flashing lights skidded this love train to an immediate halt.

"Excuse me? You want me to kick my best friend in the whole world out of his home?" The words came out tight. I tried to step away from his comforting embrace. I felt anything but comfortable right at this moment. He wouldn't let me move an inch.

"Yes. I'd like for the two of you to not live with one another, but I know that would be exceedingly difficult on you."

"Difficult? Talk about life-altering." The mere thought made me nauseous.

"Right, life-altering. Exactly what I'm proposing with you. A life-altering arrangement. I don't want you as my fling, my backdoor trollop, London. I want you as my mate. My girlfriend. And in the future, more." The word "more" had my skin beading with a cold sweat. I opened my mouth to respond, but he moved on. "I understand you're afraid, so we'll start small. First, we'll be exclusive. You will be my significant other and I yours. We will spend evenings at one another's homes as desired. No requirements, no set dates. Just when we have the ability."

A giant weight lifted off my chest, fully understanding what he was proposing. This I could work with. A little more time for him, a little less time at work and with Tripp. I'd make Tripp understand.

"I can see all of this swirling around in that beautiful

head of yours. Do you think you can try?" His tone was sincere, so filled with love and hope that I knew for *him*, I could try anything.

"For you, for me..." I placed my hand over his heart. "For us, I will try."

"I can't wait until this pomp and circumstance is over, and I have you back at the hotel, in my arms." Collier nuzzled my neck and slid his hands around my waist, holding me close.

I whispered in his ear, "It doesn't matter where we are, Collier. When I'm near you, it's the only place I ever truly want to be."

As we kissed, a door behind us slammed.

"The evil bitch better back off or so help me God!" Oliver screeched as he tore down the hallway. When he got to us, his face was flame-red and his hair a mess.

"What's wrong?"

"Your mother. That's what's wrong! She's making my princess cry and not in a sweet 'I love you, you're getting married, this is the best day of your life' way. No, she's in there trying her best to talk Aspen out of marrying the cowboy."

I looked at Collier in apology.

"No, go. We have plenty of time to catch up later. Do your maid thing."

"It's not maid. I'm the Matron of Honor." I rolled my eyes and laughed. Ollie grabbed my arm and pointed me down the hall.

"Go get that evil woman out of the dressing room and do damage control. Aspen's crying. I'm going to get Aspen a glass of sparkling cider and a hunky cowboy to sooth all that ails her."

"Aspen's crying her eyes out right now. She can't see Hank before the wedding."

"The hell she can't!" Hank roared as he ran up the stairs near us. "What's this about my angel crying? Where is she?"

"Hank, relax. I'll handle it," I tried to assure him. He wasn't buying it. I grabbed his arm and took him down the hall. Collier waved over his shoulder and then went down the stairs to join the rest of the guests. "Now look, even if the she-bitch is messing something up, I'm her sister. I can fix anything."

"I'm her man, about to be her husband. My power trumps yours," he gritted.

"Oh, don't you pull your macho cowboy bullshit on me. Just stay right there. I'll have her speak to you. Just let me see what's up, okay?"

He nodded and sat on a long red bench facing the room, positioning himself like a sentinel on guard. He crossed two massive arms over each other. Fury expanded in the space around him. Lord help the next person stuck in his presence while he waited to see my sister.

Once I made my way into the bridal room, I found Aspen wiping her eyes and our mother sneering in my direction.

"Can you speak some sense into her? She won't listen. This has gone on long enough. She cannot marry below her class like this. It's uncivilized." Mother's voice was tight and cold.

"Are you fucking insane?" Funny. That's the second time I asked someone that today. "Aspen loves Hank. She's having his child." Our mother swallowed as if she had something disgusting stuck in her throat. "Hank loves Aspen, Mother, and there really isn't anything left to do, but get your happy ass down to stand next to Rio and be escorted to the front of the line. If you so much as say one more word that is hurtful to my sister, I'll have you removed. It won't be hard. I've got a really pissed-off groom sitting right outside the door ready to barrel in and sweep his bride off into the sunset."

"But…" she tried again.

"No buts, Mother. None. Shut up. Keep your trap shut, put that plastic surgery-induced smile on your face, and get down there and watch your eldest child get married." She didn't move.

"A pregnant bride, how cliché," was her last dart in Aspen's heart. That was it. I grabbed her by the arm and yanked her to the door. I pulled it open and threw her and her diamonds out.

"Hank, close your eyes and come in." He immediately closed his eyes and let me lead him into the room. Aspen ran into his arms, her sleek strapless wedding dress swishing around his legs as he held her. "Keep those eyes closed. You've got two minutes. I swear to God I'm in no mood to be messed with."

"Angel, are you okay?" he asked, placing random kisses along her neck. True to his word, he kept his eyes closed tight.

"I am now." Aspen sniffed. "With these pregnancy hormones, I wasn't able to hold back the tears. She really got to me this time. Normally I can handle it, but not today." She took a deep breath. "I guess I just wished she was coming to tell me she was proud of me. But, no, she had to tell me I was making a mistake. Do you think we are?"

"Darlin', no. Marrying you is going to make me the happiest man in all the world. Nuthin' that hag could say would prevent me from doing so. Now how's my baby doing? She comfy in there?" Hank's large hand fit between their bodies where he covered her bump.

"Stop saying she. It could be a boy, you know!"

He shook his head. "Nope, I'm going to have me another little angel with golden hair to love and protect. Now can I make it official with her mommy?"

I should have left but I couldn't. Seeing them together, knowing how right this union was gave me hope for a future I didn't think I deserved after James. Maybe it would be okay to want more.

Aspen nodded into his neck. "I love you, Hank."

"Oh, darlin', wild horses couldn't prevent me from marrying you today. Now finish up. I'll be the man in the tux at the end of the aisle."

We both laughed and Aspen hugged him tighter. "I'll be the one in white, stud."

"Forever my angel in white."

★ ★ ★

"Isn't she the most stunning woman you've ever seen?" I whispered to my brother as we sat a few rows back from the front where Hank and Aspen were saying their vows.

"Yes, she is, but women getting married always are."

I hit his shoulder. "Not her, London." My beauty was stunning. Her long black hair hung down her back in sexy waves. Her tanned arms were sprinkled with something sparkly that kept catching the light like a beacon calling me home. She was my home. Soon, I'd get her to accept it, too.

Nathaniel rolled his eyes. "Shh, listen," he whispered.

"Angel, I mean Aspen." A hundred guests laughed at Hank's slipup. "Oh hell, you'll always be an angel to me. When we met, I knew there was somethin' different 'bout you. You bring men like me to their knees with your beauty and intelligence. I know as long as we're together, I'll forever try to make you happy. In doing so, I'll always be happy right along with ya. Today, I marry my friend, my lover"— he waggled his eyebrows and Aspen giggled—"the woman of my dreams." He placed a hand over her slightly rounded baby bump. "And the mother of my children. And I plan to have lots of 'em, because the world will be a better place if there are more people like you in it." Aspen blotted her tears away. "You're everything I'll ever want and need and I promise to be that in return. I love you and all your pieces."

Oliver and London both blotted their eyes. His words hit home as I stared at London, knowing with my whole heart that she would be the woman I'd spend my life with. One day, she'd be my wife, and both of us would move on and heal together.

"Hank, you not only saved my life, you saved my heart and soul. You've made me realize there is more to life than being successful. Now, I have new goals: to be the best wife to you possible." She clasped her hands over her belly and Hank covered hers with one large paw. "And to make the best mother to your children. To teach them to never judge a book by its cover and to always follow your heart, because the one you love might just be wearing jeans and cowboy boots instead of Armani and wing tips." She smiled and everyone laughed. "I'll love you until my last breath. Thank you for fighting for me, for us. Today, you're making me the happiest woman on Earth because you've chosen me to be your wife. I love all your pieces, too."

They finished the rest of their vows and when the minister said to kiss his bride, Hank had already hauled her up in the air, spun her around, and then sealed his lips over hers in a rather vulgar public display of his affection. Finally, his brother pulled him away from the poor thing. But she was grinning wide and holding on to Hank just as tightly. Hank lifted Aspen up and carried her down the aisle as he exclaimed, "This here is my wife, people!"

The audience cheered and hooted and hollered. Well, Hank's side cheered. Aspen's side of the aisle were quite a bit more reserved in their suits and cocktail attire.

Just went to show that regardless of where you come from, you never know who you're going to fall for. Sometimes, opposites do attract and when they do, watch out. Explosion!

The wedding continued in standard fashion. The bride and groom did all the fundamental things one did at a wedding. Cake cutting, bouquet toss, garter toss… Now was my favorite part. I held London in my arms, and we swayed to the lovely music the small orchestra played. The soulful notes of Etta James's "At Last" had the room melting away to nothing but London and the dance.

I swirled London out and brought her spinning back to me. She was a stellar dancer and followed my lead magnificently. "You know this is our first dance, right?"

She closed her eyes, thinking about it. "You're right. It is. And the song…"

"How apropos. I agree."

"Wasn't the ceremony lovely?"

I nodded. "I think you're lovely. I can't wait to get you alone. When is all this maid stuff complete?"

She twirled in a circle and dragged her arm from around my waist, to my back, then around to my chest once more. Once there, I pulled her in tightly so she could feel the effect her nearness was having on me.

Her eyes widened. "Hmmm, well, I think my duties are officially over." She looked over the dance floor and saw Aspen and Hank forehead to forehead, swaying with the music, completely oblivious to everyone watching them. Good for them. They deserved to be happy. But another part of me really wanted to reconnect with my mate. And soon.

"Well, fancy a lift to my hotel, Ms. Kelley?"

"Don't mind if I do," she joked. "Let me get my suitcase from the guest room and tell Aspen and Hank."

"I'll check in with Emma and Nathaniel."

When I looked around for my siblings, I caught a sight I would not have expected in a million years. Emma was leaning against a wall, looking dazedly into the eyes of a man. The man had his hand on her hip and the other on the wall, caging my baby sister in a very intimate position. That man was none other than Tripp Cocksucker Devereaux. Before I could make my way over to them, Nathaniel stopped me.

"Whoa, hold up, brother mine. You about to go apeshit on Emma and Tripp?"

I gritted my teeth and nodded.

"Nope, not going to happen. She's a big girl. The sooner she gets over that daft prick, Evan, the better. This is just one in the line of many flings she'll likely have to get over the smarmy bastard. Let it go. Besides, I'm here. I won't let her leave with him. No worries, mate."

"Fine. Don't let him fucking touch one hair on her head. I mean it. He's no good for her!"

"Actually, I know him a lot better than you, and she could do a great deal worse. That slimy husband of hers is a hundred times worse."

"Yeah, well, I don't like it."

"You never like any man dating our baby sister. What's the difference between the who?"

"It just is. Okay?"

"Fine, fine. Whatever. I'll make sure he doesn't get out of hand with her. I'll keep an eye on things. Go, you've got a raven-haired beauty hovering behind you, waiting. Lucky sod!"

I turned to see he was right. London was standing next to her case, ready to go, a wrap of some sort over her shoulders.

"I'm going to take the car. Will you and Em catch a ride with Dean and Oliver?"

"Sure thing. No worries, mate. Go. Make up with your beautiful American girl. See you tomorrow."

"Hey, Nate." I used his nickname because I wanted him to know I was serious.

"Yeah, brother mine?"

"You deserve to be happy, too." He nodded and took a long drink of his beer then looked off into the distance before meeting my gaze.

"I am happy. What more could I possibly need?"

"I'll let it go for now. Just know that I'm rooting for you to find the one."

"All you blokes who fall in love are always trying to get us single mates married. Piss off. Go shag your girl and stuff it!"

I laughed and put my arm around London's shoulders. She hugged me and smiled up at me. "This, Nathaniel, is what you're missing out on. The best thing ever." I left it at that, turned my girl around and led her to the car.

It was pitch dark, leaving Hank's ranch and driving on country roads. The second we were on the open road, that thing between London and I popped and cracked making it hard to focus on the road ahead. It was a long stretch of nothing, all the way to the small hotel about fifteen minutes off the beaten path from Hank's ranch. I was eternally grateful.

London's hand crept up my leg as she nuzzled into my neck. "God, I want you. Do you feel it the same way I do?" she asked as she cupped and massaged my hardening package. Her hands were straight from heaven. When they were on me, I could barely focus on anything else.

"Beauty, you have no idea. But seriously, we have to make it back to the hotel first." I nipped at her lips. She pulled away and moved to sit back, then buckled her seatbelt. As I turned my head to say something filthy, her eyes widened and she braced herself on the dash in front. Her mouth opened on a scream.

It happened so fast.

I turned my head back to the road just in time to see that I was about to hit a ginormous black-and-white cow standing stock still in the middle of the road. In a split second, I knew if I hit the cow, we'd be in a world of hurt. I swerved left. London's scream pierced my eardrums a second before we plowed through a wooden fence. The car bumped and scraped along the rocky terrain.

"London!" I yelled as I lost control of the car and fishtailed. In a blink of an eye, we were barreling toward a huge oak tree, too fast for me to correct the car's trajectory. I reached out to grasp London's hand. Her warm embrace was the last thing I felt as I heard her blood-curdling scream. Then the world went black.

CHAPTER SEVENTEEN

This is not happening. Not happening. It can't be. Not my life. A dream.

"You are in a dream, sweetie pie."

I stood and twirled around. The hospital room was dark, aside from the small night-light above Collier's head, but not so dark I didn't see him standing there. Alive. In front of me, as real as the day I'd married him eight years ago.

"James." My voice broke and I was unable to form additional words.

"Yes, sweetie pie, it's me."

"But…b-but…you're…"

"Dead. Yes, I know. But you're not and neither is he." He pointed to the bed where Collier lay unmoving. My heart broke, seeing him there, completely still. His head was bandaged from slamming into the window. Had we been driving a more sophisticated vehicle, side airbags would have prevented the swelling in his brain from the impact, possibly eliminating his comatose state.

"Are you here to take him?" I could barely form the words but I had to know.

"Right now, no. I'm here for you."

"Me?"

His smile spread and reminded me of so many happy days, long ago, that I'd never have again.

"Yes. I've watched you these past years. Wanted so badly to help you through your destructive path. I'm here now though, to

make sure you make good on your promise."

"My promise?"

"At my deathbed, you promised you'd love again. You've done nothing but push his love away. He's the only one since I left who has been worthy of your love. And now, here he lies, not knowing your feelings for him. Withholding your love from him is an unbearable torture."

"But...you. I loved you so much. With everything I had. When you died, that part of me died, too."

"No, it didn't. You just lost it for a while. He's bringing it back to you. If he makes it through this tragedy, you must tell him."

"If? You don't know?"

"Oh, sweetie, all things get worse before they get better." He used an old saying that used to piss me off. Mostly because it always seemed to be true.

"I can't lose him. I already lost you!"

James shook his head and his form flickered.

"Don't go!" I screamed.

"I'm sorry. I only get to do this once. Those are the rules. I love you, London. Always have and always will. Please, don't keep your love to yourself. It's the most precious thing in the world to share. He deserves it."

"Will I see you again?"

He shook his head. "No, sweetie, but I'm never far."

"James, I love you."

He winked, a gesture he'd done a thousand times before. It warmed my heart and made me feel loved.

Then I blinked awake, still sitting in the chair next to Collier's bed. I looked around. The room was shrouded in darkness and the only sound was the beeping coming from

Collier's heart monitor.

I set my broken arm on his bed and took his scratched up hand in mine. Exhausted, I laid my head on his hand, praying, hoping against hope that he'd wake up. That I could keep my promise to James and finally tell Collier what I should have said. What he needed to hear. Fear and love. The only two things in the world that can break you and I'd let one prevent me from enjoying the other. I closed my eyes and prayed.

A warm hand rubbed along my back.

"Bridge baby, wake up!"

Oh, thank God! It was all a sick dream. I was home in my bed and Tripp was waking me up for coffee and a morning chat. When I opened my eyes, the ease I'd felt in the dream was obliterated. I was still in the hospital, clutching the hand of an unmoving man, one who I'd recently admitted I loved. One I never told. And now, I may never get to.

Tripp hauled me out of my seated position and into his arms. "I got here as quickly as I could. My phone was on silent. I called everyone else. They should be here any minute. None of us knew. God, are you okay? Your arm is in a cast!" His eyes filled with tears.

"Yes, I'm fine. Well, pretty much. A few bruised ribs, bumps, and scrapes, a conk to the head."

Tripp rubbed his finger lightly over the egg-shaped bump on my forehead, then over each scrape on my face and the cut down the side of my lip. "Collier took the brunt of the accident."

Tripp looked at my sleeping Englishman. "I can see that. He's been through the wringer for sure. What's his prognosis?"

Before I could respond, Aspen, Hank, Oliver, Dean, Emma, and Nathaniel all came to the doors of the ICU. The walls were glass, and I could see them yelling for an orderly even though I couldn't hear them. Aspen put her hand to the glass as if reaching for me. Tears poured down my face as I stood and silently connected with my big sister. Nathaniel pounded on the glass like a madman, which prompted me into action.

I made it to where they were waiting. Aspen hugged me, and I winced as the several bruised ribs screeched in protest to her embrace. Tears welled in her eyes at the sight of my bruised face and broken arm.

"What's going on? What happened?" she asked. Hank put his arm around her and waited. Nathaniel didn't.

"What's wrong with my brother?"

"We need to see him!" Emma practically yelled.

"Guys, I don't know everything. I woke from the accident a couple hours ago. All the night nurse could tell me was that he was in a coma."

Emma started to cry and Nate pulled her into his chest. "What happened?" Nate asked again.

I took a deep breath and leaned against the wall, feeling nauseous and woozy from the pain meds. Hank brought a chair and helped me to settle.

"We were driving back to the hotel. It was really dark. Pitch black. Then, out of nowhere, standing in the middle of the road was this huge cow. It stood there, unmoving, and Collier swerved and we missed the cow but went through a fence. It was so dark…" Tears leaked down my cheeks, and Dean handed me a handkerchief. "Then all of a sudden, there was a tree. Collier grabbed my hand and everything went black. I woke up here a couple hours ago with this." I gestured to my arm. "Then I left my bed and found Collier here. The night nurse told me he was in a coma. That's all I know." Tears poured down my face, wetting the hospital gown I wore.

"There you are!" A nurse ran over. "We've been looking all over for you. With that knot on your head, you shouldn't be up and about. It's dangerous."

"I'm not going anywhere until the doctor tells me what's wrong with Collier Stone."

A man in a long white coat approached us. "I'm Doctor Johnson."

Hank jumped in. "What can you tell us about Mr. Stone? He's a friend of ours."

"Friend?" the doctor asked.

"Brother," both Emma and Nate answered.

"Can I speak with the two of you in private?"

"No. Whatever you have to say, you can say in front of them. We're all close. This is his girlfriend. She was in the accident with him."

I stood shakily and the Doctor eyed me, probably assessing my wounds. He didn't seem to like the look of the one on my head. He came and inspected it. "You should be in bed. Have you had an MRI yet?"

I swatted his hands away. "I don't care about me. Tell me about Collier."

"I'm not going to sugarcoat things. His internal organs have experienced great trauma. He has several broken ribs, a broken clavicle, a dislocated shoulder, and some issues with his kidney."

"That's all fixable. Why is he in a coma?"

The group mumbled all in sidebar conversations, but Emma was a wreck. She dropped to her knees and cried out. "No, no, no, if he dies, it's my fault!" she screamed. Nate immediately helped his sister find her legs and embraced her.

"Mr. Stone only has one kidney. Due to the accident, it has completely shut down. He's going to need a transplant and soon. We've got him in a medically induced coma while we assess how to best treat him until a donor match can be found."

The words "transplant" and "donor match" were like a knife shoved directly into my heart. I backed away, not capable of hearing more until I hit the wall and slid down into a crouch. My ribs and broken arm screamed in pain, but it was nothing compared to the hell that ravished my mind. Aspen came and tried her best to comfort me as the doctor continued.

"We've got him on a donor list, but in times like these, when siblings are accessible, they tend to be the best possible match."

"But we're only half. Ten years ago, Collier donated his kidney to Emma here. That's why he only has one. I wasn't a blood type match for her, but Collier was. Does that matter?" Emma shook and sobbed into his chest as I stood against the wall, listening to my worst nightmare, one I'd lived through already, come back to haunt me again.

The doctor's eyes slid down and then closed. "Yes, it does. I'm sorry. If you're not a blood match, you can't donate an organ. Is there anyone else in your family?"

Hope sprang as Nate's eyes filled. He shook his head and that glimmer of hope plummeted. "No. Collier and Em.

Let me make some calls, see what we can find with extended family. There's got to be someone, somewhere willing to save my brother's life. Whatever the cost. We'll pay!" Nate's strength broke and tears slid down his scruffy cheeks.

"Me, test me!" I asked.

The doctor nodded. "First, we'll see about blood matches and let you know. I'll have someone brought over to schedule the tests."

Over the next few hours, I sat by Collier's side. The nurse informed me that I was not a match. She might as well have told me the sun was gone and the moon would forever light the earth because without Collier, I would be in perpetual darkness. Collier had B- blood. In the US, only two percent of the population shared that blood type. Organ donation by a live donor was rare. With a percentage that low, the odds of a deceased donor were small also.

I sat by Collier's bedside in my hospital gown. I was cold but I didn't care. If Collier couldn't be warm, couldn't live, then I didn't care what happened to me.

James was right. Hell, everyone was right. I should have told Collier how I felt. Stopped being a scaredy-cat and admitted I had strong feelings for him. I outright loved the stubbornly sexy Englishman. Now I feared I'd never get to tell him. What then?

That would be two men I'd loved and lost.

What was the saying Collier mentioned on our first date? It's better to have loved and lost than to never have loved at all? Whoever said that was full of shit. They obviously never truly loved someone because it wasn't fucking better. It was easier to go through life not loving someone. Then you didn't feel mind-numbing, all-over body pain when you lost them.

It was official. I was cursed. If London Kelley fell in love with a man, he was taken away. Twice. What are the odds of that? Really? Does God hate me? He must. I can't understand why he'd take such beautiful men away from the world so young.

"Collier, I'm sorry. If you can hear me, I'm so sorry. I should have told you." I looked at his face and swept that stray lock of blond hair off his forehead. He had cuts and bruises on his face but in his sleep, he still looked peaceful, as if he was going to wake up and melt my heart with his delicious accent. He'd call me beauty and everything in the world would feel right again.

★ ★ ★

London? Where are you? Why can't I see you? My eyes won't open. Fucking open! I screamed but no sound came out. It was like being underwater, so deep that my screams never made it to the surface.

Her lovely voice pierced the darkness as I treaded water, submerged under a cloak of blackness. I tried to move a finger, a toe, my face. I just couldn't. Nothing worked. Then her voice continued in a soft lilting tone, comforting, like salve on an open wound.

"Collier, I'm sorry. If you can hear me, I'm so sorry. I should have told you."

Told me what, beauty? What? I can hear you. I just can't reach you!

"I have so much to be sorry for. Pushing you away—" Her voice cracked. I wanted to reach out to her, comfort her. Tell her it would be okay. That I'd take away her hurt.

Make it better.

"You never deserved my leaving, running off after we'd shared beautiful evenings together."

She had a point, but if I could just sodding reach her, I'd tell her, hold her in my arms and pet her hair, explain that we were past all that. It was different now. We made amends and had full lives ahead of us. Ones we'd spend together. Christ! Why can't I fucking move?

"Every moment with you has been the best moment of my life." I could hear her sobbing and it gutted me. "I just want you to know that no matter what happens, I'll be here for you. I love you, Collier."

She loves me. My beauty admitted she loves me and I can't reach her. Jesus, I'm tired. So sleepy.

I love you, London. Please don't leave me.

★ ★ ★

The bed jostled and I woke instantly, looking at Collier to see if there had been any change. Another day had passed, and the nurse was shifting Collier and moving things around.

"You need to leave," she said hurriedly.

"What? Why?"

"He's going in for surgery in the next thirty minutes."

"He has a donor?" That evil bitch Hope came right back to the surface, and I hugged her for all she was worth.

The nurse smiled. "Yes!" I hopped up and ran out the door as I saw Tripp being wheeled on a hospital bed around a corner. Confused, I made it to his side, trying not to fall. Running in my condition was not a good idea. My stomach swirled and tightened with the effort of not vomiting. My cast was like an anchor, tugging my balance to the right.

"Tripp, oh my God. What happened to you?"

His hand squeezed mine. "Nothing, Bridge. Everything is great!"

I followed the team as they wheeled him down a long hallway. The light hurt my eyes and I faltered, but nothing was keeping me from following.

"I don't understand, what's going on?"

"Today's your lucky day!"

"I know! Collier's got a donor!" I half-yelled in glee.

Tripp smiled the mischievous one that told me he was up to no good. "How does that explain why the hell you're in this hospital bed? What is going on?"

"Guys, give me a second?"

"We need to go, Mr. Devereaux."

"I know," he answered. "Just give me a moment with my girl so I can say good-bye."

"Good-bye? What the fuck, Tripp. You're scaring me!"

"None of this makes sense right now, but Bridge, I'm a match." It took a few moments for what he said to sink in. The second it dawned on me, my smile turned into a frown.

"No, no, no, you can't be! You can't do this, Tripp!"

"Yes, I can and I have. Collier's going to have a piece of me in him. I can't wait to give him shit about it either!"

"Don't make light of this. This is not fucking funny. You could die and I'd lose you both! There has to be another way. Tell them no. You can't. It's not…" A sob broke me and I leaned over the bed. He held me. I held on so tight I worried I might have finished off those severely bruised ribs.

"Bridge, there's no other way. All of us were tested. Miraculously, I'm a match. Go figure."

"No," I cried. "You can't. I'll lose you both. I won't survive if something happens."

"Bridge, baby, you're going to be fine. I'm going to be fine. Dr. Nicholls, an excellent surgeon, was flown in. Aspen made sure we had the best transplant team. She was throwing money at the crew, trying to get random people to sign up to be donors and get checked. The doctors had to shut that down quick before they received a lawsuit." He chuckled.

"Oh my God. I had no idea." A lot seemed to have taken place while I was standing guard next to Collier's bedside.

"Yeah, she and Hank had words because she's actually a blood match, too, but with the pregnancy…"

"Oh no. They'd never let her." He nodded and pointed to his nose. "Yeah, she wanted to be tested anyway. Hank fucking lost it. It was kind of funny." My frown deepened. "Guess you had to be there."

"Tripp, seriously. Why are you doing this? You don't even like Collier." My tears fell and dropped on our combined hands. He rubbed our hands with his fingers.

"I love you. And you love him. I heard you last night, Bridge. Telling him how sorry you were for not admitting your love. I had just found out that I was a possible match. I was waiting for the rest of the tests to see if I was a sure thing. When I came to find you, you were hunched over his bedside, and I'd never seen you so gone for a man. Even James. I had to help. And now I can." Intense emotions jumped off him and slammed into me, proving his love and gratitude. "I want to give you back your life. Exactly what you've given me over the past few years. You saved me. Now it's my turn to save you." A tear slipped down his cheek.

There weren't words, but I reached for them anyway. "I love you."

"More than anyone?"

"Right now? Yes!" We laughed.

"All right, driver, I'm ready. Let's go get my girl her man back!" That actually made me smile.

"Tripp, thank you." His eyes closed and he let go of my hand. The team wheeled him away to the surgery bay.

"See you on the flip side, Bridge."

Moments later, Collier's body headed toward the same door Tripp went through.

Please, God. You've taken James. Don't take Collier or Tripp. Please.

I stopped Collier's bed before it went through. Before the team of medical professionals could say anything, I leaned over his bed and pressed my lips to his. I detected a small pressure back before I pulled away.

"I love you, Collier. I'll be waiting for you," I whispered in his ear. With one last kiss, I let them take the man I loved away.

CHAPTER EIGHTEEN

A standard kidney transplant takes approximately three hours if you have a living donor. Three hours doesn't sound long, unless you have a room filled with freaked-out Brits who spoke a mile a minute.

Meeting Collier's parents, sister, brother-in-law, and nephew under normal circumstances would have sent me barreling to the hills. Under the peril of their son possibly dying, right along with my best friend? Unconscionable.

Slipping away from the British Invasion, I made it over to where my sister sat primly, beautifully put together even after two days of crazy. As I sat next to her, she held my hand and I cuddled into her side. No matter who she was in the business world, no matter how much money poured into her bank accounts, she was first and foremost my big sister. She could make me feel better when I was hurting.

"How you holdin' up?"

"Holdin'? Did you just drop the 'g' on that word?"

Her blue eyes twinkled as she smiled. "Hank's rubbing off on me. I'll try to put it in check. Must be the country environment."

"It's okay. I think it's cute. How's my baby doing?" I leaned over and put my ear to her belly bump. All I could hear was the swish-swish of her body, but it made me feel better knowing I was so near to new life. Aspen tunneled her fingers through my hair, massaging my scalp as the events of the last couple days sank in.

"I'm officially at seventeen weeks." I heard the rumble of her voice against her stomach and tilted my head so that I could hear her but continued to appreciate her soft touch against my hair.

"Does that mean we get to find out what it is?" God, I love my sister so much right now. She was purposely talking about the one and only subject that could take my mind off the fear of what was going on with the two men I loved and adored in a sterile room not far from where I sat. "Three more weeks."

I pinched my lips together. "I have a friend who went to a place called Peek-a-boo Baby where she got to see a whole month earlier than that."

Aspen's fingers scratched along the crown of my head, soothing and lovingly. "London, if God meant for us to see our children, he would have covered our bellies in glass instead of skin and tissue. No, Hank is also adamant about not doing that." She laughed. "He actually said, and I quote, 'Ain't no way in hell some fruit loop is going to wave a wand over my baby and give her radiation or some shit. Nuh-uh.'"

A giggle eased the tension and it felt good. "I can totally see him saying something like that. He's the fruit loop."

Aspen nodded and looked over at her husband. My sister was sitting next to me, comforting me instead of Fiji bound for her honeymoon.

"Thank you for staying," I whispered and tried not to cry again. I was so tired of crying.

"There's no place I'd rather be than here with you, making sure our extended family is okay." She kissed my forehead and I lifted up.

"You mean Tripp?"

"Yes, and Collier too. I can see how much he means to you. A blind man could. It's written across your face and sealed into your essence. I could feel it at the wedding when he showed up. I just knew then that you were finally going to be okay. You have found your mate…for the second time."

Traitorous tears built again, but I pushed them back. "Yeah, but I never got to tell him. I'm so afraid I'll never get to."

Aspen grabbed my hand and put her other one on my cheek. "It's not going to happen twice, London. I know it. I feel it in every bone in my body. Have faith. Just have faith."

I closed my eyes and sent a silent prayer to the big guy upstairs once more.

Aspen hugged me and settled back into her chair. We watched as Ella, Collier and Nate's other sister, handed her baby over to a willing Hank. The boy was screaming bloody murder, but Hank put out his big hands and clasped the baby to his large chest. Immediately, he snuggled the baby into his embrace and rocked him from side to side. The mother gave him the pacifier the baby wouldn't take previously, and Hank wiggled it into the baby's mouth. Instant quiet fell over the room. It was heavenly.

I nudged Aspen in the shoulder. "Looks like your husband has the magic touch."

"Yes, he does." She grinned and had the stunning look of a woman in love shining behind her blue eyes.

After what seemed like days, Dr. Nicholls entered the waiting room. The entire room went completely quiet as the good doctor smiled. "Okay, the dean tells me I can blow through the medical privacy and just spill the details." He winked at Aspen, and she grinned proudly, obviously having made another donation to another hospital to get her way, besides sending her jet to fly the man from New York to Texas to do the transplant. Man, I owed my sister big. "First and foremost, I want to say both patients are doing well. There were a few dropped heart rate moments in Mr. Stone, but he's healthy and strong. We suspect most of that had to do with his body's trauma leading up to needing the new kidney. Mr. Devereaux flew through the surgery with flying colors and will be awake soon. Mr. Stone we're keeping sedated to allow additional time for his body to mate with the new organ. I'm sorry to say only one of you can see him at a time."

Aspen cleared her throat and lifted two fingers, making her expectation clear. The little woman standing behind Dr. Nicholls with the ugly suit and hair pulled tightly in a bun must have been the Dean of Medicine. She nodded her acceptance of Aspen's silent request. Money talks.

"I mean two will be allowed in at once. Just remember, folks, they have both been through a lot. Especially Mr. Stone. He'll likely be in the hospital a solid ten days. Mr. Devereaux will be able to leave in three or four, provided everything goes well post-surgery. This is good news, everybody. They're both going to live long and healthy lives."

The phrase "long and healthy lives" sent me to my knees on the cold laminate floor. Collier would live. He wasn't taken from me. Unlike James, both he and Tripp were spared. *Thank you. Thank you. Thank you*, I chanted over and over again until someone lifted me and helped me into a seat. The scent of cookies surrounded me as I sobbed and shook. The past day's events came to a head. The two men I loved most in the entire world were going to live.

"He's going to live," I choked out.

"Yes, sweet girl. My boy and your friend are strong men with a lot to live for, you being a good reason for my son."

I looked up into Collier's deep brown eyes, but they weren't his. They were his mother's. Eleanor's smile filled me with light, and her touch made my heart beat again. The man I loved was an extension of her, and I could feel his presence being so near to her. "I love him," I admitted.

"Of course you do, sweetie. What's not to love? My Colly is special indeed." She pulled me into her embrace. "And look how pretty she is…my boy's girl. Oh, I hope we get raven-haired grands. Wouldn't that be lovely, Walker?" she addressed Collier's stepfather over her shoulder. It was interesting that she called him by his last name. Maybe it was a British thing.

"Absolutely, dear," he said in a perfect English gentleman's response. I was happy to see him in person. Made me certain his heart attack scare was mild. Had to be if he could fly overseas a short couple of weeks after having it.

Fear must really change you. If any other woman in the world hinted to me that I would have children with their son, I might have fainted on the spot. But when this woman said it, I just accepted it. If children were in my future because Collier wanted them, I'd give them to him. As long as he was alive, I'd give him just about anything.

★ ★ ★

Once I'd cleaned myself up, it was my turn to go see Collier.

I let his parents go first because they didn't get to see him prior to surgery, having just arrived at the hospital from the airport when he went in. I also wanted to get myself together.

Oliver had sorted through my suitcase and found a pair of jeans and a blouse for me to wear. I swear, the man thought of everything. Guess that's what made him such a good personal assistant to my sister. Hell, I'd bet a great portion of her success was due to that man. He seemed on top of every detail at all times, personal or otherwise.

I made the slow walk to Collier's room. His sister Ella and her husband, Ethan, had just left. Ethan held onto his wife as she cried, but they both seemed happier after having seen her brother.

I entered silently and sat in the chair next to the bed, clasping his hand in mine. It was cool to the touch, so I used my breath and the energy from our hands to warm it. I pressed my lips against the soft skin and silently thanked whoever would listen that this man would be okay. He'd live another day to humor, love, irritate, and cherish me. All the walls I had built around being with him crumbled and slipped away, completely forgotten. After facing losing him forever, I'd do anything to ensure he stayed in my life.

Once I'd looked my fill, touched him enough to send him healing vibes and my love, I decided it was time to see my BFF.

The second I walked around the corner, I knew exactly which room was his. It was the one the laughter and giggles came from. I rolled my eyes and entered.

Tripp's grin as he saw me was priceless. "Bridge, come join the party. These lovely nurses were keeping me company until you got here. Aspen and Hank just left."

I shook my head as the two bubbly nurses turned to leave, all smiles, waving at Tripp sexily and swaying their hips to and fro.

"What am I going to do with you?" I asked and sat on the space he left.

"Love me?" he ventured.

"Well, yeah, that is a given. How do you feel? Really?" I pointed a brow, giving him my serious look, one he knew well after years of friendship and living together.

"Truth?"

"Truth."

"I feel like I've had a man digging inside my body and playing pickup sticks with my organs."

I laughed and he grinned. "Seriously, it hurts but it's bearable. I'm not letting them give me much in the way of pain meds aside from ibuprofen. I'll deal with the pain," he said firmly.

"Worried about a relapse?"

He nodded but didn't say anything. With me, he didn't have to. I knew his fears. We'd both been dealing with our demons and his were drugs and feeling out of control.

"Tripp, I don't know how to thank—"

"Bridge, don't." He gripped my hand and interrupted me. "You've saved me a hundred times over. It seems drastic, but Bond is the one for you. He's made you happier and more alive in the past few months than I've ever seen you. I've tried to put that happiness on your face. Even when we thought we could cure each other physically, nothing worked. Friendship helped. Caring for one another definitely put a huge dent in the problems in both of our lives but him…" He paused and then shook his head. "He's the shit, Bridge."

"Yeah, he kind of is." I held both Tripp's hands and kissed each knuckle.

"I want that for you. No one in this world deserves to be happy like you do. You're the most honest, kind, loving woman I've ever known, and he sees it too. He saw it the first moment he laid eyes on you. Hell, remember how you practically jumped him in the street after barely meeting him? That told me the connection between you was like lightning, something that went through the body from start to finish and ended in the heart. I just knew he'd be around for good. The way he has been looking at you, the man is head over heels in love with my girl, and I couldn't fucking be happier."

I snort laughed. "See, even your ugly piggy laugh is cute. Just try not to do it in front of him." He grimaced.

"Oh shut up. You make that weird gargley sound in the back of your throat when you sleep sometimes. Sounds like you're choking on your own spit. It's disgusting."

"Tell me how you really feel," he retorted.

"I just did!"

"I love your more than anyone, Bridge."

"I know. I love you, too." There would be no more saying that I loved him more than anyone because it wasn't the truth. A tall, muscular, lean, sexy Englishman with chocolate-colored eyes and a roguish smile had stolen my heart and a huge portion of my love along with it.

★ ★ ★

The smell of cinnamon permeated the air, filling my nose

with the scent of the only person I wanted to see. My beauty.

Slowly, I opened my eyes. They were blurry, but I could make out a fuzzy dark shape leaning over my bed. Her hand held mine, her forehead planted along my arm. Soft snuffling sounds filled the room. She was fast asleep, hunched over my arm. London's hair spilled over the white linens like black oil.

After a quick assessment, I found I was able to move my hand and my toes, though it hurt to do so. I couldn't really lift up and didn't try to. A heavy weight lay on my chest, even though nothing was there. I had no idea what had happened. The last thing I remembered was narrowly missing a cow and then barreling toward a large oak tree. The only other thing I recalled was hearing London's voice, apologizing to me. For what, I didn't know. I do remember she finally admitted she loved me. That I'll never forget. And here she was, sleeping alongside me.

Once my vision cleared, I really looked at my beautiful New Yorker in all her glory. And Christ, was she beautiful. So much so that it almost hurt to look at her. Her full pink lips were opened slightly, puffing out small bursts of air. Her button nose had a smattering of the lightest freckles, almost as if they'd been dusted on. The one thing I needed to see but couldn't were her eyes.

People say that eyes are the windows to the soul. For me, looking into London's eyes was like looking into my future. I wanted my children to have those eyes and that blanket of thick dark hair.

It took a bit of effort, but I slid my arm from under her head and tunneled my fingers into her lovely hair. Slowly, her eyes blinked open. When she saw I was awake, her eyes opened wider and she smiled.

Tears filled those ocean eyes and leaked down the side of her face. I shook my head. "No… don't cry." The words were featherlight, barely making a sound at all.

My beauty bit her lip and clasped my cheek. "Would you like a drink?"

I nodded, and she got a pink cup and gave me a sip of water. I sucked it down as if I were in a drinking contest.

"Better, thanks." My voice sounded scratchy, but I didn't know why.

"What happened?"

"You remember we hit that tree, right?" I nodded and she continued. "We were taken to the hospital, and you spent the last couple of nights in a medically induced coma. Then your kidney was going to fail. You needed a transplant." Her voice caught on that last word, and I knew it was bringing up seriously painful memories for her.

"But I only had one kidney, I gave mine…"

"You donated one to your sister. Yeah, we found that out." Her eyes squinted in what looked like irritation. "They had to add you to the national list, but your blood type is rare."

"Yeah, B negative. So a kidney came through?"

My girl smiled wide and held my hand, bringing it to her cheek and then rubbing it against her warm skin. "Yes, one did. A living donor."

"Huh? How? My family? Only Em and I have the same blood type." Things were not making sense.

"It wasn't a family member."

The information floored me. It didn't add up. "I don't understand?"

"Well, all of us tried. Me, Aspen, Hank, Oliver, Dean…"

"Aspen's pregnant. They would never let her."

"Yeah, she was pretty pissed, too. She actually has B negative blood, but they wouldn't operate on a pregnant woman. I think she just didn't want to feel useless. But it turned out one person did match perfectly."

I thought about the people in my life who would potentially be willing to donate a kidney in such short notice. Whoever it was, I sure as hell owed them a lot. My life for one.

"Tripp."

"What about Tripp?" His name sent tingles through me, bringing my fighter instincts to the fore. We'd made amends, but it would still be a while before I would consider him a good mate.

"He gave you his kidney this morning."

You know that moment where a balloon is filled to the extreme and there's no possibility of pushing more air into it, yet you blow harder, forcing, and then it explodes? That happened when those words left her sweet lips. My bloody head fucking exploded.

"You're pulling my prick," I said, deadpan, trying to assure her I didn't think her words were funny.

"No, I'm not. Believe me, if I was, you'd know it." She grinned and winked.

"I… There aren't words. I…I'm, uh, surprised. Tripp?" I searched her face to see any hint of humor or joking. There wasn't any. "Why?"

She took a deep breath and visibly swallowed. Her hand pulled a thick lock of hair, and then twirled it around her finger. Nervous, even with me. Such a sweet woman. God

I loved her. "He said he wanted to give me back life. That he owed me for helping him all these years. He didn't want me to lose you."

"But, he could have died…"

"You *would have* died, Collier. I can't bear the thought that I'd lose you, too."

"Come here." I held out my arm and she laid her head in the crook of my neck. She smelled of cinnamon and sadness. "Baby, I'm not going anywhere. But it looks like I'm going to have to do some serious groveling to your best mate."

She chuckled and sighed. "I love you, Collier. I'm sorry I was scared to admit it before."

"Oh, beauty, I love you so much. Forever more, my dear. Forever more. Now get that sweet arse up here and let me hold you. I'm so bloody tired. Having you near will help me sleep."

"Won't it hurt?"

"It hurts me not having you closer. Besides, you're tiny. There's plenty of room."

And there was. She fit right along the length of my body. Her arm cast over my waist did hurt, so I moved it between us.

"How bad were you hurt, love?"

"Not bad. Just the arm. Sore ribs. Bruises and bumps mostly."

"When we get out of here, I want to kiss every last one of them. And then you can kiss mine. We'll make each other better, yeah?"

"I'm already better. You're alive, here with me. That's all I'll ever need." Her eyes closed as she snuggled into my chest. I played with her hair until we both fell blissfully asleep lying next to one another.

EPILOGUE

Two months later...

During those moments when you're faced with death, we humans are compelled to make promises to ourselves, to God, to whomever will hear our pleas. I did that when presented with the possibility that I'd lose the first man I'd loved since losing James.

Then again, when confronted with losing my best friend in the entire world. No woman should have to deal with those things. So yeah, I made promises to God, to Collier, to Tripp, but mostly to myself. I think I've stuck to them. But I deserve a fucking medal of honor for spending the last two months playing nursemaid to two very opinionated and outspoken men in pain.

Between Tripp's incessant whining about pain because he only allowed himself a half a pain pill every eight hours instead of the requisite two every four to six hours, he's been a regular thorn in my side.

Then there's Collier, who spent more time than not fighting with me about helping him. Finally, the cavalry showed up.

Aspen sent a sexy-assed nurse in to take care of Tripp while I took care of my man. Honestly, I'd almost rather take care of Tripp. At least with him, I didn't want to kiss him as much as I wanted to throttle him.

And Collier's been the handsiest patient in the entire

world. Every time I try to re-tape his ribs, he grabs a handful of ass, bites at a nipple while I'm leaned over him, or skims those sexy full lips along my neckline. It's maddening.

Not being able to act on this newfound love has been complete and utter torture of the worst kind. At week four, I couldn't take the sexual tension anymore and held him down while I sucked him off then let him reciprocate by leaning on his side and kissing me while fingering me into oblivion. It barely took the edge off. It's not the same as having your man fully joined with you. Today, eight weeks into his recovery, I'm taking my man and riding him into the sunset.

Enough is enough. His ribs have mostly healed, just a bit sensitive. My cast was removed two weeks ago. His casts were removed last week. He's been living with me and Tripp for two solid months. It was easier than going back and forth between his apartment and ours. Even with the professional nursemaid for Tripp, I still needed to see my guys through this. It's been a hard two months, but now I feel things have turned around.

Aspen has visited every three or so days. It's been wonderful watching her belly bump get bigger, Hank's protectiveness get stronger. Her sonogram showed that she's going to have a sweet baby girl. That has made recovery a lot easier, knowing we had something to look forward to.

Tomorrow, I'm bringing Collier back to his apartment.

Emma's apartment opened, and she's decided to move to it and stay in the United States awhile. The guys are working on her business green card. According to Tripp, she's finally committed to filing for divorce. She's actually been a regular visitor, visiting her brother every couple days and becoming pretty close friends with Tripp. I suspect she has a bit of a crush on him, which I'd be thrilled to see. Both seem to be cautious of showing anything more in front of Collier, but I see the looks they've been giving one another and can feel the sexual tension flying off them the second they're in the same room. I've kept that bit of information to myself.

Tripp is aware but has made it a point to not discuss it with me. He only says some sparks did fly at the wedding. I'd like to see him with a good woman…or man, for that matter. I want to see him happy and content with his station in life and the place he has in everyone else's life, including mine.

It's taken a lot of talking and natural progression with the guys being cooped up with one another, but they've almost become better friends with each other than Tripp and I have been over the years. Maybe once you leave the physical side out of a relationship you end up with a deeper bond. Aspen and Ollie are like that and those two are barely separated.

I haven't gone back to work yet, though I have a client set up for next week. Thank God, Nate was scheduled during this timeframe. We were able to postpone his until later next spring. And one of my clients had to cancel their design at the end of March because of a job offer that moved them to Los Angeles—which worked out fine for me. I received a fifteen percent cancellation fee, which was a cool fifteen thousand for no work at all.

So I'll start work on Nate's Manhattan apartment then. I'm looking forward to getting to know him and digging into his world and psyche. He's a bit of an enigma. Good-looking, has a British accent that makes a girl swoon, yet he's alone. He's fit and muscular like his brother, makes a shit-ton of money, is extremely successful and a family man, but doesn't have anyone? When I asked Collier about it, he shrugged and said he's a piss-poor judge of character.

I finished packing most of Collier's clothes to go back to his apartment. He's been acting weird about it all day. You'd think a man would want to go home after being held up in my master bedroom for two months and sharing a space with my best friend. Hasn't made for a lot of privacy or intimacy for that matter. At least with him going back home, we'll be alone. Finally.

"You bloody cocksucking Yank!" Collier screamed from the other room. Yeah, space would be great.

"Blow me, Bond!" Tripp yelled back.

"That doesn't even make sodding sense, you half-wit imbecile!" Collier roared back.

I rolled my eyes and made my way into the living room.

The two of them were deep into some first-person shooter video game. Apparently, they were not on the same team during this particular match. When that happened, insults flew freely, mostly pertaining to Collier being British and Tripp being American.

"What the hell? You shoot like a pansy-assed little prick!" Tripp shot off.

"Arsehole...stuff it before I stuff it for you!" Collier moved his shoulders left and right. Tripp followed as if they were actually sniping and hiding out avoiding predators. It was hysterical to see two grown men resort to being teenagers when they had a controller in their hand.

"Oh wait. Ah ha! Gotcha, you bloody wanker. You can't

hide from me!" Collier jumped up in victory, then winced, and grabbed his ribs.

I ran to his side to lay my fingers along the taped ribs. "Hey, baby, be careful. You're just now feeling better. You can't be jumping around like that."

"Ha ha. Your woman told you!" Tripp looked at Collier smugly and made his way into the kitchen. "Must suck to answer to a woman all the time!"

"At least I have a woman to suck on me, you sore-losing bastard!"

"Guys, stop it. Jesus. I hate these video game wars. I'm so glad you're going home tomorrow."

"Really?" Collier's eyes crinkled tightly together. "Why wait until tomorrow then?" Collier said in a huff. "I'm well enough now." He slung the words over his shoulder as he stomped into the master bedroom.

"Bridge, what the fuck?" I whirled on Tripp, eyebrows arched to the sky. "Can't you see he's sensitive about leaving you?"

My shoulders slumped as I leaned against the arm of the couch. "That hadn't dawned on me. It's not like he's leaving *me,* exactly. I mean, he's just going back home."

"Maybe he doesn't want to go?" Tripp shrugged. "Talk to him. Go see what's up."

"Yeah, okay. You good?"

"Bridge, I'm fine. Stop nursing me. I'm practically perfect. Now, go after your man. Fix your stupid comment."

"Okay, okay. Jeez, Louise. Sometimes I forget whose best friend you are."

Tripp shrugged and smiled, and then took a drink of Gatorade. "I'd have to say now that it's both of you. I still love you more than anyone though. But I'm rather fond of our James Bond." He swatted my ass and turned me toward my bedroom. "Go get your man. I'm heading for a walk to the local bookstore. Emma's meeting me there for a coffee. Or tea and a biscuit." He snickered and rolled his eyes. Tripp loved to make fun of Collier's accent and now Emma's. I think he did it to Emma more for personal reasons and to flirt than to admonish.

Then it dawned on me. Alone. Completely alone. Shit. For the first time in two months, Collier and I would have the apartment completely to ourselves. And I've gone and pissed off my man. Just my luck.

Once I heard the front door click and lock, I half ran to the master bedroom. I found Collier unceremoniously tossing clothing into a box. Some of it was mine, but he didn't notice, obviously having something important on his mind.

"You realize you're throwing my clothes in that box. You movin' me out of here?"

He stopped and gave me the most heated look I'd seen in two long months. Instantly, my heart hammered, my blood thrummed, and that sexual connection sizzled in the air.

"Would you consider moving?"

I nodded. "Guess it depends on who's asking and what they're asking for."

In two strides, he was in front of me, our bodies a scant inch from each other. It was like two magnets fighting to seal against one another. His hand tunneled into the hair at my nape, pulling out the tie to let my hair tumble around my shoulders. He loved my hair and wanted his hands in it constantly. The other hand gripped my hip and urged our lower bodies against one another. I gasped. Instant warmth spread over me as we touched.

"If I asked you to move into my flat, would you consider it?"

"Maybe."

His eyes closed at my answer. A sense of peace, along with the twinges of desire and lust filled the air. One of his hands trailed up my spine and pulled me into his body. His lips barely touched mine as we breathed in each other's air, alternating and matching our breaths perfectly.

"Move in with me, beauty. I don't want to be without you."

"Prove it," I whispered as his lips slanted over mine.

I licked the seam of his lips and deepened the kiss. It was the first full-bodied standing hold we'd had in months. It was everything we needed and more. He ate from my mouth and devoured my kiss. His hands held my face where he wanted so he could plunge his tongue farther, leaving no part of me unkissed. Slowly, he walked us back to the bed. The moment my knees hit the mattress, I took advantage and twirled around him.

My greedy hands unbuttoned his shirt, trying desperately to get to bare skin. Collier was a sight to behold on a good day. Right now, when I was finally about to have my man the way I needed him, he was a masterpiece. I couldn't wait any longer and yanked at the fabric, the last two buttons skittered along the wood floor. I leaned away from his lips and ripped my shirt over my head. I wanted nothing but skin on skin.

"Christ, you're beautiful," he said, his mouth moving

down my neck toward the exposed cleavage. I shook my head, not wanting him to hurt his healing ribs.

"Collier. Pants. Off. Now," I said, each word in staccato. "Then get on the bed naked as the day you were born. I've waited two long months for this, and I'm not going to let you hurt yourself in the process. That will delay us more in the near future, and I'm not a risk taker."

"Bossy bird." He pretended to be affronted, but I was getting to him. If the sheer size and swelling of his cock when he released it from his jeans was any indication, he was most certainly not unhappy. Quite the opposite.

I clasped a hand around his silk-wrapped steel appendage and was rewarded with a groan and a tilt of his head. It was impossible to resist tasting the corded muscle along his neck so I took advantage, running my tongue from his clavicle to his ear. He tasted of salt and sex, and I couldn't wait for more.

"Bed. Now. Please, Collier."

He slowly prowled along the bed and leaned back against the headboard. The thick length of his cock strained proudly against his abdomen as if it was reaching for its mate. My sex wept with need at the sight. I licked my lips and imagined putting my mouth across the velvety head of his shaft, already anticipating his musky scent and spicy flavor. Collier let me look my fill as I shucked my pants, along with my underwear. Unclipping my bra, I let it fall to the floor. His intake of breath at seeing my bare body was the only indication that he was affected as strongly as I was. His cock twitched at the sight of my bare breasts. Even with his ribs taped, he was my own personal sexy-assed Englishman, and I physically itched to take him inside my body.

★ ★ ★

"Come here, beauty. Be with me." I licked my lips as the sexiest woman alive crawled up the bed. She straddled my lap, hovering just over my prick. Those blue eyes of hers were almost black, and I knew what she wanted.

Slowly, I encircled her waist and slid just my fingertips over each delicate rib, thankful that they were only bruised in the accident. She sighed as I completed the journey up to cup the heavy weight of her glorious breasts, swiping my thumb along each peak in the little circles I knew she liked.

"Take what you want from me," I told her as I placed my mouth over one nipple, making it pebble and swell like ripened berries as I milked it.

She hovered a moment as I teased and laved at her luscious tits. I could spend all day fondling them, sucking, nibbling, biting. I told her so.

I felt her warmth encase just the tip of my cock. "Look at me," she requested. I couldn't deny her anything. As my eyes met hers, she slowly sank down, inch by inch. From tip to the bloody root, she took me into her tight wet heat. We both exhaled when we were mated completely. The moment was so strong, I knew nothing else could ever compare to it. She was my world now, and I'd do anything and everything to ensure she'd be a part of it forever. I was never going to let her go.

London leaned her forehead against mine. "For once in my life, I feel as though I'm right where I belong."

"Wherever I am is where you belong. I love you, London. Move in with me. Be mine every day."

She lifted her sexy hips up and slammed down, bringing

a rough groan from my lips. "Yes, I will. It's time."

Another lift and with this one, I thrust into her. She gasped. Another thrust as she came down once more, then she ground into my pelvic bone, giving that sweet little clit a good bit of pressure. I held her hips and pressed her harder against me, going as deep as possible, enjoying the little moan she made each time I did.

My girl had the gift of riding cock. Her legs strained and her body bowed as she rode me hard. She planted those delicate hands along my shoulders for leverage and gave me everything. It was the most spectacular vision. Her breasts bounced, skin shone, lips glistened, and the sound. Oh, Christ, the sound of her body sucking my cock in and out of her swollen cleft made me insane. I looked down, and the petals of her sex opened wide around my prick, hugging me, taking me into her body, her heart, and her soul, sending a spiral of pleasure through every ounce of my body.

A fine sheen of sweat misted our skin and the coiling of tension in my boys was so close to bursting I bit my lip hard to prevent release. My girl wasn't quite there yet. Mewling sounds left her lips as her breath came in hefty pants. Her body flowed up and came down hard, pounding as if she was trying to force herself to let go, releasing all of the anxiety, the fear, everything and just falling into me… into us.

"Baby, let go," I urged and thrust hard into her. I gritted my teeth as the pain in my ribs added to the pleasure in my lower half, coalescing and mixing into a stew of bliss.

"I'm still afraid to fall…" she whispered and bowed her back. I took a nipple into my mouth and bit down. Her body shook with the exertion.

"You never have to be afraid to fall. Not with me, London."

With that, her entire body tightened, her sex gripping my prick in a vise as she soared. One, two, three more powerful thrusts, and I fell right along with her, gripping and hugging her slick body, keeping us intertwined while we both roared above the heavens through our combined release. Once we came down, I felt tears pelt my back.

"Beauty, why?" I rubbed her spine, worried I'd asked too much, forcing her to drop that last wall.

"You caught me," she breathed against my neck and ear, tucked tightly against me. I wouldn't have her anywhere else. Couldn't bear to be away from her ever again.

I hugged her tight, chest to chest, skin to skin. Cupping both her cheeks, I kissed her lips lightly and then waited until her gaze aligned with mine. She was the most precious thing in the world to me, and she was all mine. I was never letting her go.

"When my London falls…it will always be me there, waiting to catch you."

THE END

The Falling Series is continued in...

Justice Falling

ALSO BY AUDREY CARLAN

The Calendar Girl Series

January (Book 1)
February (Book 2)
March (Book 3)
April (Book 4)
May (Book 5)
June (Book 6)

July (Book 7)
August (Book 8)
September (Book 9)
October (Book 10)
November (Book 11)
December (Book 12)

The Falling Series

Angel Falling
London Falling
Justice Falling

The Trinity Trilogy

Body (Book 1)
Mind (Book 2)
Soul (Book 3)

ACKNOWLEDGEMENTS

To my husband Eric—You and our boys will forever be my everything. Even if I spend too much time writing and reading and pretending I'm in another world. My real world is pretty damn great and in my life, I will always love you more.

To my mentor Jess Dee—I'm going to continue to thank you because you continue to help me. Everyone, please read her books. They're amazing and so worthy of a read. www.jessdee.com.

To my soul sisters Nikki, Dyani, and Carrie—Without the three of you, I don't think I'd survive even one bad review, or that one "Did Not Finish" or that one "I didn't like the hero's accent." I may have convinced myself those naysayers were right. You three keep me sane.

To my editor Alfie Thompson—You prevent me from sounding like an idiot. That puts you high up there with the people I place on pedestals. Thank you.

To my beta readers:

Jeananna Goodall—Your emotional connection to my characters blows me away. Thank you for keeping me focused on the emotional side of my writing and for loving my characters as much as I do. You read each chapter in the raw without an edit or a read through and still you cheered me on. Incredible.

Ginelle Blanch—Your eagle editors eye saves my arse

(as Collier would say) a hundred times over! Without your beta help, friendship and support I don't know that this novel would have made its appearance so quickly. I owe you girl.

Niki Davis—You e-mailed me asking to be a beta. That's the first time that's ever happened to me. Then to find out we live in the same tiny town in California? If that's not fate I don't know what is. Your comments were lovely but your editing eye a dream!

To Begmeforbeta, Ms. Tara Sharland—Thank you for double-checking all of Collier, Emma, and Nate's phrasing and British terms. Without you, they'd all sound like Californian Yanks using words like, "Dude" and "Sweet." You're a life savior! I plan to be begging again really soon… Justice Falling is next and it's another English hottie!

ABOUT AUDREY CARLAN

Audrey Carlan lives in the sunny California Valley two hours away from the city, the beach, the mountains and the precious…the vineyards. She has been married to the love of her life for over a decade and has two young children that live up to their title of "Monster Madness" on a daily basis. When she's not writing wickedly hot romances, doing yoga, or sipping wine with her "soul sisters," three incredibly different and unique voices in her life, she can be found with her nose stuck in book or her Kindle. A hot, smutty, romantic book to be exact!

Any and all feedback is greatly appreciated and feeds the soul. You can contact Audrey below:

E-mail: carlan.audrey@gmail.com
Facebook: facebook.com/AudreyCarlan
Website: www.audreycarlan.com